To Eve
An Bormon -
Bb Flanigin :)

JACK PARKER SAVES THE WORLD

A LOVE STORY

BILL FLANIGIN

For mom, who told me this book was better than the latest John Grisham novel.

PROLOGUE

2029

THE MAN HATED the long days of summer. The shorter the daylight hours, the better. Occasionally, in his former life, he had heard complaints when the sun sank early, before people could even make it home from the office. Jack Parker would always smile to himself and say nothing. Now, the recluse treasured the long, black nights. They gave him cover, concealment. What good was so much sunlight anyway? Texas. Florida. Mississippi. The misery of living in scorching heat and choking humidity was not appealing to Jack in any way. Southerners eager for summer eventually sought comfort inside air-conditioned buildings and gallons of iced tea.

Michigan's Upper Peninsula was the perfect place for Jack. Vast and scarcely populated, its largest city, Marquette, has a population of around 22,000 people, many of which are students attending Northern Michigan University. Go Wildcats. Yoopers, as the good people of the Upper Peninsula are often called, learn to drive snow-mobiles before cars. Strong and resilient, folks in the U.P. seem like foreigners in their own country. They have a language and culture all their own. The shores of northern Michigan are a secret treasure hiding in plain sight, easily discovered if a person just bothers to look a little bit.

Winters were harsh. Jack Parker loved them. No one could live in the Upper Peninsula if they just tolerated winter, counted it as a bridge to the rebirth of spring. Here, winter fed Jack's soul like a trip to the beach did for most everyone else. That's not to say Yoopers don't like a sunny beach trip now and then. They do. Jack believed all beaches were the same: Sun. Water. Sand.

Jack Parker's well-hidden and isolated homestead was situated on the Keweenaw Peninsula, a stretch of land that stuck out from the U.P. like an outstretched finger pointing toward Canada. Surrounded by Lake Superior, the area held great history and a handful of beautiful cities that most people in the United States didn't know existed. Houghton, the crown jewel of the Keweenaw Peninsula, blossomed on the back of the copper metal mined from the Earth's crust, and it later became an important port city when a waterway was dredged connecting Houghton to the largest freshwater lake on the planet. Gorgeous 19th-century architecture and the Portage Lift Bridge give the town a mini-San Francisco feel to it.

Because of its latitude and unique geography, the Keweenaw landmass averages 220 inches of snow a year. On occasion, fierce winds over the lake create what is called "lake-effect snow," cold northern air strong enough to whisk water off the surface of Lake Superior, take it to altitudes that freeze it, then dump it on the good people below. It is doubtful that the folks in Dallas or Phoenix would consider such a thing possible. Locals joke that there are two seasons, "winter, and winter's coming."

Planning is essential to a man hiding from the world. Jack's late model Polaris Titan, an absolute beast of a snowmobile, needed a stockpile of fuel and extra parts for the winter months. The machine was essential, even more so than Jack's Ford F-250, rendered mostly useless by mid-winter and stored in an outbuilding that served as a garage and workshop. Perfectly tidy and well equipped, Jack's shed gave him a place to work both wood and metal, which came in handy if he needed to build a piece of furniture or fabricate a metal part or two. Primarily, though, the work gave him something to do and helped keep him out of the city and away from human eyes. The only set of eyes that regularly cast their gaze in Jack's direction were those of Lily, his dog.

Lily was a shelter dog, a heeler-terrier mix, and she was incredibly striking. Her coarse fur seemed to swirl with splotches of grey, brown, and white. Sky blue eyes sat in the center of dark chocolate ovals of fur that spun up and around each ear. Lily's feet, flour white, gave her the appearance of a dancer in go-go boots. Physically, she was gorgeous and impressive. Although Lily looked intimidating, her sweet demeanor rendered her completely harmless. She was the perfect dog for Jack Parker. She gave him balance. Lily moved quickly and with boundless energy; Jack moved about methodically and with deliberate measure. One of the pair was usually happy, the other often sullen.

Lily loved people and was a social animal; her master was anything but. There was a time when too many people had followed Jack wherever he went. He felt their stares like pinpricks stinging his skin. As a coping mechanism, Jack simply chose to avoid people altogether. He figured he had been a member of society long enough, and now, the cold winters of northern Michigan assured him the isolation he desired. However, functioning in that type of climate took an enormous amount of preparation.

Firewood was an essential commodity. Twenty pulp cords delivered on a tractor-trailer each September provided enough fuel to keep his cabin toasty warm during the long winter months. Jack would not bother plowing snow off the two-mile stretch of road between his front door and the road into town. What was the point?

Jack kept a satellite phone charged and at the ready in case of an emergency. On sunny days, which often scarce, he charged commercial-grade Tesla batteries whose primary function was to heat water and run his kitchen appliances. Long, hot showers were one of the few luxuries Jack Parker allowed himself.

Keeping the solar panels clear of snow was a full-time job. Occasionally, when he felt the need, Jack had the government send a military drone over his property to drop various supplies. The drops were an expensive luxury. Hand-milled soap, thumb drives loaded with electronic books, light bulbs, fresh batteries, even queso and chips from the great state of Texas, could be delivered within hours. Whatever he needed, or wanted, was at his disposal. Running out of resources was not an issue. Getting recognized by people was.

Jack Parker could leave his cabin and go anywhere he wanted. But leaving meant problems. While most people would consider Jack's lifestyle a prison of sorts, he thought of it as ultimate freedom. Hundreds of square miles of terrestrial playground. Rivers. Lakes. Forests.

A few years back, Jack had gone to lunch with a few people from the Jet Propulsion Laboratory. As the group was finishing the meal, a server casually walked up behind Jack and yanked a handful of hair from his scalp. As if stung by bees, Jack jerked his head around in time to see the backside of a young woman crashing through the back door of the restaurant and out of sight. The group sat frozen in shock. Jack learned later that on the secondary market, each follicle of his hair was worth around ten thousand dollars, triple if the root was still attached. After that sorry episode, Jack decided it was best to keep his dark hair buzzed short.

A year later, during a book launch at SXSW in Austin, Texas, an overflow and enthusiastic crowd of onlookers surged so forcefully toward the table where Jack sat signing books that he became wedged between the table and the wall behind him. The crushing force from the crowd broke two of his ribs. It could have been worse. A larger mob would have most definitely squeezed the life from his body. Security and a handful of good Samaritans saved him. After that chaotic event, Jack hired bodyguards whenever he ventured out in public. But all that bother became terribly restrictive.

In the end, it wasn't any one extraordinary event that caused Jack's decision to leave public life. It wasn't the scores of rude adults wanting to shake his hand in the middle of a restaurant. It wasn't the bags of mail the post office dropped at his door every day. It wasn't the women that propositioned him at every turn. It wasn't any of that.

One October 31st, through great pains of secrecy and security, Jack Parker was able to take his eight-year-old niece Alice trick or treating near the upscale neighborhood of Houston's River Oaks. His niece, appropriately enough, dressed as Alice from *Alice in Wonderland*. Jack, in keeping with the holiday's theme, dressed as... Jack Parker. Decked out in a rubber mask and blue jumpsuit, Jack roamed the streets completely anonymously...dressed as himself. Who would ever guess that under the costume that was Jack Parker was the *real* Jack Parker? (A little laugh escaped him, but the irony didn't.)

You see, Jack Parker was the most famous human being on the planet. But he wasn't a famous Hollywood actor or musician. Jack Parker didn't hit home runs in crowded ballparks or dunk basketballs in packed arenas. Jack Parker wasn't a tech billionaire, nor was he ever on *The Bachelor*. So, what did Jack Parker do? Well, Jack

Parker worked for the federal government. Most recently, he had been an astronaut. And, in an age when most astronauts can walk the streets of this or any country unrecognized and in complete anonymity, Jack Parker was different. He was different for one simple reason:

Jack Parker had saved the world.

CHAPTER 1

2021

IN 1998, an asteroid the size of Texas was on a collision course with Earth. NASA director Billy Bob Thornton explained the danger of the massive space rock's impact this way, "Damage? Total. It's what we call a global killer. The end of mankind." Fortunately, Bruce Willis and his band of misfits nuked the asteroid just in time and saved the planet.

Although the movie *Armageddon* was universally panned by critics, audiences loved it. *Armageddon* earned over half a billion dollars at the box office. Hardly a week goes by that the film doesn't run somewhere on cable. It's one of those movies that, if a person stumbles onto it while flipping channels, the channel surfing usually stops. A few minutes of *Armageddon* tend to stretch into hours. Viewers can't seem to escape the intrigue.

Scientifically speaking, *Armageddon* is so fantastically unrealistic it is laughable. Nevertheless, the movie's main premise was spot on. An asteroid's impact on planet Earth is not just a possibility, it is a certainty.

The asteroid belt located between Mars and Jupiter contains millions of pieces of our solar system's left-over cosmic ingredients. From the massive to the minuscule, almost all of these space rocks orbit the sun harmlessly and are of no consequence to life on earth. But over billions of years, some are jostled by outliers and galactical passersby. The collisions of those rocks with Earth are mostly harmless. Mostly.

In April of 2018, a private nonprofit for planetary science named the B612 Foundation released a global warning that there was a 100 percent certainty that the earth would eventually experience a devastating asteroid impact. Of course, the group couldn't tell the world when or where exactly that collision would occur, so few paid much attention. But scientists did not ignore the threat completely.

Astrophysicists have been mapping and cataloging the orbits of asteroids since 1947. Naturally, the bigger the asteroid, the easier it is to find and track. But size is relative.

Arizona's Meteor Crater is perhaps the most famous impact crater on the planet. The circular scar on the Earth's surface looks as though it was formed by a giant ice cream scoop. The crater measures over 560 feet deep and is over three-quarters of a mile across. The surrounding rim rises 150 feet above the desert floor and can easily be seen from space. The asteroid that created that crater was traveling at an incredible eight miles per second but measured a mere fifty meters across. The blast associated with the meteor's impact was estimated to equal ten million tons of TNT, or six hundred times the energy of the nuclear bomb dropped on Hiroshima at the end of WW II. When the top of Mount St. Helens blew off in 1980, the generated force was equivalent to approximately one-fourth of the energy that created Meteor Crater.

In 2021, an amateur astronomer did what amateur astronomers often do, she *discovered* something. A young, brilliant college junior named Brody Falls was searching the west Texas sky when she located a space rock. Brody's interest in astronomy began with a field trip to McDonald Observatory when she was in the third grade. Years later, her skillset had advanced to the point where she was on a first-name basis with the folks at LINEAR (Lincoln Near-Earth Asteroid Research).

On a chilly February evening, Brody had been searching the night sky as she routinely did, looking for nothing in particular. With support from her parents, she had managed to set up a top-flight observatory in the desert. The twenty-year-old had arranged a cozy astro-lab, complete with a minifridge and space heater. Following a routine she had established in middle school, Brody pecked away on her laptop, which she kept fully charged and completely integrated with her telescope. The set-up provided access to high-res images of the night sky and, of course, high-speed internet for the necessary research.

Brody, munching on a protein bar and sipping hot tea as was her custom, took a moment to peek in on the International Space Station (ISS) and then focused her telescope on the craters of the moon, whose shadows near the terminator line (the line where day meets night) revealed fascinating depth and detail. Finally, Brody turned her attention toward the asteroid belt and lost herself in a hole, the kind of hole where an hour turns into three, then four. Evening became night. Brody's parents had learned long ago to ignore their daughter's late nights of stargazing. They accepted the fact that she was, as Brody often described herself, a *nightcrawler*.

After scribbling several lines of notes in her journal, Brody stared out at the dark Texas night, her brain bouncing around in thought. She had been credited with discovering seven numbered asteroids, but locating and mapping new, undiscovered "plane-toids" was getting more difficult. That did not stop her from looking at least once a week. Brody's search was driven by a touch of OCD, which served her passion well.

Finally, just as she was getting ready to call it a night, a faint hazy dot caught Brody's attention. She blinked and rubbed her eyes, then made a couple of adjustments to her telescope.

"What do we have here?" she muttered to herself.

Brody continued to manipulate the image on her laptop, refining the picture on her computer. The amateur astronomer's copper hair fell in curly ribbons around her shoulders. Slightly tangled, Brody pushed it out of the way, save one strand that traveled around her right cheek and into her mouth. Chewing nervously, she opened four more tabs on her browser and started checking various charts and maps. Then Brody checked them again. After another hour of online research and comparing photos in LINEAR's database, she was satisfied. She touched her telescope lightly, tapped her laptop three times, then repeated the ritual twice more. A long sigh escaped from her chest when Brody realized she had been holding her breath.

Smiling, the girl born with relentless drive and insatiable curiosity said aloud to nobody, "This looks like number 8, bitches."

Brody liked to cuss. She figured everyone else could just deal with it. In celebration, the amateur astronomer rewarded herself by pouring skim milk over a large bowl of Cinnamon Toast Crunch cereal. It was tradition and yet another private ritual Brody enjoyed just before she would gather up important data to send to her friends in the field. The cinnamon and sugar tingled her taste buds and settled her analytical mind. Once relaxed, Brody crafted an email with all the necessary attachments including detailed photos and charts. Verification was important.

The young West Texas prodigy had no idea that her discovery would set off a chain of events that, years later, would culminate in so many tributes. Hundreds of Brody Falls Avenues and Streets would be so named in cities around the world. Dozens of public schools would be built in her honor. The second most common baby name in the U.S. would include either her first or last name on a generation of birth certificates. Brody had no way of knowing how much that one night of stargazing would change the trajectory of her life, but it would, in the very best of ways.

Asteroid 2021CF02 would become the most famous asteroid ever seen from earth. Why? Because after Brody's data was emailed to LINEAR and their scientists cataloged the find and ran the numbers, the many calculations and recalculations determined that 2021CF02's trajectory was problematic. LINEAR sent their findings to NASA. NASA checked and rechecked the orbital math. NASA put in a frantic call to their private sector partner, ORBIX. Scientists from all three agencies used high-speed, supercomputers to run the numbers and dissect the data. Their conclusions were confirmed, and the collective reaction was universal. Utter disbelief.

Asteroid 2021CF02 was on a collision course with Earth. The impact would be cataclysmic. Most importantly, the world had only 179 days to stop that from happening.

CHAPTER 2

2029

"C'MON, GIRL. LET'S GO!" Jack tossed the words over his shoulder at Lily who was bundled up under a pile of blankets near the wood-burning furnace. The cold never seemed to bother her all that much; even still, she had spent several minutes perfecting a cozy tangle of blankets, pawing at them, moving and fluffing the material to her satisfaction. Her steely blue eyes gazed out at Jack from underneath the top layer of her makeshift den. The dog, in an uncharacteristic move, had decided to stay where she was. Normally, she followed Jack Parker's commands instantly and with enthusiasm. Today, however, was different. She didn't move.

Jack was headed to his shop to do some work. The former astronaut needed to get out of the house, and the twenty yards between his cabin and the shed served as a commute of sorts. Even though he wasn't going far, the systems of preparation involved in even the smallest projects gave Jack a sense of routine. Today, he was going to play with fire. Melting scrap metal was almost entertaining for him. Watching chunks of cold aluminum turn into a fiery, silver liquid was uniquely satisfying, almost fascinating. Smelting was the perfect project to take on during winter, as the furnace kept the workshop toasty warm. The aluminum bars he made, each weighing two kilograms, were shined and stamped with an Earth-shaped logo, along with "JP" in block letters underneath. It was a skill Jack had perfected with lots of practice. Dozens of brick-shaped ingots lay stacked in the far corner of the shed. Eventually, Jack thought, he'd find a purpose for them.

Most of the time, when Jack called Lily's name, she'd beat him through the threshold and into the mudroom before he'd fully opened the kitchen door. This time, however, Jack was standing on the mud room's linoleum floor reaching for his boots when he realized Lily was nowhere in sight. No sweet girl waiting on him by the back door. No excited tail sweeping the floor behind her.

"Lily, c'mon girl!" Jack hollered again as he finished tying the tops of his snowmobile boots. Jack waited and listened. All was quiet. Jack wrinkled his brow and waited for the familiar sound of Lily's paws pattering across the hardwood floors of the cabin or the slurps of her drinking from her water dish. Still not a sound.

"Lily?"

Jack traced his steps back through the kitchen door, his eyes immediately cast in the direction of Lily's bed. Lily had shaken the top blanket off her body and was attempting to stand up, but Jack could see at once that something was wrong. Lily's head and body tilted to her left side as she struggled to stand up. Attempting to right herself, she lost her balance and fell awkwardly. Lily's legs trembled unsteadily as she tried to stand, but she fell back heavily onto the cabin floor.

Jack rushed across the room.

"Lily, what's wrong, girl?" Jack cradled Lily's head in his hands and stroked her neck. Jack's heart pounded and his breath quickened. Lily was family, and for years, she had been his only companion. If not for Lily, Jack would never have a reason to speak, but he talked to her all the time. She always responded. Her replies were of the canine variety, of course: tail wags; a nose under his hand, guiding it back to her belly for more scratches; lots of kisses. Sometimes Lily would snuggle up next to Jack in the early evening as he read a book. It was her way of saying the day was over. No more work allowed, no more moving around. Lily always knew when Jack had done enough for the day. If it weren't for Lily, his world would be quite different.

Quiet.

Alone.

Jack looked at Lily. Her eyes were vacant and darted around as if watching an invisible tennis match.

"C'mon, sweetie. Let's go."

In one motion, Jack scooped up his dog and wrapped several blankets around her trembling body. As he left the cabin, he grabbed his winter gear from the mudroom and flung himself into the cold winter air. The subzero temperatures stung his hands and face as he made his way toward the snowmobile. Lily needed medical attention, and the nearest vet was twenty miles south. Jack strapped on his helmet, thrust his hands into a pair of mittens, and fired up the Polaris. The machine hit the snow and was flying down the path as he worked to situate Lily securely between his legs. A fresh plume of snow shot skyward behind his trail, carried off by a slight breeze and deposited on the already laden boughs of the birches and pines that populated the area.

"It's okay girl, just relax." Jack croaked as he held Lily close against him with one hand and steered the snowmobile with the other. It was no small feat, but the former astronaut had picked up the skills needed to navigate the snow of Northern Michigan after a few years of practice.

Astronauts, who were often former aviators, loved their toys. Many owned either a boat, a motorcycle, or a sports car of some kind. Several had Jeeps. It was in their DNA. Jack's snowmobile was less toy and more necessity.

Lily, now resting quietly on Jack's lap, seemed exhausted. Her breaths were short and heavy against Jack's body.

"Lily girl, you're such a good girl. You know that don't ya? You're a good girl."

Jack reached the highway, turned swiftly, and raced toward town on a path parallel to the road. Snow blasted out from behind him and dusted the morning sky white before it fell gently back to the ground. Jack whisked across the terrain and the miles between his property and the veterinarian's office shrank quickly.

"It's okay now, just rest. It's all gonna be okay," Jack whispered to Lily, but the words were intended to calm his own worries more than anything.

In his former life, Jack had been well-trained to remain cool under pressure, calm, and always collected. Pressure-filled situations were part of his job, and Jack's nerves were rock steady. He compartmentalized tasks, and no matter how dangerous or rigorous the situation, Jack handled them as if they were ordinary household chores. Loading the dishwasher was as systematic as debriefing higher-ups or memorizing a critical space procedure. Raking a yard full of fall leaves became as strategically efficient as time in a simulator. One flight surgeon referred to Jack as "Sundance," Robert Redford's cool under pressure gunfighter from the movie, *Butch Cassidy and the Sundance Kid*. Most people thought of Jack's calm demeanor as a gift. It wasn't. Over time, he had rewired his brain to think of the complicated as ordinary, the spectacular as commonplace.

Jack Parker was no longer an astronaut. His life was as far away from NASA and the government, both literally and figuratively, as it could be. Right now, he was just a guy worried about his dog.

In less than an hour, Jack had unexpectedly left the isolated world that protected him and emerged into a place where he rarely set foot any longer. He knew the area well enough, and there wasn't much to it. Small, rectangular houses and a smattering of businesses popped out of the mountains of snowdrifts as Jack made his way down the town's main road. He steered his snowmobile around the side of a light blue, two-story home with a wraparound porch. The sign to the right of the front steps read, "Copper Valley Veterinary Clinic."

Before the snowmobile had come to a complete stop, Jack was flying off the seat and carrying Lily across layers of packed snow and onto the salted stoop of the entrance. Lily nestled her nose in the crook of his arm as if seeking the safety and comfort of her human.

Jack twisted and pulled the clinic door open, then quickly snatched his goggles off his face and let them hang loosely around his neck. The office receptionist, startled by the stranger's sudden entrance, bounced up in her seat. Jack walked straight toward the young girl behind the front counter whose attention was now squarely focused on the man. Snowy icicles clung to the bottom of Jack's bushy beard and a hint of matted gray fur stuck out from a bundle of blankets in his arms. Jack gulped for a breath. His lips quivered underneath pleading eyes as he spoke.

"Something's wrong with my dog."

CHAPTER 3

1957/2021

ASTEROID-SIZED SECRETS ARE hard to keep. Information that travels through any government agency, such as NASA, is monitored by a deeply covert government program named Guardian. In the 1940s, as scientists in Los Alamos raced to beat Germany to the atomic bomb, government officials in the executive branch worried to no end that the Manhattan Project would fail and that New York or Washington D.C. would be destroyed by a nuclear weapon. Hiroshima and Nagasaki, two Japanese cities now historically paired most unimaginably, could have easily been any two American cities on the Eastern seaboard.

Roosevelt knew the importance of not only nuclear research but US intelligence associated with the threat of an atomic Germany. Any information that mentioned Hitler's nuclear obsession was gathered through streamlined channels, sent straight to the Oval Office, and delivered by Guardian. The Guardian program had been established by an unknown previous president and triggered only during events that could, in theory, end our democracy.

Threats at the highest level. Guardian had direct access to whomever occupied The White House, and the intel was disseminated very quietly and always strictly contained. Before long, the man in charge of the secret program became known simply as *"The Guardian."* The Guardian did not make appointments. He came when he deemed it necessary to brief Roosevelt, and later, President Truman.

By the end of WW II, when the Allies' path to victory became a certainty, The Guardian's briefings with the Commander in Chief became quite rare. Truman received one last briefing in 1947 after an alien spacecraft crashed in the New Mexico desert. The intergalactic visitors wanted their comrades' bodies and spacecraft returned. The Guardian brokered that exchange. Whatever deal the Guardian had made was satisfactory. It was also a well-kept secret.

More than a decade passed before The Guardian made his next visit to the Oval Office. On October 2nd, 1957, President Eisenhower received a visit from a man in a grey suit and hat. He was trim but muscular, and his starched white shirt was in stark contrast to a thin black tie garnished with a silver clasp. The Guardian had been escorted through the West Wing by the Secret Service. Several of the same agents that served the presidency during the war had recognized the man, looking remarkably unchanged even after so much time had passed. Newer agents, who had only heard of The Guardian's existence as rumor or speculation, flanked the mysterious visitor, stealing sideways glances of him as if they were in the presence of Marilyn Monroe. Nevertheless, after The Guardian entered The Oval, his visit to the White House was strictly top secret. No agent ever spoke of him. Ever. Not even in private.

"Mr. President."

The Guardian extended his arm as if to shake Eisenhower's hand, but in one quick motion rotated his forearm and hiked up his sleeve to reveal the raised and reddened scar of a brand. The mark, shaped like a cross inset in a knight's shield, met with the President's approval.

Eisenhower escorted the man into his private study off the Oval Office, where he motioned for The Guardian to have a seat on one of two thinly padded wooden chairs. The President, who had been verbally briefed by Truman about Guardian's existence before he left office, felt slightly apprehensive about the man's sudden appearance. As Eisenhower was well aware, The Guardian only brought the kind of news one never wanted to hear.

"What do you have for me, sir?" Eisenhower asked as he lowered himself to his seat, not wanting to waste a moment with unnecessary pleasantries.

"Mr. President, in two days the Russians will be launching an object into space on top of the most powerful rocket the world has ever assembled. The object will take orbit around the Earth, traveling across the United States, from one coast to the other, with unknown but quite probably a precursor to hostile intent. Although the Soviets have boasted about the upcoming launch, most in the scientific community doubt their ability to be successful."

The President did not hesitate, "Will they be?"

"Yes," Guardian said in a whisper, "Almost certainly, barring a catastrophic event. Their testing has been vetted and successful."

Eisenhower listened intently, his eyes studying the stranger's stoic demeanor. Guardian's salted black hair, pressed firmly against his scalp and held in place by a thin layer of lightly scented tonic, gave him the look of a Madison Avenue executive. His expression never changed.

Eisenhower responded, "Intelligence on the Soviets' space capabilities has been spotty. There has been speculation as to whether their launch rockets can function as ballistic missiles, or if they plan to develop low orbit satellites that can drop atomic bombs on any target they choose," the President paused, "Is either possible?"

"Mr. President, they do *not* have that capability. Yet. They are ahead of the game and the time has come for the United States to muster every resource it can to get to outer space, and even to the moon. In two days, when the American public sees a Russian machine fly in space, right over their heads, they will be alarmed. A massive population of scared people is unpredictable, as you are well aware, so you will need to address their concerns, calm the financial markets by touting our technological advancements, and ready Americans for a race to space that they can support with enthusiasm. The Soviets *are* moving toward intercontinental ballistic missiles and low orbital launches from space. That is their goal." The Guardian stopped and held Eisenhower's gaze. "Mr. President, if they get there before we do, I'll be back. There will be nothing to stop the Russians from global domination."

Eisenhower rose and nodded, "Understood."

After The Guardian had departed, President Eisenhower and his next two successors initiated a chain of events that changed the course of history. Technical advances by the Mercury, Gemini, and Apollo programs, plus the massive amount of money that fed into the space program, relegated the Soviet space efforts to a footnote in history. A communist government could not possibly compete with the drive and funding fueled by the free enterprise system. Today, unless you were alive to bear witness, there is little appreciation for the Soviet launch of Sputnik. That harmless, basketball-shaped beeping hunk of metal could have marked the beginning of Russian dominance and the unfettered spread of communism.

In 1962, The Guardian would visit the White House to meet with President Kennedy during the Cuban Missile Crisis. The man in the grey suit would never meet with President Johnson, but he did have three meetings with Nixon regarding a radical anti-government group planning to detonate bombs in Boston and New

York. President Jimmy Carter ignored The Guardian's warning on the instability of global oil production and resulting geopolitical destabilization in the Middle East. It would take Ronald Reagan and the United States of America years to recover and, in the end, the political climate in that part of the world turned against America in a way that would drive policy in the region for decades.

About the time disco was taking its last breath, The Guardian had finished preparing his successor, who was a near carbon copy of himself except that he was two generations younger. Now nearing seventy years old, the man in the grey suit was looking forward to his pension of untraceable gold bullion and a luxury villa in Malta, complete with an impressive library and sizable vegetable garden he could tend to at his leisure. The Guardian had aged well and planned to enjoy retirement.

The "new" man in the grey suit had hair to match his predecessor, but his broad shoulders reflected the swagger of a man twenty years younger. No matter, The Guardian had spent years training his successor, who was eager to meet the challenge of leading America's most secret government agency.

So, with no fanfare whatsoever, the Old Guardian shed his suit for a pair of faded Levi's and a Budweiser t-shirt and boarded a Lear jet to Malta. The New Guardian filtered every major threat to American democracy with quiet diligence, dedication, and determination to keep his country safe.

Twenty years would pass before the New Guardian would make his first visit to an American president. During an early summer meeting in 2001, The Guardian spoke about strange happenings at American flight schools and internet chatter regarding a coordinated terrorist plot. President Bush regarded the stranger in the grey suit with casual regard despite The Guardian's serious demeanor. Perhaps the societal shifts of the 80s and 90s, along with the prosperity and sense of invincibility that accompanied them, gave the President a false sense of security. Technology was exploding, but the Guardian Program was always ahead of the curve.

A cloudless morning in September marked the only failure in the program's history. To be fair, it wasn't as much The Guardian's fault as it was the embedded and systemic distrust that had formed between government agencies. After the events of 9/11, the man in the grey suit vowed such a devastating blow would never happen again.

The Guardian Program continued to expand in its secret, underground location. A small group of patriots, heavily vetted and dedicated to the cause, monitored every relevant piece of data that could hurt, or help protect the United States. Experts in corporate espionage, the technology used by Guardian was always better than that which existed outside the program.

The guardianship transferred authority to a new Guardian, only its third, in 2010. The outgoing Guardian retired to a penthouse suite atop the infamous Dakota Building, a prime location adjacent to New York's Central Park. The man in the gray suit had always wanted to see a Broadway show and the city's numerous museums held his fascination for years.

On a late February evening in 2021, still weeks away from the cherry blossoms spattering Washington DC with the welcome colors of spring, yet another but now seasoned Guardian was making an official visit to the West Wing. He sat across from the President of the United States on a lightly padded wooden chair in a private office adjacent to The Oval. The Guardian held the President's gaze. Square jawed, dimpled chin, and with jet-black hair parted neatly to one side, the man spoke firmly and without passion.

"Mr. President, we have an asteroid problem."

CHAPTER 4

2029

LILY'S DISTRESS had caused Jack to ignore the fact that he was entering a public building where he would most certainly encounter other people. Jack's focus on his dog had carried him through the front door and into an examination room. The glossy yellow walls surrounding him echoed with a buzz from the fluorescent lights on the ceiling, and slowly, Jack eased back into his reality. It's not that the astronaut was unnerved by *where* he was, it's just that he hadn't prepared to be there, or planned his trip out in advance.

Lily, now resting comfortably on a stainless-steel exam table, had been given a thorough examination by the vet, who was busy scribbling notes on a pad of paper held in place by an old wooden clipboard. The veterinarian, a petite woman in her early thirties, paused to push a pair of black-framed glasses up onto the bridge of her nose, then quickly rerouted a strand of curly black hair around her left ear.

Jack stared straight at the woman, who was finishing her notes and had now turned her attention toward him. Other than an occasional delivery to his property, it had been years since Jack had had a face-to-face conversation with another human being. Even then, those encounters usually consisted of no more than a couple of short replies or hand gestures.

"How old is Lily?"

"You know, I'm not exactly sure," Jack paused. "Um, she's a rescue dog. Got her in Houston about six years ago, and she wasn't a puppy then." Jack's throat felt dry and scratchy from lack of use. "She was young though, no more than a year or two." Jack gently stroked Lily's fur as his attention ping-ponged from the vet to his dog and back to the woman holding a clipboard.

The veterinarian noticed Jack's uneasy manner. He was unsettled, but she dismissed it as concern for his pet, which was normal. The stranger, still bundled in his heavy winter gear, had sweat beading down his temples, and he appeared oblivious to the sixty-degree difference in temperature between the exam room and the Michigan winter outside.

"Um sir, I'm sorry, what's your name?"

"I'm," Jack hesitated. "My name is Jack."

"Jack, I'm Dr. English, but you can call me Emily, okay?"

"Yes, of course, it's nice to meet you."

"Jack, why don't you sit down for a minute so we can talk about Lily. Maybe take off your coat and get comfortable, okay?"

Jack peeled off a couple of layers of clothing and laid them on the exam table next to Lily. He pulled his beanie down on his forehead a tad, hoping that it, along with his scraggly facial hair, would help maintain his anonymity. Without breaking contact with Lily, he pulled a nearby wooden chair close to him with his foot, and then sat down.

"What's wrong with Lily?"

"It looks like Lily's had a stroke," Dr. English said in a sympathetic but reassuring tone. "That's why she's having trouble keeping her balance. It's also why her eye movements seem abnormal. But, I want to run a few tests to rule out any underlying conditions and give her a liter or two of intravenous fluids. That way, we can help her maintain oxygen and nutrient levels in her brain and flush any waste products from that area. Does that sound okay to you?"

Jack responded almost before the vet had finished speaking, "Yes, whatever you need to do. Absolutely." The astronaut, whose right hand had never broken contact with his dog, tensed with worry at the news. "Will she be okay?"

"Well, I can't be certain, but normally around seventy-five percent of dogs who've suffered a stroke are back to normal in a week or two. Lily is in remarkable shape so that ups the odds considerably. Jack, dogs can live years after they've had a stroke and have a happy, healthy life."

Jack flinched slightly at the sound of his name, but at least he was getting what seemed like good news from Dr. English. His hand left Lily's body and he covered his face and sighed. The tension left Jack's shoulders and rolled down his body, and he finally let himself relax.

Lily would need to stay overnight so that Dr. English could keep an eye on her, which wouldn't be a problem since the upstairs of the building served as her living quarters. It made for an easy commute. Dr. Emily English carried Lily out of the exam to start treatment as Jack slid his chair back against the wall. He stood still in the center of the room, the yellow walls failing to brighten his mood, but the encouraging news about Lily's recovery chances had provided extraordinary relief.

Pacing around the room, Jack studied Dr. English's framed credentials hanging on one wall of the exam room. Undergraduate work at Northern Michigan University. Doctor of Veterinary Medicine at Michigan State. Displayed on the wall across from her diplomas was a collage of pictures showing the smiling faces of people posing with their pets, along with various community citations thanking the good doctor for the clinic's support. Youth hockey league. Garden club. Community theater.

Several minutes passed before Dr. English returned to the exam room to give Jack an update. She smiled broadly as she entered, which Jack took as a good sign.

"Lily is doing well. She's already perking up a little and I've got her snuggled up nicely in one of the recovery crates." Dr. English looked at the man in front of her curiously. "Jack...you said your name was Jack, right?"

"Yes, that's right."

"Are you visiting or passing through? I'm only asking because, well, I don't know you, and around here at least, everybody knows everybody."

"I have a little place north of here, but I pretty much keep to myself. I don't get out much...by choice."

Emily English studied the man. There was something familiar about him, about his eyes, his mannerisms. She didn't want to be rude, but strangers didn't just appear on the Keweenaw Peninsula out of nowhere, especially during the winter months. Regardless, she couldn't quite place him.

"Interesting. Okay, well, if you want to check out at the front desk and leave your phone number, I can call you later this evening with an update on Lily. I don't see why you wouldn't be able to pick her up tomorrow and take her home. Sound okay?"

"I'm staying here with Lily," Jack answered matter of factly.

"Sir..." Dr. English began but was cut off.

"Look, I'm sorry, but I'm not leaving my dog."

Dr. English sighed but saw that Jack was resolved. "I understand you're worried, but trust me, I can't see any reason Lily won't make a full recovery. And besides..."

"Dr. English...Emily?"

"Yes?"

Jack stood frozen briefly in silent debate, his brain cloudy with uncertainty. Suddenly, a thought came to him.

"Is there such a thing as doctor-patient confidentiality, you know, for veterinarians? Like, you can't talk about your animal patients *or* their owners to anyone else? Is that a thing?" Jack asked.

"That's correct. It's all privileged information."

"And what we say here today won't leave this room? Nothing about me? Nothing about Lily?"

Dr. English looked slightly confused. What was going on with this guy, she wondered? "Sure. Of course, nothing leaves this office." The veterinarian looked at Jack amusedly. What was the big deal, she wondered. What was happening?

"Emily, look at me closely."

"Listen, sir, I don't have time..."

"Please," Jack interrupted as he pulled off his beanie, his long hair falling around his neck. "Take away this silly beard. Add a proper haircut. Maybe flesh out some color on my cheeks as well."

Emily studied the man. She leaned in closer, furrowing her forehead slightly.

"I've been up north for years now, and there just isn't enough sunshine here to give me much color these days." Jack stood still, then turned. Posing.

Emily English continued studying the stranger, either out of curiosity or irritation, she wasn't sure. She looked over the man calling himself "Jack" and rearranged his face in her mind. She leaned in even closer. Closer. Jack turned from one profile to the other, then he looked straight at her and stood still. Gears turned in the veterinarian's mind, light switches flipped, and bulbs brightened. A small knot twisted in Emily's stomach as she began fitting the pieces of the human puzzle in front of her together.

"Jack. As in...*Jack Parker?*"

"That's correct."

"Well, I'll be damned."

CHAPTER 5

2021

THINGS MOVED QUICKLY after The Guardian left the White House. Phone calls were made, nondescript government jets took flight, and twelve hours later a meeting was beginning in one of an unknown number of underground bunkers deep beneath the West Wing. Richly padded leather chairs, each adorned with a finely embossed presidential seal on their back, sat in place around a mahogany conference table. The table, void of the usual White House fare of bottled water and keepsake pens, was situated in the middle of a room about the size of a typical suburban garage. Walls of light grain wood paneling surrounded a group of people shuffling around on forest green, low pile carpeting as they each settled into one of six empty chairs.

The President's seat had no special designation but, since the table was oval, he had a favored position as he started to speak. The Guardian, who had pulled his chair away from the group and positioned it near the door, quietly took his seat. The man in the gray suit looked as he always did, except for a faint five o'clock shadow.

The group of people, although well aware of the reason for the meeting, felt uneasy by being hundreds of feet underground, but the moment passed quickly. There were things to sort through. Important things.

Other than the President, and of course The Guardian, the group consisted of Robert Blane, NASA director; Philip Chernier, ORBIX CEO and chief scientist; and LINEAR director Andrea Clark. Those three had earned enough advanced scientific degrees between them to cover the walls of the room. Directly across from the President sat the Vice President, an African-American woman in her fifties. For now, she was an observer. The President had insisted she be in the loop, which wasn't customary, but he wasn't taking any chances. He could drop dead tomorrow and, if an unlikely health event rendered him unable to fulfill his duties during the months ahead, she would need to stand ready. The President knew he had to cover every contingency, and The Guardian had agreed. Still, the Vice President had no idea who the man in the grey suit was, nor how he had gained such important access to the Executive Branch.

The President began, "First things first. As all of you know, we are on the clock. Before we discuss the problem at hand, we need to strictly contain the intelligence circle. No one that doesn't already know about 2021CF02's orbit is permitted to learn about it without prior authorization. That would only occur if their help is required." The President stood to his full height and paused. He rubbed his chin and chose his words carefully. "Anyone with whom you've communicated, either by phone, text, or email, anything that leaves an electronic trail, we know about it. Don't ask how, but if you've so much as chatted with your mother through *Words with Friends* or suggested she travel to Antarctica, that communication has already been intercepted and flagged. Luckily, that isn't the case here, but you get my meaning. That said, there is no way to monitor private face-to-face conversations which might have occurred in the last 36 hours. Each one of you knows what's at stake here. If one person outside our net starts talking, well, let's just say last year's run on toilet paper would be the least of our worries. We'd have a complete breakdown of our society."

Eyes nervously shifted around the table. The people in the room were patriots, but they were also human beings. No one had said anything to anyone outside of their respective circles, but the president wasn't taking any chances.

"Is there anyone in your loop that may have been overlooked? I want to confirm containment on this," the President looked directly at Andrea Clark. "Andrea, your team at the Lincoln Center had the first heads-up on this asteroid. Who knows what over there?"

Andrea Clark spoke without hesitation. "There are four people total connected to LINEAR, two orbital mathematicians, you know about them, and me of course. We're tight in house." Ms. Clark paused, "And then there's Brody Falls, of course, although she doesn't know the orbit is problematic. There is no way she could."

"Let's swing back to her in a minute," the President replied. "NASA?"

"Just me and my director of operations, we ran the computer program ourselves, checked each other's calculations. We were triple-checking the data when a team in black suits escorted us out of the building and onto a plane to come here. I can't see any breach of intel by way of NASA." Director Blake added without amusement, "Unless, of course, you're not counting the people looking over our shoulders."

The President smiled but said nothing, then turned his attention toward Dr. Chernier. He had saved ORBIX for last. As a private company, all information, data, and development were regarded as trade secrets, safe within company walls to be sure. The problem was that usually information inside the company spread casually and without any fanfare. ORBIX's collaborative concept meant every employee was vested in the company's future...there *were* no secrets. The President hoped, at least in this instance, that only a small number of ORBIX employees needed to know about a killer asteroid.

"Philip, what kind of containment can I hope for with this, outside of the usual electronic channels? Tell me ORBIX wasn't brainstorming orbit shifting ideas around the Friday morning doughnut table? Did you all practice trust falls on your bean bag chairs while sipping your lattes?" The President was noticeably irritated.

"Mr. President, electronically, as you know, there are eighteen higher management and engineering personnel that know of 2021CF02's trajectory." Chernier swallowed. Sweat beaded on his forehead. It wasn't his place to control data or information inside the company. LINEAR sent them the data and they ran the numbers; that's it. Yes, in hindsight he should have contained the intel about the asteroid's problematic orbit. But in his defense, he never really thought the good citizens of Earth were in any danger. It was a billion to one shot.

"Go on," urged the President.

"Seven family units, our top-level brass. Every single one of them tried to intervene and shelter their families in some way, but they also didn't explain the details of the situation, I can assure you. There would be no point in scaring loved ones. But several people decided to take 'vacations' to Australia."

"Australia?" asked the President.

Robert Blane interjected, "The asteroid will most certainly hit somewhere in the northern hemisphere, but we aren't sure of the exact location, hence the vacations to Australia." Chernier nodded.

The President sighed, "I was hoping for one break to fall our way and that was a big one. Jesus Christ." There was a measured pause, and the President took his seat. "It doesn't change our efforts as a nation. We are the only country positioned to try to avert this catastrophe, and that's what we're going to do." The Guardian and the President exchanged glances and he continued.

"All of you in this room; every ORBIX employee and any of those direct family members we just mentioned; any gifted engineer, mathematician, or physicist that you think can help us and contribute to our mission, is moving to Kennedy Space Center. We will contain the science and intel there, and we are planning for a camp of sorts within the gates of the center. We are either going to eliminate 2021CF02's threat or toast it as it comes crashing down on our heads."

Andrea Clark started to ask a question, but the President held up a hand and stopped her before she said two words. "Consider this our way to both quarantine information and to create a centralized command center. We are in this together and if for some reason you think otherwise, you are grossly mistaken."

The President took a handkerchief from the breast pocket of his suit jacket and wiped his mouth. The notion to tighten the circle of people that knew about a potential doomsday event was the correct response. It was step one of an exceptionally long to-do list, one that had thousands of potential mistakes waiting at every turn. The funny thing about saving the world is that, if you failed, there wouldn't be any critics left to annoy you. The President smiled at the irony.

"Any thoughts?" the President asked.

The room was silent for a moment. Collectively, the minds in the room had already been working on the problem for nearly two days. They all had plenty to say and, suddenly and in unison, those thoughts filled the room in a salvo of ideas, theoretical hypotheses, and still unknown variables.

POTUS held up both hands and nodded vigorously, "Okay, okay. Save it for Kennedy. Your response is...encouraging. Everything we have, every resource, will be at your disposal. It will be waiting on you when you get there."

Andrea Clark raised her hand and waited for the President to acknowledge her.

"Andrea?"

"Mr. President, about Brody Falls?"

"Yes. So, will Brody Falls be able to figure all this out on her own? Is she a containment threat?"

Ms. Clark responded without hesitation, "There is no doubt in my mind that she will continue to observe the asteroid out of sheer curiosity. It's hers, she found it, and she'll keep peeking in on it. But she doesn't have the computing skill to put anything together just yet. However, I wouldn't underestimate her. She's relentless."

"Alright then," the President said, "she comes with us. And her family. We are ready with cover stories for all the civilians so there aren't folks thinking they all just suddenly went missing."

The Guardian, who had watched the meeting play out with great focus, stood up and nodded at the President.

"Before we leave, there is something you need to know." The President waited for the group to set their eyes on him. It was a habit he had formed during lengthy cabinet meetings with the Joint Chiefs, and he wanted for their full attention. "There are things at play that I may, or may not, be able to share with you all. If it's important to the mission, you will know. Otherwise, you're going to have to trust me. That will be hard at times, so I'm telling you now. We have the same goals here. Every resource at my disposal will be available to this team."

The President then nodded at The Guardian.

The man in the gray suit, still standing near the door, cleared his throat, which startled the group since, up to this point, he

JACK PARKER SAVES THE WORLD

hadn't made a sound. His voice carried a confident weight as he spoke. "Mr. Chernier, will you please make arrangements to get Pegasus I and II to Houston. Under the cover of night of course."

Philip Chernier was stunned. "How do you know about Pegasus?"

CHAPTER 6

2029

JACK SPENT the rest of the morning and afternoon sitting next to Lily's crate. His heavy winter coat and inner lining padded the floor where Jack sat leaning against a paneled wall. A wooden chair sat nearby but unused, even though Lily spent most of the day sleeping. The sweet little girl was exhausted, and the meds did their part in keeping her comfortable. Earlier, Dr. English had given Lily fluids and medication intravenously, but right now, there was nothing Jack could do but wait.

The afternoon came and went, and the dinner hour approached. The girl at the front desk left early. The forecast called for heavy snow and, at any rate, it was a slow day. Northern Michigan was dog country, and the veterinarian's light day included nothing unusual. A Labrador retriever puppy had chewed up and eaten a piece of plastic, which the good doctor extracted by using an endoscope. An old German shepherd needed a couple of decayed teeth extracted, an easy enough fix. Another dog had gotten into and eaten…something, and now had an unpleasant case of diarrhea. And then, there was Jack Parker and his dog.

Emily had enough to do to keep herself busy, but Jack Parker sitting on the floor next to his dog had the vet stealing glances in his direction whenever she could. The former astronaut was a household name, think George Washington mixed with a little Jesus Christ. And even though as a rational human being she knew Jack Parker was just a man, the combination of his fame and his DB Cooper-like disappearance had fascinated the world, and her as well. Yet here he was, right here, in her office. The urge to phone her parents came and went, usurped by pity. Yes, that was the right word. She felt sorry for Jack Parker.

Astronaut Jack Parker had fascinated the world since he returned from space eight years ago. After his successful mission to redirect *the* asteroid, Jack's life had become unbearable. Initially, the world had gotten to know the man by way of magazine covers and late-night talk show appearances. But poor Jack had no idea that his fifteen minutes of fame would continue...forever. Paparazzi had followed him incessantly. Dozens of unauthorized biographies, most including sources Jack had never met, sold out in stores and online by the tens of millions. A college roommate, one old girl-friend, and dozens of minor acquaintances waxed on and on about Jack, dissecting details from his life that were trivial, embellished, or outright fabrications. No one knew the real Jack Parker.

An internet story convinced certain people, as crazy as it sounds, that God had sent Jack Parker to save the world. The JP Church of the Second Son had become the fastest-growing church in America, with devoted followers around the globe. Online services raked in millions in donations every week, and church leaders soon drove Ferraris and roamed massive estates in South Florida. As silly as it all sounded, Jack Parker had united a desperate populace looking for answers to questions they never knew existed.

Six years earlier, Jack had left public life, reportedly for good. At the time, the President had issued a press release, again thanking Jack for his service, and announcing that Mr. Parker would be retiring from public life to a place where he could live simply and in peace away from the spotlight. The President then respectively added, almost begged really, for the press to leave Jack alone so he could live the life he wanted and, thanks to his efforts, had earned. And that was that.

Emily stood in front of Jack, her mind separating the myth from the man that had fallen asleep on the floor next to his dog. Most people considered Jack a good-looking man, but that man had been replaced by a bearded castaway in a flannel shirt. Jack's long brown hair fell around his face, hiding the features that made him so recognizable. As he slept, Emily heard his soft, gentle breathing, which seemed louder in the stillness of the recovery room. Lily, sitting in her crate like a good girl, watched her master with curiosity and concern. Their roles had been reversed.

"Hi sweetie, how ya' doing?" Emily asked as she bent down to open Lily's crate. Jack woke at the sound of Emily's voice and righted himself. As soon as the door opened, Lily stepped out of the crate and began licking Jack's face, something he ordinarily resisted, her tail wagging excitedly.

Beaming, Jack greeted Lily, "Look at you, pretty girl!" Jack stroked the sides of his dog's face as Lily stepped onto Jack's lap. "You gave me a scare, little girl. I was worried about you." Jack let Lily clean his face a little more. He laughed softly and scratched her neck. "Look at you!"

Emily smiled and laughed, "This is great, Mr. Parker. Really." Emily paused, then added, "I'm not surprised, but she'll need to take it easy for a while. No heavy lifting."

Lily filled Jack's lap as he continued to throw his full attention all over her, scratching and rubbing her fur.

"Let's step out back and see if we can get her to pee," Dr. English suggested.

Slowly, and with a little urging, the pair got Lily to follow them out the back door of the clinic and into a fenced area adjacent to the back of the building. Large snowflakes filled the air and had begun stacking themselves on the world below. The light of day fell below the horizon and the early darkness of winter covered the world beyond the porch light. Lily squatted and turned a patch of snow bright yellow, then immediately retraced her steps toward the warmth of the clinic.

"Good girl," praised the astronaut and veterinarian in unison. The two exchanged friendly smiles and closed the door behind them. Lily was unsteady but walking on her own.

"Doc, I can't thank you enough. I'm so relieved that Lily is okay."

"She needs a little time like I said, but I don't see anything that would prevent her from a full recovery. Before long, you'll probably never know that she'd had a stroke." Emily was encouraging, "Dogs are resilient, but we need to keep an eye on her the next few days."

"Okay, for sure. I'll watch her every second."

"Listen, Mr. Parker. Lily really needs to stay the night. She's doing very well, but I always like to err on the side of caution with these types of things."

"I understand," Jack agreed, nodding his head but saying nothing more.

"Why don't you go home, and I can call you in the morning. You can take Lily home then, I'm almost certain."

Emily English looked at Jack, who seemed to be turning something around in his head, thinking, crafting his next sentence. Jack, for his part, stood searching for a way to continue the conversation. As limited as the exchange had been with Dr. English, it was Jack's first in-person conversation of length in years. She had reminded him how important facial expressions and body language were in simple communication.

"Dr. English…"

"Please, you can call me Emily. No one in this town calls me Dr. English."

"Emily," Jack looked at his watch. "This will sound awkward, but I'm a little out of practice dealing with people so please forgive me."

"Sure," said Emily.

"Um, do you have anything to eat? I'm sorry. I haven't eaten anything since yesterday and in all the excitement it's just now hitting me." Jack looked at the floor, then at Emily.

"Well, I have food upstairs, I guess, but…"

Jack interrupted, "Oh, I'm not asking you to cook me dinner. Oh god, no. Geez, that came out wrong."

"That's good because I sort of hate cooking." Emily laughed nervously. "I barely cook well enough to keep myself alive. But I do have the basic food type ingredients needed for cooking, I'm just not a fan of putting them all together correctly," Emily stated unapologetically.

Emily, surprised by Jack's demeanor, giggled. The cool and collected guy she had once seen on television was quite different in person. Right now, at least, he was almost stammering. Jack ran his hand through his hair, pushing it over the top of his head and around his ears. He pulled his beanie from his back pocket and held it with both hands. His eyes seemed a little sad despite Lily's improvement.

Jack wasn't a tall man, slightly over average height around six feet even, but he towered over Emily who was just a hair over five feet. She'd removed her glasses and put them in the breast pocket of her lab coat. Jack had barely noticed earlier but was now fully aware that Emily English looked quite adorable. She was book smart nerdy beautiful, perfect in Jack's opinion, and he couldn't stop staring. Her big brown eyes waited for him to respond.

"Is that a pocket protector?"

"No, it's an eyeglasses protector in my pocket"

Jack thought, "I guess there is a distinction."

"Most certainly."

Emily, amused, continued, "You were saying?"

Jack was silent for a moment. He wanted to spend more time with Emily English for two reasons. First, he was truly enjoying the conversation. And second, Emily English, Jack happened to notice again, was really quite adorable.

"I'm an excellent cook," Jack said with a certain grin his face had long forgotten about.

CHAPTER 7

2021

KENNEDY SPACE CENTER is the most storied and state-of-the-art space flight facility mankind has ever constructed. In the 1960s, NASA's Project Mercury introduced seven space travelers to the world. Alan Shepard became the first American to touch the heavens, and John Glenn, who orbited the Earth on a metal stallion, became an American hero. From then on, generations of children could say they wanted to grow up to be doctors, firefighters, ballplayers, and even...*astronauts*. Aboard Faith 7, the last Mercury mission, Gordon Cooper circled the Earth twenty-two times and spent over thirty-four hours in space. He was the last person to fly in space alone.

Project Gemini successfully launched ten pairs of astronauts into space. When Ed White left the safety of his capsule and danced in space with Earth's majestic blue marble as his backdrop, the citizens of the world were held breathless.

In 1969, Neil Armstrong humbly took a "giant leap for mankind" when he descended a ladder outside of a strange-looking lunar lander named Eagle, leaving man's first footprint on the moon's ancient, dusty surface. A little over three years later, Gene Cernan would leave behind mankind's last. Between them, ten other men of character and courage would earn the title of "moon-walker," forming the most exclusive explorer fraternity the world had ever known.

Later, when the fickle people of Earth grew tired of command modules pushed through the sky atop massive rocket ships, NASA ushered in a new era of living and working in space via airplane-like shuttles and orbiting space stations. After twenty years, the program produced 133 successful missions, along with two horrific national tragedies. By turning the magnificent into the routine, NASA was rewarded with shrinking budgets and a segment of the populace that believed some of mankind's most historic accomplishments had been faked.

But exploration continued. As private-sector space ventures grew, and probes gathered information from comets, asteroids, and other planets in the solar system, the fortunes that traveled silently around our Sun proved too enticing to ignore. Whoever could successfully find a way to mine the rare earth minerals of asteroids could, without question, become the world's first trillionaire.

Money is an excellent motivator, and the United States' future as a superpower, as well as the position of its global economy, would be cemented for generations if the government could partner in such a venture. De Beers had created a diamond monopoly that lasted for over a century. The United States wanted to find a way to monopolize the supply of platinum, osmium, ruthenium, rhodium, and other rare earth elements (REEs). To do that, a mining operation would need to travel to an asteroid. A better option would be to find a way to somehow move an asteroid from deep space into orbit around Earth. Mining an asteroid there would be far easier than running an operation from beyond Mars.

Asteroid redirection, at least in theory, had been argued and discussed among scientists and physicists for years. Today, in a portable building much like those outside of an elementary school, a dozen scientists were speaking all at once.

"One at a time, goddammit! Listen, as brilliant as all of you may be, and you are no doubt, a few of you have awful people skills. So, here's what we're going to do!" an exasperated Robert Blane raised his hands in the air and put one hand across the other as if he were calling time out. His neatly cropped grey hair fell just above his collar. A pale yellow, short-sleeved dress shirt and brown tie was Blane's homage to the NASA of the 1960s. It was, unofficially anyway, the uniform of mission control personnel back in the day. Blane paused and took a breath.

"No more yelling. Put a sock in it because it's not helpful."

All eyes were on Blane. He was running point, because, well, Kennedy Space Center was *his* turf. Not only that, but all the funding for the mission was coming from the US government. ORBIX was represented by Chernier, of course, and three of its most brilliant engineers, all MIT graduates. Blane had his team of four, not counting himself. Rounding out the field was Andrea Clark and an orbital engineer from LINEAR. Last was the unnamed man in a gray suit, sitting by the door taking notes.

Blane went on, "Nuclear options?"

The room collectively shook their heads, "No."

"What are the obstacles?"

A portly NASA engineer with flaming red hair raised his hand. Blane nodded in his direction.

"There are many," the engineer started, but paused to collect his thoughts. "I assume you're talking about putting a thermonuclear device on top of a rocket packing tons of highly explosive fuel. That's a risk, of course, but even still, assuming launch was successful, there are other, larger issues."

Blane waved his hand, "Launch is not my concern."

Chernier spoke up. "First, it's the physics. Mass equals force times acceleration. You have a tremendous mass moving at an incredible speed. Think of the asteroid as a moving locomotive pulling a hundred cars. Anything you put in front of that mass would be demolished. Stopping a moving asteroid like that would be no different than shooting a bullet at a locomotive. Assuming, of course, that you had aimed the nuke perfectly and didn't miss it altogether. Your best bet would be nudging it off course, not destroying it, but moving it out of Earth's path."

An ORBIX physicist interjected, "If you guided a nuke to the asteroid from Earth, there would be no margin for error, zero. And any course correction would be delayed slightly while the information is transmitted through space to the vehicle carrying the explosive. Wouldn't be much though. Bottom line, you *can't* miss. Even if you hit the asteroid directly, the nuke might not detonate. We have never detonated a nuclear device in space; in fact, it's against international law. Not that anyone would care by that point."

The man in the gray suit stood up and cleared his throat. Necks swiveled in his direction. "Believe it or not, some would care." The Guardian waited a moment, smoothed the wrinkles from his jacket, then continued. He had the room's complete attention.

"Depends on where this thing hits. All of you have a singular focus on trying to move this asteroid, that's all good; that's what you're paid to do. But the geopolitical ramifications surrounding this event are not something any of you have considered...at all. That's what *I* do."

The Guardian held the gaze of each person in the room for a moment, then continued. "China and Russia would love to see this asteroid hit the United States. The event would collapse our economy and break supply chains. Our inability to grow food and feed our populace would create massive famine. No one can predicate how long those dire effects would last. The resulting climate shift could be, well, permanent. I'm talking about lawlessness and desperation. And let me remind you, there are more guns in this country than there are people.

"Some Americans have prepared for this kind of thing, almost hoping for an apocalypse of sorts. Rouge militias would move to protect small towns all over the country. Larger cities would be in chaos. Local law enforcement and the armed forces would be overwhelmed. Make no mistake, life would be anarchy. Not to mention, of course, the tens of millions that would die from impact-related events alone, perhaps more. Massive firestorms. Earthquakes and tsunamis. Billions of tons of pulverized impact debris would be forced into the stratosphere only to rain down on all of us.

"Our country would be weakened dramatically, a shaky-kneed boxer waiting for a knock-out blow. Computer hackers could ruin what was left of our energy grid and water supply. Reliable communication would be lost. It would all be over, let me assure you."

The people in the room sat slack-jawed in their seats.

The Guardian drove the point home. "Make no mistake. If this asteroid hits land within our borders, or even close to us, or just off the Pacific or Atlantic coasts, the United States could be reduced to a third-world country. And then, of course, there are the secondary effects of such a blast. Bridges and dams are gone. Nuclear power plants compromised." The Guardian snapped his fingers. "All gone. And there would be no one who could or would be willing to help us."

The room fell completely silent as the scientists absorbed what had just been said. Of course, they had considered most of the aftereffects already, but hearing them aloud was a sobering reminder.

Chernier, the only person in the room who understood the private sector and free enterprise, spoke up. "He's right. Neither the government nor the private sector could handle the problems created by such an event. ORBIX, like most all companies, would be finished. The only thing of value after such a cataclysmic event would be clean water and the food you could grow in your garden."

Andrea Clark, who hadn't said much during the meeting, wanted to get back on topic. "What is the rendezvous time frame here?"

Blane checked a computer printout and took a breath. "We are at 174.5 days. Our intercept needs to be done as quickly as possible. The faster we can get to the asteroid and start a redirect, the better shot we have at a successful orbital change. The closer the asteroid gets to Earth, the harder it is to redirect enough to make a difference."

Blane grabbed a pencil from the table and held it up parallel to the floor. "Think of us as having to redirect a bullet traveling to a target at six feet versus six hundred feet." Blane pivoted the pencil in his hand. "At six hundred feet you don't have to move the rifle much to miss your target. At six feet, the rifle needs to be moved considerably more to miss what you're targeting. The faster we start a new orbital path, the more time we have to keep nudging the asteroid away from Earth." Blane tossed the pencil back on the table and looked to refocus the group.

An ORBIX physicist raised her hand slightly, and Blane nodded at her.

"Let's assume all collision avoidance strategies are out, what are we left with here? I mean, reasonably speaking, there are only a handful of other options."

"Let's go through some," Blane said. "Gravity Tractor?"

A gravity tractor was an artificial mass set in orbit around an asteroid to slowly move the asteroid's trajectory using gravitational forces.

LINEAR's mathematician beat the others to the punch. "Not enough time, the tractor could take years, maybe decades, to make any difference in an asteroid the size we're dealing with here." Several others nodded in agreement.

"Agreed," Blane answered. "Solar arrays? Can we use focused solar energy to heat the asteroid's surface enough to create thrust?" Blane knew the theory behind this idea was solid but had some logistical issues.

The NASA engineer with the red hair spoke quickly, "The issue is hardware. Physically setting up the mirrors and adjusting them would probably take months. You're talking about setting up a workstation on the asteroid, which we could do, but again, time is the limiting factor here. By the time the solar arrays would be operational, the asteroid would have traveled past terminal, so to speak, the point of no return."

"I'm afraid you're right. So that, more or less, leaves us with propulsion," Blane added. "A conventional rocket engine fastened to the asteroid would need fuel—fuel that would have too much mass to transport," Blane said rubbing his chin. Of course, he knew this already, but he wanted to hear someone else in the room suggest the idea he had already marked in his head as the prime solution.

Chernier cleared his throat and spoke quietly, as if he were thinking out loud, "We could attach an ion thruster. Well, we'd need more than one, but if we attach a series of ion thruster engines to the rock, it would move a little and that's all we need. Current generation ion thrusters are nuclear powered of course, but that's far different from a bomb."

Early versions of ion thrusters used solar power gathered from rather large collectors unfurled in space. The acceleration they provided was small and took weeks to build. Nuclear-powered ion engines, on the other hand, were much more powerful and provided greater acceleration.

Blane looked at Andrea Clark, "What's the rotation period?"

"The asteroid spins once every seventeen hours. Not too fast. Of course, the thrusters would have to be positioned near one of the asteroid's poles; otherwise, the thrusters would be working against themselves as they rotated with the asteroid."

Chernier and Blane nodded in agreement.

The group collectively flipped through sheets of data until each scientist was looking at a computer-mapped, three-dimensional illustration of the asteroid. Hubble had provided multiple views of the spinning space rock. "Butch"-no one was calling it that-looked like a huge potato. It measured just over 490 meters across and roughly 400 meters top to bottom. It was smooth, as far as asteroids go, except for billions of years of galactic battle scars across its surface. In a way, it was beautiful...almost peaceful as it moved through the solar system.

But the benign-looking space rock was anything but peaceful. It was a silent, unexpected killer, not unlike a sniper's bullet. An undetected aneurysm. A sudden heart attack.

If this particular asteroid hit the United States, it would explode with the force equal to nearly all of the world's current nuclear arsenal. But all at the same time. And all at the same place.

"Ion thrusters," Blane said. "ORBIX, how many operational thrusters do you have?"

CHAPTER 8

2029

OLIVE OIL, salt, and pepper. Jack had learned long ago that those three ingredients went a long way. With a small clove of garlic, two leftover chicken breasts, and a couple of other miscellaneous ingredients from Emily's cupboard, Jack was putting the finishing touches on two large plates of chicken over roasted garlic and parmesan spaghetti. After a brief kitchen orientation, Emily had excused herself to the back of the house to wash the day from her body. She returned wearing a bright red sweater over a white t-shirt and a pair of Levi's that hung loosely on her hips.

"Smells delicious," Emily said as she took a seat on the other side of the kitchen island and faced Jack. He was carefully placing an array of roasted tomatoes around two mounds of spaghetti.

"Almost ready," Jack said. His tongue stuck out the side of his mouth as he cajoled each tomato into the perfect position.

Emily smiled at Jack. The notion that this man was standing in her kitchen cooking her dinner was simply ridiculous. Jack Parker's face, although a little tough to see under his beard, had been photographed like no other in history, adorning thousands of newspapers and magazines. If an internet site needed to generate traffic, all it needed to do was post some sort of clickbait featuring Jack Parker. Bronze statues stood in front of hundreds of buildings across the country. Murals commemorating his feat decorated the sides of countless more. Yet here he stood. To Emily's credit, she wasn't entirely overwhelmed. Sure, she was intrigued by the man, who wouldn't be? But Emily English had one thing going for her that most any other person meeting Jack Parker did not. She had had the opportunity to see him as an ordinary guy, a man worried about his dog.

As a vet, Emily's benchmark for judging a person's character had always been the way they treated their pets. Was the animal simply a piece of property, something to own? Or was that animal part of the family? By this measure, Jack had passed without question. Any guy that cared about his dog the way Jack Parker cared about Lily was bound to be decent.

Still, the man himself was a mystery. Apparently, he lived almost unnoticed, somewhere quite close, which was quite odd. Questions ricocheted around in her head. Emily was curious, but she wasn't nosy. At any rate, dinner was ready and the wonderful aroma that filled her kitchen made her realize just how hungry she was.

Jack placed a plate in front of Emily, "Dig in. Hope you like it. Nothing fancy, but I do guarantee this will be better than noodles and Ragu."

Emily took off her glasses and set them down beside her; she never wore her glasses while she ate. She leaned into her plate slightly and spooned a second bite into her mouth before the first one had cleared.

"Umm," Emily moaned. "This is delicious."

Jack laughed. The vet's curly hair hung off the sides of her head, nearly dangling into her food.

"I'm sorry. No one ever cooks for me, and I'm not much of a cook myself so..."

Jack smiled and cut her off, "Don't apologize. It's fine. Really."

There was an awkward silence between the two as they ate. Jack, still out of practice when it came to conversation, looked around the room. The kitchen adjoined a good-sized living room with built-in shelves full of books on one side and a television hanging above a red brick fireplace on the other. A stereo and turntable sat on a blonde credenza in the corner. The doors underneath were opened slightly, revealing a collection of vinyl record albums neatly arranged on their sides.

"So, what kind of music do you listen to," Jack asked as he nodded in the direction of the hi-fi.

"Eighties music mostly: Madonna, The Psychedelic Furs, INXS, The Police. There is a little of everything over there. It's all my mom's old stuff, plus a few odds and ends," Emily answered.

"That's good stuff. I know those bands," Jack lied. He knew extraordinarily little about popular music, much less about bands that were in vogue over forty years ago. Sure, he'd heard of Madonna, she toured occasionally and still drew a crowd. But the others, not so much.

Emily grinned at Jack and put down her fork, "Really? Somehow you don't strike me as the type."

"Oh, yeah. I'm a big music person. Huge fan of all kinds of music. Massive fan. Big concert-goer, too," Jack said as he talked and ate at the same time.

Emily laughed, "Can you even name one Madonna song?"

"Yes, of course I can," Jack answered.

She waited. A few seconds passed. "Well...name one then," Emily said with a giggle.

"*Lucky Star*," Jack replied without hesitation. He continued to chew his food.

"Okay, name another."

"It's the only one I know. NASA has it on a playlist somewhere. It's a thing they do. CAPCOM pipes in music to the astronauts, usually to wake them up or whatever."

"Well done, anyway," replied Emily. "CAPCOM?"

"Capsule communication."

"Oh," Emily said. "Well, what kind of music are you into?"

Jack hesitated, "I'm not really a music guy."

"You never listen to music?" Emily asked incredulously in between bites of her dinner.

"I mean, not exactly. I was always so busy with work I never took the time. Of course, just moving about life you hear music. Television, radio, elevators. But never by design. I like music... don't worry. I'm not a monster or anything. I just don't know much about it."

"Do you miss your job?" Emily asked without thinking she shouldn't.

Jack finished swallowing a bite of spaghetti, "No, I don't miss it." He paused, thinking, "What I did for NASA wasn't exactly a job I planned on doing for twenty or thirty years. Space doesn't work that way. Especially for me." Jack paused and took another bite of chicken. "Do you know how many trips to space Neil Armstrong made?"

Emily thought, "I'm not sure. Two or three?"

"That's right, two. The most famous astronaut of all time flew to space only twice. Amazing, isn't it? Astronauts have short careers." Jack wiped his mouth and pushed his plate slightly away.

"Second most famous," Emily said.

"Pardon me?"

"Neil Armstrong is the second most famous astronaut of all time. No offense to Neil, mind you, but every school kid knows *your* name. Ask a high school senior who the first man to step foot on the moon was and you'd likely hear Lance Armstrong at least as much as Neil."

Jack shifted in his seat nervously. Emily continued, "But hey, I bet Neil knew more Madonna songs than you, so there's that."

Jack laughed, "You think?"

"No doubt. I know for a fact that Neil Armstrong's favorite song was *Vogue*. And, I have it on good authority that he would walk around the house 'Vogue-ing,' much to Mrs. Armstrong's chagrin."

"I don't know what that means."

"Google it."

"I'll do that," Jack assured her. "So, Emily, if I may, what brings you to these parts of Michigan? Are you from here?"

"Born and raised. College over in Marquette, veterinarian school at State. My dad started the practice and it's all I ever wanted to do. This kind of work gets in your blood."

"Are your folks still around?"

"Yes. They winter in south Texas, though. I guess at a certain age you've seen enough snow for a lifetime. And then, in the summer, of course, they come back and stay at their lake house. It's the perfect life for them."

Jack nodded as if he understood completely. "You never had a notion to leave, see what else is out there?"

"I leave all the time. I love to travel. New York. Paris. Egypt. Japan. Believe me, I get away, but you know, I'm always glad to come back." Emily reached over and grabbed her glasses. After cleaning them with the corner of her shirt, she pushed them back up on her nose and sighed. "This place isn't for everyone though, that's true enough."

"Where's one place you'd like to visit, but haven't gotten the chance?" Jack asked as he stood up and put his empty plate in the sink.

Emily thought for a second, "Bora Bora looks amazing. But I don't think I'll ever go."

"Why not?"

"It's just too far." Emily paused, "It would probably take two or three days just to get there, then two or three days to get back. Hardly seems worth it, I guess."

"Are you a beach person, then?"

"Not really. I mean, Michigan has amazing freshwater beaches. Gorgeous. I'll hit three or four every summer. So, I guess because I go to beaches on the Great Lakes, I've never felt the urge to make a special trip to one." Emily added, "But…if I ever do, I think it would have to be Bora Bora. You ever been?"

"I have," Jack answered. "Can I grab your plate? You look like you're finished. I'll clean up."

"No, no. Please, I'll do it. You cooked, for heaven's sake. Wait, what? You've been to Bora Bora?" Emily asked in surprise.

"Tell you what, you wash, I'll dry. And I'll tell you about Bora Bora."

For the next half hour, Jack and Emily stood hip to hip at the sink, their hands dancing in and around lemony scented suds and red and white plaid dish towels. Bora Bora was indeed a magical place, and Jack took his time to paint Emily as vivid a picture as he could.

Jack described the luscious green slopes of Mount Otemanu and Mount Pahia and the Valley of the Kings which lie between them. He talked of ancient kings who rest under the cascading canopies of the banyan trees, trees that are so majestic, one can't help but reach out and touch their bark, connecting, wishing the trees could reveal their secrets.

"But it's the beaches, the colors of the water that seem so impossible." Jack tried his best to explain what he meant. He dried his hands and turned to face Emily. "Imagine, if you can, an island as beautiful as I've just described, then give it a stunning necklace of pearl white beaches and turquoise water so vivid it hurts to look at them. That's what's amazing about Bora Bora. There's a barrier island around the main island, surrounding the mountains like jewelry."

Jack used his fingers and made circular motions around a closed fist. "On one side of the barrier island is a sapphire blue ocean; on the other lies a topaz lagoon filled with fish. But not ordinary fish, a rainbow of tropical fish like you'd see in an aquarium, except it's real life and you're there swimming around inside, knowing you don't belong. And honestly...you don't."

Emily smiled and stood in front of Jack. Close. She failed to catch his mahogany brown eyes as they pivoted back to dishes, now clean, dry, and stacked on the counter.

"Sounds beautiful."

"It is. The only drawback is all the tourists. But what can you do, right?"

Once the kitchen was clean, the two went downstairs to check on Lily one last time. She was sleeping soundly in her crate, snoring little doggy snores and dreaming of chasing snowshoe hares. Jack had put on his winter gear for the trip home, but only after a few more assurances from Emily that Lily would be fine, but needed to stay the night.

"I need your phone number. I'll touch base with you around noon tomorrow. I'm sure everything will be alright." Emily added as she grabbed a pen and business card from the front reception desk.

Jack took the pen and wrote down his number for Emily.

"Is this your cell or a landline?"

"Neither. It's a satellite phone," Jack answered.

"Of course it is. Why wouldn't it be?" Emily cracked.

Jack started toward the door but stopped and turned slightly back toward Emily. He sighed, then said after a moment, "Thank you. Thanks for everything. Today was, well, it ended way better than it started." Then he smiled and added, "And that's only because of you. See you tomorrow."

With that, Jack Parker walked out of Emily English's veterinary office and into the blackness of a snowy winter night.

Back upstairs, Emily took a minute to start a fire in the fireplace and, once it was large enough to paint the room in an orange glow, she curled up in a worn leather chair to read a book. After she had read the same page three times, Emily gave up and laughed aloud.

"Jack freakin' Parker just made me spaghetti."

CHAPTER 9

2021

THE GUARDIAN MET with the President, in person, to brief him on the progress made at Kennedy. But things were moving quickly in Florida and, considering travel time, face-to-face briefings were going to be problematic. The man in the grey suit had set up a secure video communications line to pass along future mission-critical information to the President, the first such line in the program's history. It had been secured through four different encrypted algorithms and was only accessible through rotating passcodes, not unlike those used on nuclear submarines.

ORBIX had quickly delivered Pegasus I and II to Cape Canaveral on the backs of heavily modified Boeing 747s, the same planes that, a decade earlier, had ferried massive space shuttles from their landing sites back to the Shuttle Landing Facility in Florida.

The engineers from ORBIX proudly gave their counterparts at NASA a guided tour of the Pegasus spacecraft. Philip Chernier himself showed off the versatility of Pegasus and could barely contain his enthusiasm over the project. He was practically gloating.

It was not lost on Chernier that ORBIX had benefited greatly from the sum of knowledge of space travel that had been accumulated by NASA over the last sixty years. That knowledge had sometimes come at an incredible sacrifice. But NASA had a political arm to it, one that understood its whole existence was dependent on government funding. Occasionally, NASA was a victim of "t-twwadi," meaning "that's the way we've always done it." If it works, don't mess with it, even when things could be better. On three occasions, astronauts died before things changed. Painful as it was, NASA's inspiring legacy included a handful of dark shadows.

ORBIX had no such restraints since the private sector worked in a completely different manner. Rooted in Silicon Valley, ORBIX engineers intuitively looked for new ways to improve old systems. And so, they did.

Pegasus had been designed to fly faster under a new type of propulsion system. And, unlike its predecessor, it was multifunctional. The space shuttle program used orbiters over 120 feet long and contained massive payload bays, along with a crew compartment designed for up to seven people. Pegasus was sleek, built for speed, and to accomplish that, it had to have less mass. Pegasus was only forty feet from nose to tail. The flight deck on Pegasus held only two people, but technically, the spacecraft could easily be operated by just one pilot. The second seat was simply a design redundancy; two is always better than one.

Most importantly, part of the flight deck became a completely detachable abort capsule. After the Challenger and Columbia disasters, NASA toyed with various ejection module designs and abort capabilities, but with the shuttle's large crews, it was impractical. ORBIX engineered the bridge of the Pegasus craft to separate from the fuselage and, if necessary, carry the crew to safety. The ejection system could operate while the craft was in Earth's atmosphere or shallow orbit. Additionally, the capsule could land on land or water. Chernier and his engineers had spent years evaluating the ejection pod functionality on Pegasus. It was a point of pride that the team could, and would, protect their astronauts in a way NASA had not.

The versatility of the space crafts was a marvel of forward-thinking and design. Pegasus I and II each had identical flight decks and propulsion modules, but beyond that, the crafts' design featured interchangeable interiors. Pegasus's fuselage opened on massive hinges so that different, but completely compatible, mission objective interiors could be inserted into the spacecraft.

For example, if Pegasus needed to swap out crews working on the International Space Station, a transport interior could be fitted inside the fuselage. The spacecraft could also deliver supplies with its cargo interior. There were even hybrid interiors that had design components of different modules. Longer, crewed missions would include spacious crew quarters and workstations connected by a vertical ladder, all running parallel to the ship's propulsion system. By using the ship's thruster engines, the steady push of Pegasus as it traveled through space would give the astronauts onboard the first-ever sense of simulated gravity. With gravity, the effects of weightlessness on the human body would be irrelevant.

Pegasus's propulsion system was the same type of engine the team was planning to use to move the asteroid—ion thrusters. Thruster technology wasn't new, but it had improved over the years. A small nuclear reactor easily generated enough heat for the xenon gas propellant to turn into ionized plasma. The energized ions exited the thrusters, thereby creating the force needed to push the ship through space. The engines are incredibly efficient and xenon gas is inert, both key factors in space travel.

ORBIX and NASA each had a version of the thruster engine, and remarkably, they were nearly identical in design. Each Pegasus spacecraft could carry four ion thrusters in the cargo bays of a hybrid compartment. Crews at Kennedy were readying the twin ships for launch as fast as they could. Even so, the team would need ten days to prepare the Pegasus vehicles and the launch site. Ion thrusters only provided propulsion in space; conventional launch rockets would still be required for the ships to escape Earth's gravity.

Robert Blane hadn't slept more than three hours in a stretch for over a week. He was up to twelve cups of coffee a day and, along with everyone else, he pushed through mostly on adrenaline. Despite that, he appeared clean-shaven every morning and continued to sport his signature short-sleeved yellow dress shirt, along with a brown tie held firmly in place by a silver tie clasp.

The NASA director had kept things moving, but there were still crucial details to work through. Blane's core group of physicists and engineers had continued with morning and evening briefings in the same nondescript portable building where they had first met six days before. The Guardian took his regular position by the door. He continued to be a topic of speculation amongst the group. Only Blane and Chernier, by way of repeated video chats with the President, understood the importance of his presence.

"Navigation? We all set?" Blane directed his question to the room in general. Navigation had been a full-on team effort and Philip Chernier was ready to present the mission design.

Chernier referred to his notes and stood up. "Technically, navigation is our least complicated hurdle. We've got to get the Pegasus spacecrafts to intercept with the asteroid at least forty-seven days before impact; let's say fifty days so any margin of error is on our side. Fifty days of thrust against the asteroid will redirect its orbit enough to push it around Earth's gravitational pull. We're talking about a redirection of only a handful of centimeters an hour, but it adds up."

"Then I'm assuming trajectory isn't a problem?" Blane asked.

Chernier pushed a few buttons on his computer and an image

appeared on a screen to his left. "We start, of course, by using the Earth's gravity to gain acceleration of the Pegasus vehicles." A computer-animated video of Pegasus I and II started playing as Chernier talked. "Earth's gravitational pull is going to slow down Pegasus early on, so we will need to get another gravity assist from the moon. That will get us more acceleration and buy us time; all the while, mind you, the ion thrusters are operating at 1g."

All eyes in the room locked on the simulation as the Pegasus vehicles left the moon's orbit and entered deep space toward the asteroid.

"Can we increase thruster force?" asked Blane.

Chernier continued, "Yes, a little. We thrust to 1.15g at first. Increasing the g-force on the astronauts for extended periods could have adverse effects on their bodies. We can't risk that. But we can increase thrust to as high 1.25g and still be okay."

"Keep going," Blane said.

"At this point in the mission," Chernier pointed to the screen with a laser pointer, "we flip the Pegasus vehicles around. They have to slow down, otherwise, they'll fly right past the asteroid. Time-wise, it's an issue because it takes weeks to slow the vehicles down, then speed them up again to match the asteroid's acceleration, but there's nothing we can do about that."

"Understood."

"After we reverse the space crafts, we increase thrust to 1.25g, which gains us a little more time. Then Pegasus pulls up alongside the asteroid and lands smoothly on its northern axis." The computer simulation showed both Pegasus vehicles seamlessly connecting with an ominous-looking asteroid on the screen.

Blane paused and thought for a moment. "If flight path control heavily monitors and course corrects Pegasus during flight, we can avoid time-consuming course adjustments while in route, yes?"

Chernier nodded in agreement.

"Break down the timeline. I want us all on the same page," Blane directed.

Chernier was ready. "We have 169 days until impact. We launch on day 160. Moon gravitational assist will occur on day 158. Pegasus spin maneuver on day 119. Reacceleration and asteroid rendezvous on day 55. That gives us five days to attach and fire up to eight ion thrusters onto the asteroid's surface. Fifty days of thrust and we're good to go."

Blane knew Chernier presented the best-case scenario, but that was expected. "How do Pegasus I and II get home?"

Chernier smiled, "They just sit on the asteroid and ride it home. As the asteroid flies by Earth, they hop off and enter the Earth's atmosphere."

Blane took a deep breath. The easy part of the briefing was over. It was time to address the elephant, or rather, the herd of elephants, in the room. He adjusted his tie clip and stood resolutely. After rubbing his chin for a moment, he continued, "Mission design looks good. We didn't have too many options so there aren't any real surprises. If something goes wrong with the mission, the President is ready to launch nuclear warheads into space as a last resort."

No one flinched. The news was not a surprise.

"If we aren't successful, the latest computer models indicate the asteroid is likely to strike the northern hemisphere. It could be a continental landmass strike, or off our coasts. That variable didn't fall our way, nevertheless, our resolve doesn't waver."

The air left the room. Although any strike in the northern hemisphere would be catastrophic, a projected North American impact was a gut punch.

"Okay, mission crew. I'm going with single pilots for each Pegasus spacecraft," Blane said matter of factly.

Everyone started talking at once. ORBIX engineers shouted their objections and NASA mission specialists threw their hands up in disbelief. Blane, peppered with a dozen questions at once, didn't flinch. Robert Chernier sat in his chair stunned and ran his hand through his hair. Only LINEAR's Andrea Clark seemed to work out the logic in her head. She sat motionless, quietly nodding.

After thirty seconds or so of complete mayhem, The Guardian stood up. He didn't have time for what he knew amounted to petty grievances and differences of opinion. The man in the gray suit spoke in a tone that commanded the room, "Everyone needs to stop talking right now."

The room fell silent.

The Guardian and Blane exchanged a knowing glance.

Blane spoke, "This mission, and you all know it, has about a thousand things that could go wrong with it. Hell, it probably won't work, but we're going to try like hell anyway. But the mission is time-critical. A crew of two in a Pegasus vehicle adds mass. Co-pilots have mass. The EVA system has significant mass. Course correcting compressed air has mass. This mission is mass-driven. Less mass means faster travel."

The NASA director's words were sinking in. He was right, of course, but piloting a spacecraft alone seemed out of the question. It hadn't been done in sixty years.

"Pegasus II is Pegasus I's redundancy. Those two vehicles are all we have."

Chernier asked, "Who have you chosen to pilot the spacecrafts?"

"I'm going with the two people with the most time in the box. The two that have logged the most successful simulator time and have managed all we've been able to throw at them. At least so far."

The room collectively held its breath. Whoever Blane announced to the room would be charged with saving the world as we know it.

"Pegasus I will be commanded by Evelyn Davis."

Evelyn Davis was a total pro. A former test pilot, she was highly regarded at Edwards AFB, home of the USAF test pilot school. It certainly made sense that this type of mission would use a pilot with that kind of experience. She joined NASA ten years before and had been a valuable asset on half a dozen missions. She had been on loan to ORBIX for months, and her credentials were impeccable. She was especially known to be cool under pressure. No one would second guess Blane's decision to pick Evelyn Davis.

"Who'll pilot Pegasus II?" asked Andrea Clark.

"The pilot of Pegasus II is a man that has flown everything from an SR-71 Blackbird to a V-22 Osprey. He has been working the simulator for months."

"There's no way he's been in the box for months. I'd know him." Chernier said with emphasis. "The only Pegasus simulator in existence is the one I have in California." Chernier looked stunned. What was happening?

"Well, your design was appropriated. There is another simulator," Blane admitted.

"Who the hell has it?"

The Guardian stood and cleared his throat. He walked from his usual spot near the door to the front of the group. A room full of eyes followed his every step. He brushed the wrinkles from his white shirt and buttoned the top button of his gray suit jacket.

"I have it," The Guardian said. "I have it, and I'll be piloting Pegasus II on this mission."

Philip Chernier looked at the man in utter disbelief. He was equally shocked and livid, "Who the hell are you anyway?"

The Guardian answered, "Let me introduce myself. My name is Jack Parker."

CHAPTER 10

2029

EMILY ENGLISH SHRUGGED off the previous night's events and readied herself for the day ahead. Technically, it was a half-day. Saturday mornings flew by quickly and today was no different as she busily attended to as many patients as she could before noon. Typically, the animals she saw on Saturdays suffered from ailments that couldn't wait until Monday, and although this Saturday morning was steady, it was mostly routine.

Sadly, a black Labrador had reached the end of the road. Emily had been treating Hank since he was a puppy, but the poor dog had stopped eating and needed to be carried outside to use the bathroom. His face, once covered with shiny black fur, had turned white over the years; his eyes, bright and observant when he was younger, were now glazed with fog. Time seemed especially tough on pets. Putting a dog down was always miserable, and Emily's heart broke every time she had to do it. She cried along with Hank's owners, a middle-aged couple she'd known her entire life, and by the time they left, she was exhausted.

Emily took a moment to compose herself over a cup of coffee before she finished her morning. As she sat on a stool in the treatment area sipping from a Scooby-Doo mug, her receptionist handed her a message.

"He's called three times but won't give his name. Says he's a friend of yours."

"Right…thanks," Emily said.

She stared at the paper in her hand, then pushed her glasses up onto her nose and took a deep breath. Emily had meant to call Jack by ten, but it was now a little after eleven. She grabbed the receiver from an old, land-line phone on her desk and dialed. Jack answered on the first ring. Emily reported on Lily's condition, which was excellent she assured him. And after a little back and forth conversation, they decided that Emily would bring Lily to Jack after she closed the clinic around noon.

At first, Jack didn't want to be an imposition, more probably though, he didn't want Emily to know exactly where he lived. The vet wanted to get outside. Yesterday, the grey sky had layered close to six inches of snow on the area. Today, the cloudless, blue sky was so bright it hurt to look at it. After convincing Jack that he was doing her a favor by letting her bring Lily to him, he relented. She scribbled directions on a notepad and told Jack she'd be there in a couple of hours.

Jack looked at himself in the bathroom mirror and decided he should shower. After spending a good hour on basic scrubbing and hair management, Jack added a finishing touch. A dime-sized bead of oil helped soften his beard and kept his bushy hair at bay so it could fall back behind his ears. After a swipe of woodsy scented deodorant under each arm, Jack leaned over the sink and studied himself in the mirror. His hair was longer than it had ever been, falling a couple of inches short of his shoulders. He ran his hands back over his head repeatedly, training the locks to stay in place. The amount of black hair on his head still largely outnumbered the gray, which was fine by him. His beard was aging faster.

Although the former Guardian turned astronaut turned regular Joe wasn't particularly tall, right at six foot even, his shoulders were broad and muscular. He religiously completed hundreds of sit-ups, push-ups, and pullups every day. The workouts kept his upper body hard. In the winter, Jack looped miles around his property on cross-country skis. When the snow melted, he ran wind sprints up a sandy hill east of the cabin. As hard as Jack tried to *not* follow a daily routine, routine was not easy for him to shake. Jack wanted to push his body, so why not exercise regularly? The activity helped fill the day.

Jack dressed, then spent the next thirty minutes straightening his cabin, which was hard to do considering he kept the place perfectly clean and tidy. He spent five minutes examining a massive wall of books. The ex-Guardian read...a lot. In his former life, it was an occupational hazard, but one he enjoyed.

"Okay, nothing to straighten up here," he said to himself. His library was perfectly organized.

The morning dishes were drying next to the sink. He returned his fork, coffee mug, and a small plate to their designated spots. There was nothing else to do.

Jack looked around the room and laughed. He had never had a guest inside his cabin before, and he was genuinely nervous about it.

The cabin wasn't huge, yet it resembled something straight out of a magazine. The walls featured exposed timber that stretched upward and around a vaulted ceiling. Wooden beams crisscrossed the space above and angled down toward one corner of the living room, where they met and surrounded a large, stone fireplace. A panel of sliding glass windows spanned one side of the fireplace and let in an ocean of natural light. On the other side of the glass was a panoramic vista so picturesque, so perfect, it looked like a Christmas snow globe.

The rest of the room consisted of bookshelves, comfortable, hand-crafted leather furniture, and a small television set tucked away in one corner. That space also served as his reading nook, complete with a recliner and floor lamp, intended for one person... and a dog.

The great room had a spacious kitchen attached opposite the fireplace, complete with top-of-the-line coffee machines-there was more than one-and every modern kitchen appliance Jack might need, all of which operated via an off-the-grid electrical system. To the right of the kitchen was a separate mudroom and restroom, near a door leading outside.

Upstairs was a massive master suite, which included an attached lounge area and a second stone fireplace. The bathroom included a number of impressive amenities such as a redwood sauna, a cement shower area with four adjustable heads, a Jacuzzi tub, and even a urinal. The floor was heated from beneath. The water was always hot.

"Where are you?" Jack muttered to himself as he moved around the living room waiting for Emily's arrival.

Finally, a snowmobile came into view through the window, its engine growing louder as it neared the cabin. Through the mudroom window, Jack saw Emily round a curve in the drive and emerge from behind a wall of pines. The former Guardian opened the door and directed Emily to park her sled next to his. Lily, seeing Jack, flew off the snowmobile before it had come to a complete stop.

"Hey, girl! Oh my, look at you!" Jack knelt and rubbed the sides of Lily's head as she stood on her hind legs and licked Jack's face. Her colorful fur coursed over and around Jack's fingers. She seemed like her old self, just moving a bit slower, but no worse for wear. Jack was surprised by Lily's energy, but incredibly happy, to be sure.

"You are such a good girl, yes you are!" he repeated, then turned to Emily asked. "Find it alright?"

"Just like you said. It's funny how this place is situated. The turn off from the main road is kinda hidden in plain sight, not noticeable unless you're looking for it."

"And lucky for you, I remembered to turn off the secret cloaking device, or you never would have found the place."

"You're joking, right?"

"Yes. And no," Jack said with a wink.

Lily nudged Jack who took the hint and invited Emily inside. Already tired from their exciting reunion, the sweet girl went straight to her pile of blankets in the living room and scratched out a nest before Jack and Emily could finish taking off their coats and boots.

"Would you like some coffee?" Jack offered.

"Sounds great, thanks."

Emily sat across from Jack at a small kitchen table and sipped her salted caramel and vanilla latte. It was incredibly delicious. It was ridiculously delicious.

"Good lord this is good. Is this what you're into? Super coffee-type stuff?" Emily asked, her brow furrowed with genuine surprise.

"Sorta, yes...but I have a good reason."

"Oh, yeah? What's that?"

"Well," Jack started, "I used to only drink straight black coffee. That's it. I was too busy for fancy coffee. Coffee, for me anyway, was a means to an end, and usually, that end was me needing to stay awake. So, I was late to the party as far as fancy coffee goes. I'm making up for it now."

Emily smiled. The hot coffee gave her lips a rosy glow, contrasting her flawlessly fair complexion, neither of which escaped Jack's notice. "It's like you have your own little coffee shop in here," she remarked.

"I do, more or less. I experiment with all kinds of types of coffee. I grind the beans myself and brew it all up. To be honest, it gives me something to do, but it *does* taste good, so there's that." Jack smiled and took a sip from a plain white coffee mug.

Emily looked around. She'd been in her share of modern cabins in her life and this one was as amazing as any. Custom. Brilliant artisanship. Modern luxuries. Flat out gorgeous.

"Your place is amazing, by the way," Emily said as she turned her head back toward Jack. "How long have you lived here?"

"Want the nickel tour?"

Jack showed Emily around the cabin, which didn't take long. Still, Emily was constantly impressed by the intricate details and finish out. Upstairs, she stared in awe at Jack's bathroom.

"I can't believe you have a urinal."

"It's the only way to go."

"And that shower? That's not a cabin shower. No way." Emily shook her head in amazement.

"It is for me." Jack grinned.

Back downstairs, Emily held her mug as she stood and examined the hundreds of books tucked into the shelves before her, the spines announcing their contents. Most had titles involving science and history. Some were biographies, books on the lives of everybody from Albert Einstein to Johnny Carson. The entire bottom shelf, Emily noticed, contained nothing but maps.

"Another cup of coffee?" Jack asked.

"Yes, please," replied Emily.

The couple moved to a pair of leather chairs in the living room and continued their conversation. They talked easily with Jack taking a keen interest in her life, asking questions, listening to her stories. Jack laughed when Emily told him about how she failed her driving test by running over the proctor's foot. And he watched her eyes turn red when she talked about a marriage that ended when her now ex-husband packed a suitcase and left one day for reasons she would never know.

Emily and Jack weren't strangers, but they certainly weren't friends either, at least not yet. There was something cleansing about telling a story without being judged, and that seemed to be what was happening, so they kept at it. Eventually, Lily came over settled on the ottoman next to Emily's feet. Jack was slightly jealous.

"What about you?" Emily asked, "I feel like your life is already out there for the world to know. That's got to be weird, right?"

Jack smirked, "You believe all that stuff? The stuff about my life?"

"Well, maybe not all of it, but the basics, I suppose."

Jack's life as The Guardian was top secret, but his time as a NASA astronaut wasn't initially meant for consumption. The Guardian program had had to fabricate and disseminate a complete backstory on the soon-to-be-famous astronaut and then give it to the world. Jack's faux identity had been in the can for years as a failsafe, just in case an unforeseen event forced him to leave the agency early, before retirement age. It was standard operating procedure. After minor tweaks to the story, Jack became the only Guardian to assume his cover earlier than planned.

Jack looked at Emily. She *was* beautiful, but so what. She was kind and smart and…safe, but so what. Jack could lie to Emily and tell her anything he wanted to and she would believe him. That was tempting. So, Jack did something he had never done before: He told a civilian something personal about himself. At this point, it didn't matter.

"Yeah, well. None of that is true at all."

Emily looked puzzled, "What do you mean? How could that be exactly?"

Jack smiled, "Well, the world was told a story. They had no reason to doubt it, but it's not exactly the truth."

Emily took off her glasses and set them on the table. She cocked her head slightly and let out a little laugh. "You mean to tell me that all the books about you, all the television programs, even the movies...none of that is true? How could that be?" Emily was genuinely confused.

Jack replied, "How do I know the stuff you told me about your life is true? Your parents are in Texas. A marriage that fell apart. Even that the glasses you wear, they could be a prop. Maybe you look good in those frames and the glass is nonprescription? I choose to believe you because I have no reason to doubt you, right?" Jack picked up Emily's glasses and put them on, then made a face. "Wow. Okay, your prescription is real. I'll admit that." Jack handed her glasses back to Emily and smiled.

"So, what's the truth? I mean, I know it's not my business, but you brought it up and now I'm curious." Emily returned the glasses to her face. "Never mind, it's fine." Emily looked away embarrassed; she worried Jack might think she was being nosy.

"Honestly, I could tell you everything about me, every detail about my life. Seriously. I could because no one would believe you if you repeated it. And even if they did, there are so many crazy stories out there about me that the truth would get lost in the static." Jack leaned over and gave Lily more scratches. Her tail wagged immediately.

"Well, then. I am curious about one thing. How did you wind up in Michigan? Why here of all places?" Emily thought that was a fair question and Jack could answer it however he wanted.

"I had to live in a place where I could be anonymous. Plus, I love it here." Jack pointed out the window. "Look at it. It's amazing."

"Yes, true." Emily paused. "But the Upper Peninsula is an acquired taste for most people." Emily reached over and helped

Jack love on Lily, who rolled over slightly to give the pair better access to her belly.

Jack looked at Emily, then leaned in toward her slightly. "It's like this. I worked for an agency that helped keep the people of this country safe, like thousands of people do, but I did so in complete anonymity. It wasn't just a job; it was my life, totally consuming. After Pegasus landed, I couldn't do that job anymore, and I couldn't walk around like a regular person either. So, I picked this place." Jack waved a hand around, gesturing to his surroundings. "I have no regrets."

"What's with all the books?"

"I read. All the time. It was part of my old life. Information. Data. Facts, figures, and calculations."

Emily got up and walked over to one of the bookcases. She scanned the spines carefully. "I don't see one fiction book on these shelves. Not one. Who has a library without fiction books?"

"Honestly, I haven't read a fiction book since I was a kid."

Emily straightened and turned toward Jack, smiled then shook her head. "I'm leaving."

"You're leaving?" Jack asked, a little surprised, then he stood up to meet her eyes.

"I'm going home," Emily announced. "But I'll be back tomorrow with some books. Fun books," Emily laughed.

"Okay, well," Jack stammered. "If you're bringing books for me to read, bring your favorites. Stuff *you* like, not stuff people are supposed to like. Okay?" Jack waited for a response.

"Sure."

"And don't leave just yet. Stay for dinner. I have steaks marinating. And two huge baked potatoes. And some wine."

Emily thought about the pot pie in her freezer, "I suppose I could do that. If you insist."

CHAPTER 11

2021

SECURITY SURROUNDING the launch of the Pegasus vehicles had held, as least as far as the true nature of the mission was concerned. However, it is impossible to hide the effects of massive rocket engines pushing two spaceships out of the atmosphere and into the heavens above. Impressive plumes of smoke and steam trail behind the launch vehicle. Anyone watching the launch will feel it, too. At first, a light rumble cascades over the land, soon replaced by the sound of the solid rocket boosters (SRBs). Their percussive roar travels *through* objects, through a person's face and chest. In this way, anyone watching a launch can feel strangely connected to the astronauts sitting atop those rockets. Witnessing a launch is simply...magnificent.

NASA and ORBIX had issued a joint press release just two days before launch, an unprecedented time frame. In it, the secretly developed Pegasus vehicles were being introduced to the world by way of a test run to the international space station. Philip Chernier, like a proud father, put Pegasus specs and a detailed 3-D computer-animated tour of the vehicle on the company website. It trended on social media immediately.

There was a problem, however. The Pegasus mission would take months, not days or even weeks. The world would expect the vehicles to return and land at some point. Even NASA can't hide a vehicle such as Pegasus leaving Earth and failing to return. With few options, it was decided that NASA would deploy the recently developed CRV (Crew Return Vehicle), a dedicated lifeboat for the astronauts aboard the International Space Station, and land it under cover of night. That way, the world could certainly see the shower of reentry in the night sky, but the craft itself could be hidden from view. Since there were two Pegasus vehicles, the other one would "stay docked" to the ISS for extensive testing of the craft's capabilities.

IMPACT: T-MINUS 162 DAYS

Evelyn Davis and Jack Parker had one singular thing in common that made them a perfect fit for each other: they were obsessively focused on their work. Not just for this mission, the most important in the history of mankind, but their job. Their calling. Their purpose. Evie, as she was called by her inner circle, had never met anyone like Jack. Like her, he had the stamina to attend to every detail, to chase and capture perfection. Jack and Evie practically lived in the simulator, or "the box" as it was commonly called. Mission engineers threw everything they had at the pair, and when they didn't get it right, they stayed until they did.

Although Jack and Evie would each pilot separate crafts, they took turns riding shotgun in the simulator, watching and learning from each other's moves and reactions. Working with mission control is a flow of movement and conversation. Arms move. Buttons and switches are activated. Console lights flash and change color. There is a rhythm to it all that is not unlike a perfectly chore-ographed dance routine. When the computer gave an astronaut a "glitch" to work around, it was as if a dancer had stepped on their partner's toes, and it was important to see what adjustments would be made to put things right. Jack and Evie did all that was asked of them.

Training was fast and impossible. Both astronauts resisted the urge to push through to exhaustion because they knew that a sleep-deprived astronaut would be useless. Jack and Evie slept six hours a night and took breaks for necessities, but that was it. Beyond the time spent in the box, the pair stayed busy attending meetings with the mission design team, practicing for the deploy-ment of the ion thrusters, and learning about NASA's EVA system.

There were only two mission-critical objectives. First, the Pegasus vehicles had to intercept and successfully land on the asteroid. Second, the astronauts had to unpack multiple ion thrusters from the cargo bays and secure them to the surface of the asteroid. NASA and ORBIX would be responsible for getting Jack and Evie to the rock, but the rest was up to them. After intercept, they were on their own, with the exception, obviously, of each other.

Spacewalks, or EVAs, are a common component of space flight. Astronauts aboard the ISS have performed hundreds of EVAs, totaling a combined time in space of almost two months, most of which had been used to assemble and maintain the space station. On the bright side, no astronaut has ever died during an EVA. But no astronaut had walked on a solid heavenly body since the era of Aldrin and Armstrong. Evelyn Davis and Jack Parker were rehearsing for something that had never been done before: completing multiple tasks on a large asteroid in near-zero gravity.

Although the asteroid was large enough to do immense damage on Earth, it was tiny as far as heavenly bodies go. The asteroid itself would create no significant gravitational pull on the astronauts or the Pegasus crafts.

Davis and Parker spent hours dangling on lines and floating in the Neutral Buoyancy Laboratory, or NBL. There, they rehearsed the maneuvers needed to leave the Pegasus vehicle, attach themselves to the rock via a computer-controlled tether, and use Pegasus' robotic arm to remove each ion thruster. Once each thruster was released from the crane, Jack and Evie would attach it to the asteroid using six, pneumatic anchors that would drive titanium posts into the surface of the asteroid. Once anchored, they would make a few leveling adjustments and turn on the ionic engine. The engineering team decided to engage each thruster as it was deployed, starting with the outermost deployable engine and working back toward Pegasus. That way, the maximum amount of thrust against the asteroid would be achieved over time. The deployment sequence had been practiced over and over and over. Both Jack and Evie were proficient enough with the maneuver to feel confident, which was excellent considering its importance to the mission.

After another go-round in the tank, Evie and Jack sat in the cafeteria talking over a plate of grilled chicken and fresh fruit. They had a fourteen-minute break.

"You tired?" Evie asked.

"I'm not tired, are you tired?" Jack replied smiling.

"I think I'm running on adrenaline, but I'm afraid I may run out," Evie said while spearing bits of melon and strawberries with her fork.

"Well, I figure once we launch, we can both catch up on our sleep. It'll be weeks before we reach the asteroid with not a whole lot to do in between."

"Agreed," said Evie as she chewed. "Can I ask you a question, though?"

"Of course," Jack answered as he cut his chicken breast into bite-size pieces, therefore reducing the need to repeatedly pick up and put down his knife. Again, systems.

"What do you figure our chances are?"

Jack stopped cutting his chicken and put down his utensils. He grinned and looked at Evie, then took on a more serious tone. Her green eyes looked to hold his gaze. She didn't look vulnerable as much as she wanted to hear his honest opinion. He took a breath and was measured in his response. "Well, we're flying a relatively untested spacecraft farther into deep space than anyone in the history of space flight. We're intercepting and landing on an asteroid traveling at great speed and deploying multiple objects on its surface. Then we have to make it back safely to Earth, all along, hoping we don't face any mission-critical problems."

"Correct."

"I'd say our chances are 50/50. If we intercept and deploy without any glitches, 60/40, maybe 70/30."

Evie nodded but was quiet. Jack and Evie had spent hours together getting ready for the mission, but the simple fact remained, there was so little time to practice, to prepare. Most astronauts trained for months before they went into space. In comparison, this mission was like cramming the night before a big test. On the bright side, Evie and Jack had to repeat only one distinct operation several times over once they had attached their crafts to the asteroid. All they had to do was deploy the ion thrusters.

"One more question?" asked Evie.

"Shoot."

"How come I didn't know you a week ago?" This had been Evie's burning question. The one she wanted to ask since the moment she got paired up with Jack Parker for the mission. It made no sense that an astronaut she didn't know was selected for the most critical space mission in human history. Who was Jack Parker?

Jack had been waiting for this question. It was more than fair, and he was surprised it took this long for Evie to ask. "Are you dissatisfied with how it's gone so far?"

Evie answered quickly, "Not at all. Quite frankly, you're a machine. We mesh well together. But, that said, I should have met you years ago." Evie, not knowing what to say or do next, took another bite of fruit and stared at Jack.

"Does it matter?" Jack asked.

"Yes, it does. It does to me. It doesn't make sense."

Evelyn Davis was a career pilot. Military elite. Who was Jack Parker?

"Are you married?" Jack asked already knowing the answer. As Guardian, he had access to every detail of Evelyn's private life. Interestingly enough, she didn't have much of one. Like Jack, she was solely committed to her work. No family. No relationships. No hobbies. Nothing but complete focus on her career. Evie looked like an athlete, strong and fit. Her blonde hair was cropped short and spiked up a little on top. The assumption around NASA was that she was gay, not that it mattered. No one would have cared. It only struck people as odd that Evelyn Davis never talked about her private life, ever.

Evie stopped chewing and swallowed, "Why would you ask that? What does that have to do with anything?"

Jack tilted his head slightly, paused, and then spoke like he had rehearsed his answer, "Because you're like me. You are singularly driven for success in your field. People like us do not have families or get married or go to PTA meetings. Oh, maybe someday, when we've mounted enough accomplishments to think about other things, then perhaps we can try to make up for what we've pushed aside. I've done that. Just like you. My whole life has been about my job, just like you. The only difference is that I worked in the shadows where no one could see. You worked out in the open. My job was very much under the radar. My accomplishments were achieved in complete anonymity. That's why you've never heard of me."

"You don't have a family?"

"I have one sister that I haven't seen in a decade. My parents are long deceased. No wife. No girlfriend. No friends, just work associates. They're people I like and admire, but they are not my friends. Not really."

A corner of Evie's mouth curled up in recognition of what Jack had said. She understood completely. She took two more bites of food, nodded at Jack, and said, "We're two minutes late."

Jack grinned. "Did we just have a conversation, Evie?"

"Shut up, we have to go."

Jack stood up. "Aye aye, Captain."

IMPACT: T-MINUS 160.5 DAYS

The last thirty-six hours had been a frenzy of activity. The Pegasus vehicles had been mounted and stood on either side of a set of massive SRBs. Although the ships would use ion thruster technology in the vacuum of space, they needed massive amounts of solid rocket fuel to escape Earth's gravity.

Jack and Evie were as ready as humanly possible. They spent the last few hours of training rehearsing the thruster deployment over and over again. NASA and ORBIX checked and rechecked data and prepared the computer systems onboard the Pegasus vehicles. Overall, the team was cautiously optimistic. Robert Blane continued to perform a song and dance for the media, and Philip Chernier found time to give *Popular Mechanics* an interview expounding the greatness of Pegasus.

Jack had kept the President informed on the progress of the mission with daily briefings and, in their last video conference, the President had given Jack his best wishes and blessing. The Guardian turned astronaut almost felt sorry for the man. He could sense the hope, fear, and helplessness in the President's voice.

It was midnight. Jack was lying in his bed waiting for the next three hours to pass so he could get up and ready himself for launch. The launch process alone took hours. He wasn't nervous, but he was anxious to get going. Blane had insisted Jack and Evie unplug and relax prelaunch, so Jack lay staring at the ceiling in a nondescript bedroom in the crew quarters area, running through various procedures in his head. The room was dark, save for a small night light coming from the bathroom. Jack tried to shut down his mind, but that seemed impossible.

A light knock came at the door.

"Come in," Jack said.

The door opened slowly. It was Evie. He could tell by the outline of her body. She wore a black tank top and boy shorts.

"Are you asleep?"

"I'm just lying here. I can't sleep."

"Me neither." Evie paused. "Jack, can I ask you another question?"

"Sure."

"Have you thought about this mission turning south on us? You know, maybe not coming home," Evie stopped for a moment. "It's not out of the question."

"I have."

"Are you scared?"

"Yes, you'd be crazy not to be," Jack answered.

Evie moved closer to Jack, now propped up on his side, trying to focus on Evie's face in the dark. Evie was as strong a woman as Jack had ever met. But, like Jack, she was human. Humans have human thoughts. Jack and Evie, as robotic as they may have seemed to everyone else, were still people. People that had been given the impossible task of saving the world.

Jack lifted the corner of the blanket nearest Evie. She took off her tank top and crawled in beside him. When they were finished, the astronauts collapsed beside each other and fell asleep.

CHAPTER 12

2029

EMILY DID RETURN to Jack's cabin the next day, but only briefly. Lily practically danced when Emily walked through the door. She hopped up and down at Emily's feet and then rolled on her back so the good doctor could scratch her spotted belly. It was apparent that Jack's dog was far more social than her owner. He felt another tiny ping of jealousy.

Emily gave Jack a stack of books and made him promise to dip his toe into some fiction for a change. He agreed, then talked her into one, then two, cups of coffee. But Emily had told herself that she wouldn't get sucked into a lengthy visit. She had things to do, and it was Sunday, her only day off. The two exchanged awkward goodbyes and Emily headed back home.

The wind stung Emily's neck as she raced down the drive toward the main road from Jack's cabin. Jack kept the snow on the path tightly packed with daily runs up and down the roadway on his Polaris. Emily had gotten her snowmobile license when she was in seventh grade. Her dad's Ski-doo, which he'd essentially abandoned, had become one of her favorite toys and she used it as often as possible. Scenic trails stretched up and down the Keweenaw Peninsula, and she had seen the beauty of Lake Superior from every angle the region had to offer.

Emily pulled her jacket collar up around her neck and tucked it in under her helmet. What was she doing? As she headed south back to town, riding on the shoulder of the main road, she thought about Jack Parker. The whole thing seemed both surreal and completely natural. She liked talking to Jack; he listened to her. He was also sweet and thoughtful, but in a way that seemed effortless.

As she got closer to town, friendly waves from passing cars and trucks became more frequent. Although her snow gear and helmet hid Emily's identity, the familiar make, model, and color scheme of her sled gave her away. The lava red Expedition model was sleek but rugged, built for trails and comfort. A snowmobile served a variety of purposes in the upper peninsula, but for Emily, it was just plain fun to drive one. Emily returned the friendly waves as the buildings ahead of her got closer and more frequent.

Several hours later, Emily was nearing the end of her regular Sunday routine. She had made her usual grocery store run, had sorted through the week's stack of mail, and had begun working on the pile of laundry that lay heaped on the sofa in her bedroom. Her bedroom sofa was not for sitting, its sole purpose was to hold clean laundry. The actual washing and drying of laundry were easy; the machines did most of the work. However, folding and putting away laundry was another matter. Normally, Emily listened to true crime shows on *Investigation Discovery* or *A&E* as she did the housework, referring to those networks as "The Murder Channels." But today she hung clothes and folded sheets in silence, completely lost in her thoughts.

Emily felt lonely. Her loneliness was not the sad and melancholy kind though; it was the kind of loneliness people feel when everything is quiet, when the days are spectacular but there is no one around to share them. Emily knew plenty of people, but her friendships had changed over the years. Some faded away during the time she attended college and vet school. A few of her closest friends had gotten married and started families, which was always Emily's plan as well...until it wasn't. After her divorce, she felt expelled by her inner circle. It wasn't a conscious decision by her friends, at least Emily didn't think so, but a newly single friend, especially one as cute as Emily English, simply didn't fit in anymore. Smart and adorable can be very threatening. Girl's night out had slowly been replaced with "we have to get together soon" whenever she crossed paths with an old friend. Those false promises evolved into simple "hellos" and oversold smiles. Of course, if any of her friends had a dog that needed veterinary care, the overblown smiles and false promises of drinks or dinner were always mentioned but somehow never materialized.

Friendships are a funny thing. More often than not, friendships are built on convenience and proximity. If those two things change for some reason, friendships can die easily. Fair enough. But when you lose a friendship that had roots, one that survived good times and bad, one that connects people like family, it hurts. Pile that misery on top of the pain you feel when a husband kisses you good night one day and packs his bags the next, and it just doesn't seem fair.

Chores completed, Emily decided to trudge three blocks south and one block west to Sal's Pizzeria. Sal's served New York-style pizza and meatball subs that were incredibly delicious and completely out of place given the location in the Upper Peninsula. Emily ordered a meatball sub and a Miller High Life and grabbed a seat in a booth with her back to the front door, the only place left to sit. Like most every Sunday night, Sal's was a treat for Emily, one to be savored and not rushed.

Emily let out an audible moan when the flavor of tangy tomato sauce slathered over the homemade meatballs and melted provolone cheese hit her mouth. As was customary, Emily ate her sandwich with a fork, so she could strategically mix the combination of bread and cheese with the perfect amount of meatball. A large sip of cold beer washed down every other bite. She looked at the bottle of Miller in her hand and attempted to peel the label off the glass without tearing it. Slowly, gently, her thumb rolled the label down bit by bit until finally, she'd completely removed the paper from the bottle. Using the condensation from the cold bottle, she plastered the label onto the wooden table like a sticker and wiped away the excess water from the area. She smiled and rewarded herself with another bite of the sandwich.

"Hey Em, how ya doing?" The voice seemed to come out of nowhere. Emily looked up to see a woman holding a kid on one hip with another slightly older kid pulling at her free hand.

"Hey Flynn, I'm good. How ya been?"

Erin Flynn had been Emily's closest friend since fifth grade. Their teacher that year, Mrs. Potter, seated her students in alphabetical order, resulting in an instant friendship. Emily became "Em", and for some reason (the girls couldn't remember), Emily had always called Erin by her last name.

"Oh, you know. Chasing kids and keeping busy. Jimmy made the basketball team this year, so there are games to go to and my turn to run the concession stand is Tuesday. Big Jim is busy at the brewpub, as always. So busy. And then there are these two little ones," Flynn nodded to each side of her body.

Amy, the little girl Flynn held on her hip, was exploring her mother's ear. The older kid, a boy whose name Emily couldn't remember, buried his head in Flynn's jacket. "What are you up to these days?"

Nothing much. Jack Parker, remember him, he saved the world a few years back? Well, he brought his dog into the clinic one day, a super nice guy. Anyway, he's cooked me dinner a few times. His cabin, man, it looks like something out of a magazine. He secretly lives out here. Who knew? I sure didn't. He'll probably swing by this week and hang out some. That's about it.

"Em? You okay?"

"Yes, I'm sorry. Right. Um, same here. Super busy at work mostly. Mom and Dad are in Texas, of course. I'm guessing they'll be back end of May. Other than that, same ol' thing." Emily took a sip of her Miller and smiled at Flynn.

"We just have to get together! I know we always say that, but I mean it this time. The brewpub is always fun. They have trivia on Wednesdays and we're always looking for someone to play on our team. Interested?" asked Flynn.

"You know, that sounds like fun. What time on Wednesday? I can meet you there."

Flynn stammered a bit, "Oh well, this Wednesday we're full up. The maximum number of players on a team is six. But we almost always need someone to fill in. I can call you for sure."

Emily smiled, "That sounds great Flynn. Let me know."

Just then, Sal called Flynn's name from behind the counter. Her freshly baked pizza had saved her from more chatter.

"Oh, that's my order. I gotta go, but it was so good to see you, Em." Flynn flashed one more smile and turned to leave before Emily could even reply.

"Same, here," her voice trailed off.

It was a conversation the two had had a hundred times. Flynn wasn't being mean necessarily; the two ladies had just grown apart. It wasn't anyone's fault, but it still hurt Emily's feelings. Emily took her time and finished her sub. She even enjoyed one more High Life, then walked back home as the last bit of sunlight hit the western edge of the horizon.

Emily spent a few minutes downstairs readying the clinic for the coming week. She stocked supplies in the two exam rooms and reordered some meds online. After turning off the clinic lights, she walked upstairs and ran a hot bath.

Emily took off her clothes and stood naked in front of the bathroom mirror. She stared at herself, then turned slightly to the side and looked at her butt. "Not too shabby," she said out loud.

Emily lowered herself into the steaming water and closed her eyes. The warmth tingled her body, especially her feet, which were always freezing this time of year. She let out a sigh of contentment and sunk lower into the tub, the water slowly reaching her chin. Her black curly hair floated around her neck and shoulders.

It was quiet.

Then the phone rang.

Jack unloaded and packed away his latest drone delivery. There were more steaks and fresh vegetables, of course. This time, however, Jack had requested the government deliver a couple of dozen CDs along with a Bose Wave music system. The CDs were mostly 80s bands, the ones Emily had mentioned the day they met, as well as every Beatles and Rolling Stones studio album ever released in the States. If he was going to read fiction, Jack figured he might as well start listening to more music, too.

Theoretically, Jack should have loved music; his analytic brain could easily break down the science and math of its composition and structure. Jack's formative years had been littered with a strange mix of popular music. At the turn of the millennium, bands like NSYNC, The Baha Men, Aaron Carter, and Moby were chart-toppers. Jack had taken a hard pass and opted to spend his time reading biographies and watching documentaries covering a variety of topics, but mostly history.

Jack consumed printed material as few people could; it was his superpower. He had finished one of Emily's novels in a few hours and had begun reading another. But he had trouble concentrating on the second book because he was too distracted thinking about the first. It had been a fascinating read.

An early sunset had darkened the outside world. Jack and Lily stepped outside so she could potty, but Jack lingered a bit before heading back inside. It was biting cold, and Jack wasn't wearing a jacket. He tilted his head up toward the stars, so many stars, and thought about his time on Pegasus. Jack didn't dwell on the mission much these days-the past was the past. Things happened. So far, Emily hadn't asked him one question about Pegasus. Jack supposed it was because most everything about the mission was public knowledge. But even still, it was to her credit, at least by Jack's way of thinking.

Jack and Lily retreated to the warmth of the cabin, but Jack's thoughts stayed on Emily. She was sexy. She was sexy in a way that Jack thought all the more adorable because she had no idea that she was sexy. He also admitted to himself that, as knowledgeable as he was about so many things, he knew almost nothing about relationships. It seemed logical to Jack that since he enjoyed Emily's company, he would try to get to know her as a friend. Since he didn't have any friends at the moment, it seemed like a good place to start.

Naturally, Jack figured, people often call their friends on the phone to talk about things. He picked up his phone and dialed.

Emily's phone rang.

CHAPTER 13

2021

IMPACT: T-MINUS 160 DAYS

NAVY SEAHAWK HELICOPTERS circled the perimeter of the Kennedy Space Center. A breach anywhere near the launch grounds would certainly be met with deadly force without hesitation. Military snipers perched atop every conceivable vantage point, as well as security personnel armed with assault rifles, who stood post on high alert. Nothing was left to chance.

No formal in-person viewing of the launch was going to be allowed from the Kennedy grounds. There would be no way to plan and prepare for such an audience. Plus, it would take weeks to vet every person in attendance. There was nothing to stop people from watching the launch from their doorsteps, however. Even from a point miles away, massive rockets exploding through the atmosphere was a uniquely unforgettable experience.

Evie and Jack sat quietly on the bus as it rolled slowly out to the launch pad. After a minute or two, Evie broke the silence.

"Never seen this much security for a launch before. I guess this is for real, isn't it?"

Jack nodded, "I suppose Blane didn't want us to change our minds."

Evie didn't laugh at Jack's joke, but not because it wasn't funny. Her brain had moved on.

The driver slowed and rolled to a gentle stop. He opened the door, then turned his head and eyed Jack and Evie as they exited through the front door. "Good luck," he said without thinking, or of course, even knowing the true nature of their mission. Jack nodded in return.

The two astronauts were visually striking. ORBIX had outfitted the astronauts with the latest generation pressure suits for launch. The image of the white Pegasus vehicles embroidered on the mission patch was in stark contrast to the sapphire blue of the suit material. A US flag had been sewn on the left shoulder of each suit, and "Parker" and "Davis" were stitched in gold on a black patch on the right side of their chests. Both carried streamlined white space helmets with clear face shields.

The Pegasus vehicles looked magnificent. Sleek. Remarkable. Otherworldly. Because they were not as massive as previous shuttles had been, the twin crafts were being launched together, attached to opposite sides of the same solid rocket boosters, a first for NASA. The SRBs stretched vertically over twenty-six stories above the launch pad. Television cameras zoomed in on Pegasus I, then cut to Pegasus II. By design, the crafts were identical except for the color schemes. Pegasus I had a white body but featured black wings, tail, and canopy bay doors. The colors were reversed on Pegasus II. The heat shield underneath both spaceships was dark grey. With their angled wings, the crafts looked like manta rays that had slipped through the surface of the ocean, taking flight.

NASA distributed an official live video feed of the launch to the networks, and the original mission objectives were provided and parroted verbatim by various cable news talking heads. ORBIX and NASA continued to put on their happy facade, hiding the true nature of the mission. No one questioned it, and why would they? Americans had been flying in space for sixty years. A single episode of *American Idol* had more viewers than NASA's last ten rocket launches combined. Several local television networks had cameras covering the launch, from quite a distance of course, but none could make out the two figures that, unbeknownst to them, were preparing to ride rocket ships into deep space to prevent the largest scale disaster in the history of humankind.

Jack and Evie walked past several members of the launch team and rode up the launch elevator with four men in white suits. No one spoke. When the doors opened, Jack and Evie handed off their helmets to two of the men and exited the elevator. They stood on a metal platform that split in opposite directions toward each Pegasus vehicle. The men in the white suits waited patiently behind them. The liquid oxygen and hydrogen, both hundreds of degrees below zero, vibrated and strained against the walls of the tanks below them. The metal creaked under the intense cold and pressure. The sound caught Jack by surprise, and he looked over at Evie. She did not react.

The astronauts stopped and looked out over the Florida landscape, flat with the ocean looming off to one side along with a half dozen vacant launch pads sitting in a row parallel to the beach. Jack Parker and Evelyn Davis turned and faced each other.

Jack started to speak but stopped. The two locked eyes and Evie sighed. As did Jack. Everything Jack wanted to say, and Evie, too, for that matter, didn't need to be said aloud, so they simply nodded at each other. But then, Evie spoke.

"Okay, Jack, we got this," she said confidently, without breaking eye contact.

"Yes, we do Evie," Jack paused momentarily. "Yes, we do." Jack smiled and nodded up at the sky. "See you out there."

The two turned away from each other and marched toward their respective Pegasus vehicles. The procedure was the same for both astronauts. Jack and Evie each made their way to the space crafts by way of the orbiter access arm that connected the tower to the ships. Entrance to the Pegasus vehicles was in the rear through a narrow hatch on the underside of the crew quarters.

Jack maneuvered his way through the hatch and up to the flight deck. He carefully lowered himself into the pilot's seat. Once settled, a launch crew member strapped him in his chair and affixed his helmet to the flight suit. The two exchanged thumbs-ups, although truth be told, the launch straps were so tight Jack could barely breathe. He checked his oxygen level, then opened his coms.

"Coms check. This is Parker to Launch Control."

"Launch to Parker: We read you loud and clear, Jack."

"Davis to Launch: Coms check, come in."

"Roger that Commander. Communication check confirmed."

"Davis to Parker. Can you read me?"

"Affirmative. Loud and clear. Communication check is a go."

"This is Davis. Confirmed. Communications check complete."

Jack stared out of his port window. On his back, the horizon looked like a vertical stripe out in the distance. He slowed his breath and got ready to wait. It would be an hour before things would get interesting.

Evie could see only blue outside her window, blue sky meeting with the blueish gray shades of the ocean. She cleared her mind and worked through the mission details in her head. Experienced in space flight, she knew a clean launch was the most critical part of the mission. Like Jack, she waited for Launch Control to go through their protocols and safety checks. For Evie, this was the only time when her excitement was mixed with any amount of fear.

An astronaut without a trace of fear is someone who should never fly in space. Astronauts have a healthy respect for the explosive power beneath them on the launch pad, as well as for the incredibly hostile environment of space.

Time ticked by. And ticked by.

Evie smiled. She was keenly aware that Jack Parker was in for a rude awakening in about...

"T-minus 25 seconds. Pegasus I and II computer systems handoff. Solid Rocket Booster nozzle steering check."

"T-minus 20 seconds. Firing chain is armed."

"T-minus 15 seconds. Go for main engine start."

"T-minus 10 seconds. All three engines firing."

"T-minus. 5, 4, 3, 2, 1, Zero. Liftoff."

Jack Parker fought the urge to yell "giddy up" over his com, but he thought better of it as massive amounts of explosive power came to life right under his ass. He felt the tower tilt slightly, then the SRBs fired, and Jack was moving. Pegasus was traveling at 150 mph by the time it cleared the tower. Moments later, Jack had broken the sound barrier. He was really flying now. Pressed against his seat as Pegasus shook and rumbled, Jack felt as though he was strapped to a wild buffalo bouncing around the center of a stampede. Jack's eyeballs felt heavy in his skull; his spine seemed to flatten out as it was pushed back into the seat.

"Kennedy handoff to Houston."

Now that the Pegasus vehicles had left the confines of the Kennedy Space Center, all mission control and communications were transferred from the launch center to Johnson Space Center in Houston, Texas. Houston, which had managed all human space flight since the Mercury Program, was ready and eager to get to work.

"Roger Launch. Capcom to Pegasus. Initiating roll maneuver."

"Davis: Copy that Houston...roll maneuver complete. Jack, how's the ride?"

"We're flying commander. All is good."

"Copy that, Jack."

Capcom: "Throttle back. SRBs, go at seventy-two percent thrust."

Jack winced. No one would ever know just how close he had come to throwing up. There is no way to prepare for going from 0 to 25,000 miles per hour in just minutes. Outside his window, Jack saw the sky turn from royal blue to violet, and then to black. The SRBs exhausted their fuel and separated from the Pegasus vehicles. Pegasus I and II then achieved orbit in parallel paths, gaining speed as they sped around the Earth.

Davis: "Thanks for the boost, Kennedy. Houston, this is Pegasus I confirming altitude and trajectory for acceleration."

Capcom: "Pegasus I, you're good to fire ion thruster on my mark. Pegasus II, do you copy?"

Pegasus II: "Copy. On your mark."

Capcom: "Fire thrusters in 5, 4, 3, 2, 1, mark."

Jack and Evie fired their ion thrusters simultaneously and both engines came to life. A blueish ring of light circled the tail end of each vehicle as electrically charged ionic charges shot out of the engine's exhaust ring. It would take hours for the engines to gain maximum output. As the Pegasus vehicles circled Earth, then departed for another gravity assist around the moon, Jack and Evie, along with hundreds of others, had completed phase one of a mission that could not fail.

In a small, windowless room, two men were wrapping up a video conference with the President. Robert Blane and Phillip Chernier were exhausted and slightly disheveled but in good spirits due to the successful launch of the Pegasus vehicles. The President looked the same as he always did, an accomplishment given the circumstances. His demeanor was steady and all business, almost comforting. He was wearing his standard blue suit and yellow tie. His puffy jowls spilled over his collar ever so slightly.

"Congratulations on the launch, gentlemen. I know your team hasn't had a decent night's sleep in a week. But all your efforts proved fruitful today." The President praised the men like a proud father.

Blane and Chernier both nodded, "Thank you, sir," Blane answered.

"Let's talk tomorrow. Keep me briefed on everything, no matter how trivial. I want to know what you know, okay?"

"Yes, Mr. President. Thank you, sir."

The screen went blank, and Blane immediately got up and walked over to a filing cabinet in the corner of the room. He pulled out two glasses and a bottle of Wild Turkey from the bottom drawer and poured Chernier a drink.

Chernier looked at the light brown liquid and swirled it around in the glass. He took a sip and felt the long-forgotten burn in the back of his throat. "Delicious," he said.

"I read somewhere that you don't drink. That true?" asked Blane.

"I rarely drink. But I'm surely making an exception today." Chernier chuckled, "What do you think of him." He nodded toward the blank television screen.

"He's fine, better than most. But he's a politician and he's looking to us to get the job done. Lucky for him we just might be able to do that."

Chernier nodded in agreement. "What are the odds we *can* do this?"

"I quit doing the math after the first day. There are just too many variables. But honestly, we did pretty well today. That said, we have a long way to go."

Chernier thought for a minute. A lot had happened in the last ten days. The events would shape modern history, one way or another. He looked at Blane, hesitated, then asked, "Parker?"

Blane thought for a moment, rubbed his hand over his chin, and measured his words carefully. "If that man makes it back alive, it will be a miracle. An absolute miracle. And make no mistake," Blane paused, "he'd become the face of space flight. No doubt about it."

"And that's a problem?"

Blane quickly downed his whisky, swallowed hard, and answered, "I don't know. Maybe. I guess we'll see."

CHAPTER 14

2029

JACK FINALLY ASKED Emily something that had been bugging him, "How come you don't have a pet? No dog or cat? That seems strange for a veterinarian. What's the deal?"

Emily smiled, "I've had plenty of pets, both dogs and cats if you must know."

Jack crinkled his nose, "I just figured a vet would constantly be rescuing some poor thing nearly all the time. Are you saying you are between pets at the moment?"

"I am between pets, yes. Not counting you, of course," Emily gave Jack a sideways glance but kept a straight face.

During the last month or so, Jack and Emily had been carefully and slowly feeling their way around a budding friendship. Jack, with Lily in tow, would regularly come to her place and whip up a fancy meal, usually involving something like roasted brussel sprouts along with meat that required a fancy rub, and Emily would thankfully savor every delicious bite. After dinner, she'd return the favor with a bowl of microwave popcorn and a screening of a movie she felt Jack couldn't live without seeing. This part of the evening often involved conversations about the film they watched or the music Jack had been exploring. Occasionally they talked about books. Sometimes they did all three. As smart as Jack Parker was, pop culture was largely lost on him. Emily especially loved seeing Jack's reaction as he watched old movies.

Tonight's movie was the 80's classic, *Vision Quest*, starring Matthew Modine and Linda Fiorentine. The film, based on a book by Terry Davis, is described as a coming-of-age movie involving a high school wrestler and his slightly older, more mature love interest. Emily liked it because the movie cast Madonna as a club singer, the emerging superstar's first-ever appearance on the big screen.

Jack and Emily sat on the sofa, bowl of popcorn between them, and watched the story unfold on the television. Jack patiently tolerated her frequent interruptions.

"See that actor there, the one playing Louden's best friend? He was Jake in *Sixteen Candles*. Have you ever seen that movie?"

"Yes, it's a classic."

"You've seen it?" Emily asked excitedly.

"No. Never heard of it," Jack said, grinning.

Emily slapped his arm playfully, and they continued watching the movie.

"Okay, here it is. This is where Madonna sings *Crazy for You*. Right here." Emily pointed to the television and then stopped talking so she could enjoy the scene.

Jack saw his chance, "That's Madonna, right there? Is that her?" he asked jokingly and in a rather loud and interrupting voice.

"Shhh. Yes." Emily was glued to the television screen. Jack smiled.

When the movie was over and the credits started to roll, Emily turned to Jack, "What did you think?"

"Epic," Jack replied.

"Really?! How so?" Emily wondered.

"Well, first of all, wrestlers have almost no body fat, so to drop down *two* weight classes is unheard of, unthinkable. Not only that, the main guy, Louden, wanted to make his mark, as he said, so to train that hard and wrestle an undefeated champion like that Shute fella, that's pretty impressive." Jack smiled, "Five Stars."

Jack turned his attention toward the popcorn bowl and started picking around the unpopped kernels and small pieces.

"You know, the book has a different ending," Emily remarked.

Jack was intrigued. "No kidding?"

"Totally."

"Did Louden lose the match at the end?" Jack asked, a little confused.

"Not sure."

"What do you mean you're not sure?" And then it hit Jack. If Louden won the match at the end of the movie version of the story, but Emily was unsure if he'd won or lost at the end of the book, then Jack had the answer. "Oh, I got it. The book ended just *before* the championship match."

"That's right! That's it exactly," Emily said, impressed.

Jack thought for a moment, "I like that ending better."

"You do? Why?"

"Because it's not about whether Louden won or lost. Not at all. The important thing was that he had the guts to try. Just making it to the championship match was huge."

Emily paused, "Well, I like that he won."

"Sure, that's cool and all, but it was a quest, remember? The guy did his best, that's all you can ask."

Jack finally gave up on the popcorn bowl. There weren't any pieces left big enough to salvage. He turned his attention to Lily, zonked out on a pile of blankets across the room. Lily's evening visits involved a lot of sleeping and wondering why it was dark outside and she wasn't snuggled up in her own home.

Emily thought about Jack's comments for a moment. He had a

point. Considering Jack Parker knew a little something about quests, he made perfect sense.

Jack abruptly changed the subject, "I've been listening to those Rolling Stones CDs a lot this week. You know, boning up on the music scene. I dig them."

"You 'dig' them?" Emily asked with a giggle.

"I totally dig them. They're a gas."

Emily took off her glasses and set them on the end table next to her. She rubbed her face for a second or two, then pushed her curly hair over the top of her head. She was tickled, but she wasn't sure why exactly. She laughed until she snorted. Her hands quickly shot up to cover her mouth, while her eyes opened wide.

Jack started laughing as well. "What's so funny?"

Emily composed herself as best she could, "I dig them? They're a gas? Really? The last person I heard talk like that happened to be in a nursing home."

"Okay, sure, but I stand by my assessment. I *do* dig the Rolling Stones and they are, in fact, a gas," Jack said confidently.

"I loooove the Stones," Emily crooned as she pulled a throw pillow into her chest and curled her legs around her body. "They are amazing, no doubt, but please, do go on. Give me your assessment of the band."

"My opinion?"

"Yeah, tell me what you like about them."

"Okay, easy. For me, it all starts with *Gimme Shelter*. That song is unreal. Raw, but polished. A little nasty. Background vocals that come on like a piledriver. And to think, that song was recorded in the 60s! But...the seventies Stones, man they had it all: *Sticky Fingers, Goat's Head Soup, Some Girls*. Then *Tattoo You* came out in 1981. After that, full stop. I'm done and there's nothing else there. Not for me anyway." Jack waited for Emily to respond.

Emily was slightly taken aback. Jack *had* been listening to the Stones. And he wasn't fooling around.

"You're a mess. But you know what, I think I agree with you." Emily nodded slowly and without realizing she was moving her head. She was a little envious of Jack Parker. Imagine, Emily thought, how cool it would be to discover decades of the best in music, film, and fiction, all at once without wasting any precious time on all the filler.

"Did you read any of the books I gave you this week?" Emily asked.

"I read all of them."

"I gave you four books five days ago. You've read all of them?" Emily asked just to make sure she heard Jack correctly.

"I did. Remember, reading is my true superpower."

From then on, Emily was never able to wrap her head around the speed at which Jack devoured books. Every week, Emily pushed her favorite books on him like a drug dealer. Often, she'd quiz him about the plotlines to keep him honest, but he was always able to answer her questions.

"One sentence responses, ready?" Emily furrowed her brow and steadied herself. This was a little game she had invented to get his quick reaction to the books she made Jack read.

"Ready."

"*A Prayer for Owen Meany?*"

Jack answered excitedly, "The Shot!"

"*Watership Down?*" Emily asked next.

"Epic adventure tale. Dude rabbits need lady rabbits," Jack said matter of factly.

Emily smiled, "*Blood and Money.*"

"Not a fiction book, but the guy didn't kill his wife, at least not in my opinion. No way," Jack stood up and walked around in front of the coffee table. "Next?"

"I agree, but only after I read it a second time. Okay, next up, umm, what was the last book?"

"You know what it is," Jack said grinning. He got up from the sofa, stretched, and walked over to Lily so he could give her some attention. Jack's long hair hung in front of his face as he lowered himself to the floor. He pushed it behind his ears and started rubbing Lily's tummy. She twisted onto her back to accommodate his familiar scratches.

Emily crossed her legs out in front of her and put her hands behind her head. She looked toward the ceiling as if she were thinking hard about something. "Was it...*The Notebook?*" Emily whispered as if she didn't know.

"Yes, it was," Jack said as his smile slowly faded from his face.

"Well, what did you think?"

"Oh, I don't know," Jack said hesitantly.

"What do you mean you don't know? Did you not like the story?" Emily asked a little worried she must have said something wrong.

"It was sweet. And I did like it. But it made me, I don't know, a little sad maybe," Jack paused, "I guess...I don't know."

Jack was being honest; he liked the book, loved it even. But the story reminded him that love and relationships were foreign territories to him. Jack's last romantic relationship was with a nerdy redhead in college named Justine, and that was light years from where he stood today. After his mission, that girl had written a book about their time together. Since then, his life as The Guardian was much like that of a monk, total dedication to a cause and certainly no time for women. It would have been impossible for Jack to do his job and have a "significant other". Secrets are horrible bedfellows. Outside of a very occasional one-night stand, he was human, Jack sacrificed love affairs for service. Jack Parker was accustomed to getting proficient at things he needed to learn. This, though, was different. Jack felt small. Helpless. He hated feeling that way.

"I'm sorry Jack, I didn't..."

Jack interrupted her, "It's fine. Seriously. Don't worry about it.

It's not a big deal. Honestly." Jack sighed. "Look, let's change the subject. It's all fine. I promise."

Emily felt awful. She'd stuck a chord somehow by having Jack read...*The Notebook*? A love story?

"Listen, Jack. The book reminded me of my grandparents. I miss them. That's all, nothing more. It's a chick book. I'm a chick."

Jack smiled reassuringly and stood up. Lily followed Jack's lead and rose from her bed, stretched, and gave her body a good shake.

Emily was a little confused. She had no way of knowing what was going through Jack's mind, but it seemed to be pinballing a little.

Emily followed Jack over to the door that led down to the clinic and watched him layer up for the snowmobile ride home. It hadn't been as cold as usual the last few days, but winter had in no way said goodbye. It was early March, a time when thoughts of warmer weather started to creep into the heads of people daydreaming about a frozen world in thaw. Jack turned to say goodbye, but Emily beat him to it.

"Jack, I'm curious. You ever think about going into town and, oh I don't know, grab a gallon of milk or six-pack of beer? Ordinary type stuff?"

"I come to your house and do ordinary type stuff, don't I?" Jack answered in a serious tone.

"Sure, right, of course. But you know what I mean, right?" Emily looked down at her feet and shifted her weight as she waited for his answer. She was uneasy but wanted to ask Jack a question.

"I have a couple of times. But rarely."

"Did anyone recognize you behind that beard and long hair of yours?" Emily's heart was thumping nervously, but she steadied herself and raised her head to meet Jack's eyes.

"No, why do you ask?" Jack replied cautiously.

"There is a brewpub in town that has trivia night every Wednesday. An old friend has invited me to play, sort of, but their team is always full so it's not exactly an invitation. But it sounds fun. I was wondering if you'd consider going with me sometime. You know, get out a little. If you feel up to it, of course. I know you may not feel like doing something like that."

Emily was talking fast now. One sentence rolled over into the next with no space in between. She immediately apologized for even asking.

"I'm sorry if that was not cool of me to ask. I was just wondering."

Jack smiled and put his hands on Emily's shoulders. Jack Parker would never intentionally hurt Emily's feelings. He could tell she was genuinely uncomfortable at the moment for having asked Jack out on…a date?

"Em, I don't think that's an option for me. I'm sorry, truly," Jack replied in a whisper. "I gotta go. I'll call you tomorrow."

And with that, Jack leaned over and kissed Emily. She wasn't expecting it but leaned into him ever so slightly. Jack ran his hands in and out of Emily's thick curls as she clutched a fistful of his flannel shirt through his open parka. The kiss lasted all of four seconds, but after hours and hours of tiptoeing around a platonic friendship, they were both crossing the line for something more.

When they separated, Jack sucked in a big breath of air.

Emily sighed.

And Lily barked.

CHAPTER 15

PEGASUS I AND II, hurling through the vacuum of space, mirror images of one another, had performed perfectly. Helped in the beginning by gravity assists around Earth and the moon, along with the carefully calculated firing of the vehicles' ion thrusters, the spacecrafts reached a maximum velocity of close to 30,000 miles an hour. But now their high rate of speed was becoming an enemy. It was time to slow down.

Unlike a mission to a planetary body where even a thin atmosphere, retro rockets, and massive parachutes can land a craft on a terrestrial surface as soft as a feather, coming to a stop in deep space is extremely difficult. Isaac Newton told the world that the Pegasus vehicles would continue in motion, in a straight line, until a force acted upon them. Jack Parker and Evelyn Davis would need to slow down their rocket ships, reverse speed, and then match the velocity of the oncoming asteroid in order to land on it. If not, the astronauts might as well look out of their windows and wave at the space rock as they flew past it toward the outer regions of the solar system.

On day 119 of the mission, the team was scheduled to complete a maneuver that would flip the spacecrafts backward to face the opposite direction. In other words, the flight deck of the crafts would need to turn so they would face back toward Earth, not toward the asteroid. It would take fifty-eight days for the ion thrusters to slow the Pegasus vehicles down and then regain enough velocity for the spacecrafts to land on the asteroid. The math had to be perfect. It was as if the astronauts were racing toward a speeding locomotive, slowed to a complete stop, and then reversed direction so they could run and jump on board. Except, this was a whole lot faster and in the cruel environment of space.

Because Jack and Evelyn were now millions of miles into deep space, farther than any two humans had ever traveled away from the confines of Earth, it took approximately two minutes for radio transmissions to travel between the astronauts and mission control. Flight adjustments couldn't be corrected instantly based on any directives from NASA, so all course corrections were built into the computer's navigation program. However, the astronauts would have to deal with any urgent problems using their onboard computers.

Evie and Jack were excited. Long-distance space travel is fairly boring, and for the first time in forty days, they would perform as pilots rather than passengers. The rotation maneuver went as planned with no complications. The ion thrusters were turned off momentarily before the inversion maneuver program commenced. Next, small onboard thruster bursts flipped each spacecraft 180 degrees. The move was synced so precisely that Pegasus I and II turned in unison like the gentle hand movements of a Tai Chi master. The spaceships now faced away from the asteroid and the ion thrusters were fired back on. After fine-tuning the procedure manually as needed, it was time for Jack and Evie to hurry up and wait some more. First, the pair waited as their spaceships gained velocity, now they waited for them to slow down and reverse course.

"It's weird. We're traveling backward even though you'd never know it," Jack remarked.

Evie and Jack used an alternate channel for their private communication. NASA, of course, monitored the astronauts' every conversation, so they weren't exactly private; "personal" was the technical word for it. Privacy for astronauts, like any other space mission, did not exist.

NASA was a public agency and required public transparency. Information was disseminated according to law, mostly. Every word spoken an astronaut uttered through a com system was recorded for the historical record. Every movement was logged by the ship's onboard cameras as well.

The only video blind spot on Pegasus (or any other NASA craft) was, of course, the bathroom, where all sorts of very personal hygiene moments took place. The waste collection system, or WCS, was always the most fascinating part of space flight for everyone below the age of twelve. The ion thrusters provided simulated gravity for the astronauts, so going potty in space was much easier than on previous shuttle missions or the ISS. Using the bathroom in microgravity is a skill that takes practice.

"Have you peeked through the scope at our visitor yet?" Evie asked.

The ships were equipped with onboard telescopes which tracked the oncoming asteroid. There wasn't much to see, not yet anyway, just a dimly lit dot in the distance. A dot that would slowly get brighter and brighter with each passing day.

"Of course, why do you ask?"

"We're going to live on it, you know, at least while we attach the thrusters. Plus, it's our ride home. It's unprecedented."

Jack chuckled, "I can see the Yelp review already. One star. No Pool. Dirty. Inconsiderate of all human life."

"Are you exercising again?" Evie wondered out loud.

"I am," Jack replied. His heavy breathing gave him away.

The crew quarters were equipped with a mini gym that pulled down from the hull like a Murphy bed. Compact and well designed, the ARED, or advanced resistive exercise device, was equipped with various resistance cables for a total body workout, as well as a rowing machine that helped the astronauts work up a sweat. On the ISS, astronauts used a treadmill, but Pegasus' simulated gravity made a huge difference in keeping the astronauts fit. Evie and Jack were going to need to be strong for the work ahead of them. Jack, Evie thought, was on the verge of overdoing it. He worked out four hours a day on average. Even CAPCOM had noticed and asked him to pull it back a little.

"The guys back home are gonna fuss at you again."

"I'm fine. I'm just a little revved up after our turn," Jack replied as sweat beaded off his stubbly chin and dripped onto his white tee. His rowing was swift and mechanical. "Besides, I've read all the manuals three times. My socks have been repeatedly organized, rearranged, and organized again. Not only that, but I'm tired of losing to you at chess. It pisses me off."

Jack and Evie had been playing chess every day, electronically of course, but Jack couldn't crack the chess code. It irritated him to no end. Evie had been trouncing him for weeks. Never mind that she played on the level of a grandmaster.

"How long has it been since you were pissed off?" Evie wondered. She had decided to give the rowing machine a go since she needed to get her work in for the day. Her body was just warming up to the movements. Heat flowed through her limbs and her heartbeat quickened.

Jack answered without hesitation, "August 7, 2013."

"Oh yeah," Evie laughed, "What happened."

"A certain president went on Jay Leno."

Jack Parker and Evelyn Davis often talked for hours through the intercraft communication system. Jack quickly concocted a story to go with the President's appearance on *The Tonight Show*. It was fiction. The real threat came from a rogue terrorist faction that had planned to detonate a dirty bomb in Los Angeles. The President certainly needed to avoid the area as a precaution. But he had faith in Jack's (back then The Guardian's) intel, and he attended the taping anyway. The President was right. The dirty bomb was found and the threat neutralized, one of many incidents the public could never be made aware of, even if doing so would make certain agencies look good. Still, Jack was angry his advice had been ignored.

Their conversation continued.

Radio waves are funny things. Most people fail to appreciate their magnificence. A form of electromagnetic energy, radio waves travel at the speed of light, which is 186,000 miles a second. Additionally, they travel outward in all directions, which was a problem for NASA. CAPCOM needed to stay in constant contact with the Pegasus crafts, and to do that, they needed to use radio waves. For security reasons, the powers on Earth did their best to scramble the transmissions. Jack's team back at The Guardian's lair continued to help with security by monitoring electronic chatter, both online and through cell phone towers, looking for keywords and phrases that might indicate a security breach. But luckily, digitally encoded radio transmissions, by their nature, are not easily hacked.

That said, an amateur radio operator on Earth would have to be extremely lucky to randomly stumble onto NASA's signal, much less decode it.

But stumble upon it someone did.

One night, on day twenty-two of the mission to be exact, an amateur radio operator outside of Beeville, Texas, sat down in his ham shack to relax and chat with friends. He enjoyed bouncing radio signals off the moon and reaching out to his contacts through the onboard repeaters of several ham radio satellites regularly orbiting the Earth. For that purpose, an impressive UHF antenna array was mounted in his backyard, along with a high-end VHF/UHF transceiver.

It was 8 pm. The single father had just kissed his little girl goodnight. Exhausted from the day, he was looking forward to a few hours to himself. As he settled into his contour chair, he noticed that his precocious five-year-old had, once again, twisted the station's various dials and knobs this way and that, randomly setting the transceiver and antenna to new positions.

"I'm playing radio like daddy," she would often say as she carefully positioned an oversized headset between her braided pigtails.

The father smiled, amused more than irritated. Before he could return the settings to their usual position, a crackled voice chirped through the receiver. Intrigued, he dialed in. The signal was coming through the 1.2 GHz ham band, but he couldn't bring it in clearly. Eventually, he gave up.

The very next evening, at exactly 8 o'clock, he tuned his IC-9700 transceiver back to the frequency from the night before. He expected to hear nothing but was surprised to pick up the same unusual transmission. Crackles would break long enough for a word or two to come through, but strange buzzes and tones garbled the sound. The transmission was nothing recognizable, but it was too tantalizing to ignore.

After several days of hearing the same thing at the same time, the man's curiosity had peaked enough to ask for help. He shared what he had discovered with some of his fellow radio pals, and the team went to work. Collectively, using their own carefully positioned ham satellite radio antennas, they discovered several interesting things about the mysterious transmission. First, because of the rotation of the Earth, the messy signal was only available briefly during the evening hours and only when the antennas were aimed in a certain direction and elevation. More importantly, they triangulated the transmissions and observed that the signals could only be originating from space.

And there it was, the flaw in the plan no one saw coming, but certainly should have. While The Guardian Program monitored modern electronic means of communication and targeted traditional security leaks, the mission's cover was blown by one of the oldest forms of communication ever used...radio.

Word about the strange transmissions spread quickly throughout the amateur radio community. Ham operators filled the ionosphere with theories and speculation, and since the transmissions were digital, it didn't take too long for someone to decode the communications.

Somebody was talking to NASA from way out in space. Much farther away than the ISS. Farther even than the moon. And from the chatter, people soon discovered it was none other than Jack Parker and Evelyn Davis, who, according to Robert Blane and Philip Chernier, were *supposed* to be testing the Pegasus vehicles in and around the ISS.

The radio transmissions repeatedly mentioned something about intercepting an asteroid. A rather large asteroid.

And before long, the world knew everything.

Surprise.

CHAPTER 16

2029

EMILY THOUGHT ABOUT THE KISS.

But she was a woman who wasn't prone to over-analyzing everything. She also happened to be busy. The clinic had been treating a steady stream of maladies. A super sweet and very senior husky had a bad case of cataracts. All Emily could do was coach the owners on how to care for her and keep her safe around the house. Dogs are resilient; they figure things out. There was a terrier mix with a urinary tract infection. Later, Emily neutered a boxer and spayed a feral cat that had been trapped by a woman near the university. The best patient was a crested gecko that needed treatment for a calcium deficiency. The last couple of days were full but mostly routine. They were also a couple of days in which she hadn't heard a peep from Jack Parker. Well, it was thirty-six hours to be exact. Emily rounded that up to a couple of days.

Screw it. He can call me. Emily thought as she walked up the stairs from the clinic to her living room. She had an hour-long break to chill and scarf down some lunch. Her receptionist ran to Sal's to get an Italian sub. Emily picked at a bowl of leftovers: stir fry chicken with red bell peppers, onions, carrots, and chili peppers, Jack's creation from two nights ago. She twisted her dark curls in one hand and spun her fork around some noodles with the other. Emily stared out at nothing as she chewed. *It was just one kiss. It doesn't have to mean everything, but it has to mean something, doesn't it?* Emily hadn't kissed anyone since her divorce, and her heart beat faster the more she thought about it.

Who the heck was Jack Parker anyway? A scraggly guy with greasy long hair and a stupid beard. It wasn't even a hipster beard anyway, that might make him sort of cool. It was a "disguise" beard, the worst kind of beard in the beard family. He could cook, big deal. Maybe he was fun to hang around. Jack could talk about any topic under the sun, except those that mattered, the ones that had to do with feelings. God forbid a man talk about his damn feelings.

Emily had been there before. She wouldn't go through that again. Grownups with feelings for each other communicate by talking things out. If that couldn't happen, for whatever reason, she and Jack could just be friends. That would be okay with her. Maybe a little disappointing, sure, but it's not like she and Jack were involved in a torrid love affair. Friends are good to have around. Emily repeated the thought in her head several times.

She then realized she had stopped eating. She was staring out the window hypnotized by the treetops swaying in a slight breeze. It was cloudy, grey. The weather matched her mood and that bothered her. Emily let out a deep sigh and returned to her lunch.

Jack had been in his shop all morning, as well as most of yesterday. He was finally getting around to melting his scrap aluminum, the very project he had planned to do the day he ran Lily to the vet. Of course, that was the day he met Emily. He was nearly finished, and several brick-sized casts of polished metal lay on a workbench near his furnace. Jack centered his stamping press on top of the ingot and stuck it squarely with a mallet. A "JP" inside of a circle was now permanently marked on the brick, stamped by the man who fashioned it from scraps of old cable, bent rain gutters, and a few beer cans.

What am I doing?

Jack's exercise in cutting down his pile of waste seemed silly at the moment. Melting scrap metal was a hobby, at least an activity, that kept him busy. Before, he had enjoyed it. He enjoyed learning how to do it and perfecting the practice of it. That was the old Jack.

For nearly two days, Jack had moved around his shop routinely, mechanically, as his thoughts drifted squarely back to Emily English. She'd changed him in a way he never saw coming and didn't ask for. And the change had to do with happiness, something Jack had never thought much about.

He had always hated the notion that people thought of happiness as a journey, some sort of noble quest. Happiness is a fickle mistress. Jack wasn't unhappy, not at all. He just never thought about it all that much. Did Emily make him happy? He wasn't sure that's how it worked; happiness provided by others was not sustainable. Jack knew that much. Regardless, he knew that when he was with Emily he liked it, and that made him happy. He was certain of it.

Jack thought about a famous quote by Yogi Berra. *When you come to a fork in the road, take it.* It almost made sense. He paused for a hot second, then picked up his satellite phone and dialed a number. His chest pinged with nerves and by the time Emily answered, he was almost out of breath.

"Hello?"

"What time does trivia start?"

"Seven," Emily answered hesitantly.

"I'll be there at six, I'll need you to brief me on the procedure."

"Procedure?"

"Yeah, procedure. What will be happening exactly? I'll need the layout of the place. Seating assignments. That sort of thing."

"Who *is* this?"

"Very funny. You wanna go or not?" Jack asked with a chuckle.

"See you at six," Emily answered.

Jack let out the breath he'd been subconsciously holding in. Lily was looking straight at him, and like all dogs, sensed something different was bouncing around inside of him. She pulled herself away from her cozy spot near the warm fire and slowly walked over to where Jack sat staring at his phone. She nosed his hand slightly, pulling Jack from his thoughts.

He bent down and rubbed her sides up and down briskly. "I know, right?" Jack said as he moved his hand up Lily's body and scratched both sides of her neck. Lily tilted her head up and licked Jack's face to reassure him. Jack smiled. "C'mon girl, let's go inside."

It was 6:15 and Jack and Emily had been going over the plan for the evening.

"Don't wear the hat backward. That looks stupid. And don't push your hair behind your ears either, let it fall on the sides." Emily turned Jack's hat around and fussed with his hair. "There, that's better." She stood back and admired her work.

Jack added a pair of reading glasses and pushed them down on the end of his nose. "How do I look?"

"Well," Emily paused. "You smell good."

"Do you think anyone will recognize me?" Jack removed the glasses and slipped them in the front pocket of his flannel shirt.

"Honestly, I don't see how. I barely recognize you and I know who you are. Besides, you look like a vagrant. You ready?"

Jack put on his coat and zipped it halfway up his chest. He

looked at Emily and nodded, then smiled broadly. "By the way, you look nice."

Emily had pulled her hair behind her in a ponytail, and a few black curls bounced around her cheeks. A vee neck cardigan clung firmly around her waist, accentuating her curves. Hiphugger Levi's and a pair of L.L. Bean boots with leather uppers rounded out her outfit. She looked cute, just as she'd planned.

"Why thank you very much," Emily replied, grinning.

The sidewalks were clear and dry for the walk over to the brew-pub. There was still plenty of snow on the ground, but the white carpet which had covered so many front yards and flower beds was slowly retreating, another hopeful sign that winter was nearing its end.

Jack pulled the front door open and held it for Emily as she made her way under a lighted sign that read, "taproom." Instantly, Jack spotted an empty table in a corner and motioned to it with his hand. Emily took the cue, and the couple found their way to a wooden table, positioned so that the entire room was in full view. Jack felt relieved at finding such a premium location, and he quickly took note of the layout of the room and his nearest exit points. He put on his faux reading glasses and grabbed a beer menu from the center of the table. Emily watched Jack pull the menu up high enough to cover most of his face.

Jack scanned the menu, "What is all this stuff?"

"What do you mean?"

"Bitchin' Camaro, My Kiss IPA, Honey Lav-beer, brewed with lavender and honey?" Jack's eyes furrowed.

"They are beers, Jack. Craft brews. Small batch breweries, like this one, make them." Emily was amused.

"Well, okay then," Jack thought for a moment, "I'll have a Lumberjack Lager. And some onion rings."

Just then a guy with a red beanie and overalls walked up to take their order. "How are you guys doing? My name is Ben and I'll be your waiter. Can I interest you in our beer of the month? It's a super select porter, full-bodied with a kick of cinnamon. It's called Monk's Beard. Plus, our food specials are on the bottom of the menu by day of the week."

Emily ordered two lagers and a platter of onion rings to share. As Ben scurried off, she noticed that the room was about half full, but the crowd of regulars seemed to know each other and mingled and talked freely all around the brewery. Just then, she noticed Flynn working her way past several groups of folks chatting, making a beeline toward her and Jack.

"My friend Flynn is headed this way," Emily whispered.

"I see her," Jack replied.

"Em! I thought that was you!" Flynn squealed as Emily rose to hug her old friend. Flynn side-eyed Jack as she hugged Emily and wasted no time in satisfying her curiosity. They turned toward Jack.

"Hi, I'm Erin Flynn." Flynn stuck out her hand as Jack stood up politely.

"Hello, I'm Ja...," Jack stopped himself. He and Emily had not come up with an alias for Jack. He caught himself, "I'm Jay. Nice to meet you." The two shook hands and everybody took a seat at the table. Flynn turned her attention back to Emily.

"So you came! That's great! Are you waiting on more people to join you? You can have as many as six on your team." Flynn's eyes bounced between her friend and the strange-looking guy next to her. Certainly, this guy couldn't be Emily's date? Flynn thought her old pal could do much better but, oh well.

"It's just us two. We're going to have a few beers and chill out for a while. Nice to just be out for a change," Emily answered.

"Well, good luck! We usually do pretty well, I must say. But listen, don't feel bad if you miss a lot of questions. It takes a while to get used to how they do trivia here and we've been coming for years now." Flynn grabbed a score sheet from the far side of the table and explained how the game worked. "It's six rounds, eight questions per round, and the last round is always worth double points. Each round covers a different topic or theme. The quizmaster will give you the category theme at the beginning of each round. Let's visit after, okay?"

Flynn headed back to her table just as the waiter brought the beer and a platter of crispy fried onion rings, along with several dipping sauces. Jack dug right in.

"I love onion rings, by the way. Oh, and…" Jack paused and raised a finger in the air so he could gulp down half his beer, then picked up where he left off, "What do you think about kicking your friend's ass in trivia?"

"Yes, please," said a grinning Emily.

A few seconds later the quizmaster's microphone sparked to life. A nerdy-looking fellow with a bald, shiny head and a copper-colored beard made a few semi-humorous quips about the weather and what happens to people who use their cell phones to look up answers. Then he rolled through the categories for the evening. When he was finished, Emily flashed Jack a smile and grabbed a tiny, miniature golf-scoring pencil from a cup on the table.

The couple whizzed through one round after another, scribbling down their answers to questions in categories, among others, "medical homophones", "presidential children", and "tools of the trade." After every round, the quizmaster announced the team scores, and surprisingly, an unfamiliar name sat atop the group of weekly regulars. "Jem," short for Jack and Emily, wasn't the witty kind of team name that was expected from the teams that regularly played trivia, but it didn't matter. As the space between Jem and the others grew, the teams that regularly finished on top began to take notice…and they were more than curious. Through observation and elimination, it became clear that Jem was the name that belonged to the pair sitting quietly in the corner of the brewery: their little town's veterinarian and a scraggly stranger.

Once again, the microphone crackled and the quizmaster spoke, "Okay everybody, it just might be a runaway tonight. Team Jem leads the pack by ten points, but the values are doubled this next time. That means the round is worth a total of sixteen points. Stranger things have happened, so it's not over yet. The last round of questions is titled, 'Is That a Fact, Jack!' Every question will cover the early life of the legendary hero, Jack Parker. So, here we go."

Emily smiled and looked at Jack wide-eyed in disbelief. Her mouth formed a perfectly rounded letter "O." Amused, Jack shrugged and whispered, "This should be interesting."

Team Jem came in second place.

Jack and Emily had a case of giggles most of the way home. The crisp air carried their laughter down the street when it wasn't echoing off of the buildings along the way. They walked shoulder to shoulder as if trying to keep each other warm.

"How is it possible that you missed so many questions about yourself?! It makes no sense!" Emily managed to ask between bursts of laughter.

Jack, still grinning from ear to ear, replied, "Technically, I didn't miss any. They're the ones that got them wrong...not me!"

"How is that possible?"

"I've already told you, you can't believe what you read on the internet. Most of that stuff is utter nonsense. Besides, my backstory is a bit, um, cloudy at best."

Emily stopped and faced Jack; her breath hung in the space between them briefly as her laughter slowly drifted away. She grabbed Jack's hands in hers. "You've said that before. Backstory? What does that mean anyway?"

"It's honestly quite complicated," Jack replied. "That's another conversation. But hey, we got second place, man! That means more lagers and onion rings in our near future."

"It does?"

"Definitely, maybe," said Jack with authority.

Emily and Jack held hands the rest of the way home. It was the best night either of them had had in years. And they both knew it.

CHAPTER 17

2021

T-Minus 55 Days

NASA DIRECTOR, Robert Blane had a lot of explaining to do. So did the President. And they did. The President gave an address to the nation, live from the Oval Office, and reassured the country that the most brilliant minds and the best technology had been used to plan for and execute the mission to redirect asteroid 2021CF02. Following his address, a live television special was broadcast to the world, detailing specific timelines and using advanced computer graphics to illustrate the mission dynamics. Astrophysicists, engineers, and even former astronauts, all dressed in crisp suits and silk ties, helped explain to the world how deep space travel worked and why ion thrusters were chosen to redirect the oncoming asteroid. The logistics and equipment involved in safely landing the Pegasus vehicles on the asteroid's surface were presented in detail. Collectively and sincerely, the on-air hosts gushed about what NASA and ORBIX had been able to accomplish in such a short period. The presentation was a comfort to the

American people, but there was another feeling conveyed to the viewing audience by the expert panel that had been assembled for the cameras. Excitement. This was exciting stuff.

Excitement is a relative term. Although there was a segment of society that loaded up on ammunition, beef jerky, and of course, toilet paper, the vast majority of the planet did what it does best: watch television. Turned out that mankind didn't want to prepare for the worst nearly as much as it wanted to be entertained. And entertained it was.

Cable news networks suddenly had massive amounts of new content, and people tuned in by the tens of millions. After the local news and before the late-night talk shows, Pegasus Mission update reports were given by broadcast news anchors who soon became some of the most famous faces on television. NASA's online feed became the most trafficked site on the internet. Radio chatter between the astronauts and CAPCOM was now a hundred percent available for public consumption through NASA's website, but it was mostly mundane stuff. That didn't matter; these were the words of Jack Parker and Evelyn Davis, now world-famous celebrities.

Jack and Evie had become the most "real" of reality shows. Occasionally, Robert Blane would release video feeds of the astronauts performing various routine tasks. All video was recorded onboard the Pegasus vehicles and only a few cherry-picked segments got sent back to NASA. The clips always went viral, not because they were cute or funny, but because they showed brief moments of Jack or Evie up close and personal. Jack, of course, gave the world a demonstration of how the ARED functioned. On one clip, he rowed strenuously, and silently, for thirty minutes while humanity watched every stroke. Afterward, there was a run on rowing machines. Evie, being the seasoned astronaut she was, showed the world the *inside* of Pegasus I, pausing in the crew quarters to whip up a meal of Salisbury steak with potatoes and leafy greens. Meal kit delivery companies immediately added the Evelyn Davis-inspired dinner to their menus. They couldn't keep up with demand.

People fell in love with Jack and Evie. They pulled for them as if they had a choice. No one can root against the people trying to save humanity from a hugely consequential event. From the time their radio transmissions were discovered nearly two months earlier, Jack and Evie had taken over the consciousness of the country in a way that was both unprecedented and hard to describe. Both were good-looking, even better for marketing departments across the country. Action figures appeared on store shelves across America-then the world-but disappeared quickly due to overwhelming demand. Pictures and models of the Pegasus crafts were sold by the truckload. Photographs of Jack and Evie, taken straight off of NASA's website, were blown up to poster size, then thumbtacked to bedroom walls and classroom bulletin boards across the nation.

Americans adored Jack Parker and Evelyn Davis. They were the world's only hope.

Evelyn Davis' background as a NASA astronaut was well established, all anyone had to do was perform a quick Google search to find out everything there was to know about her life. Jack Parker was different. His story was a combination of NASA reinventing history, and the Guardian staff planting misinformation online. It helped tremendously that Jack's name was a common one. Several hundred so-named American males made it easy for someone claiming to know the "real" Jack Parker to float a completely bogus biographical tidbit via some television show or podcast. The public did the Guardian Program's work for them, almost as if by design.

Of course, now that the truth had emerged, all of the "guests" that had been quarantined at Cape Canaveral could return home. Brody Falls and her family had stayed as Andrea Clark's guests. LINEAR's entire team was back in the loop working with NASA engineers to calculate orbit and trajectory calculations. Clark, who had taken Brody under her wing the last few months, had quickly realized that the teenager was genius-level brilliant, clearly a young woman who could absorb information with unmatched recall, and who would no doubt be an asset to Andrea, if not now, then sometime very soon.

Globally, only Russia and China met the news with any trepidation. Officially, both countries offered their help and services to the United States with any needed support or resources available on request. Privately, both governments were concerned that the US government could, and might, nudge the asteroid just enough to redirect the impact onto their soil. A North American strike was a statistical certainty due to the current tilt of the Earth's axis. In any event, nuclear stockpiles stood at the ready. If the United States could not avert the asteroid completely, there would be unimaginable consequences. Realistically, designing a Russia or China asteroid strike would be impossible. There were too many variables in play.

For weeks now, Jack and Evie had one of the most extraordinary views in space flight history. As they continued to monitor the asteroid through their onboard telescopes, it slowly became bigger and bigger and needed less magnification as the mission proceeded toward the most critical moment...rendezvous and landing. The space rock was magnificently both underwhelming and impressive. Under normal circumstances, it appeared like hundreds of others: gray and lifeless. This heavenly outlier was slightly oblong, resembling a football that had been squished in at both ends. Although most of its surface was smooth, some areas were sprinkled with shallow impact craters and scars, the result of billions of years of pinballing around other such family members. Turning slowly on a nearly vertical axis, the only threatening characteristic about this particular asteroid was imagining what it could do if it penetrated Earth's atmosphere.

2021CF02 had been monitored, studied, and analyzed by scientists around the world. When sunlight reflects off an asteroid, its composition can be determined by examining how the minerals on the surface reflect or absorb energy. The past months had proved to be more than enough time to pinpoint the asteroid's exact orbital path, its geological features, and most importantly, the probable time of impact if no human action was taken. Ponca City, Oklahoma, give or take a hundred miles or so, was calculated to be the impact event's ground zero. A surge in tourism revitalized the city's economy, temporarily to be sure, as Americans across the nation traveled to Oklahoma to "say goodbye," and to party their asses off. The good citizens of the United States needed no reason at all to have a good time. Never mind that an actual impact in the breadbasket of America would more than likely cause their own eventual demise, and degrade the economy of the nation to a position well below third-world status.

And while the world of self-absorbed humans did their thing back on Earth, Jack and Evie remained focused and unaware of such events at home. They were meaningless. As time passed, a foreboding dusty gray object slowly stretched across the onboard monitors of the Pegasus vehicles. The sight was impossible to ignore. Without remorse, the asteroid wasn't unlike a schoolhouse bully waiting for his victim after class, a confrontation inevitable. Slight and continual course corrections of the Pegasus vehicles had synced the velocities of all three objects perfectly. After weeks of waiting, the time had come to land on 2021CF02.

Because of the delay caused by radio wave transmission times, Evie and Jack were flying without guidance from Houston. CAPCOM was receiving full audio and video feeds, but could only watch the astronauts perform the landing sequence and cross their fingers. The world was holding its breath.

"Jack, I'm level on your port side. Do you copy?"

"Copy that. I show perfect alignment. Two meters above the surface and ready for tether line deployment."

"Okay, Jack, countdown sixty seconds, set auto fire on my mark...three, two, one, mark. Alright now, let's see if these anchors deploy like they're supposed to."

Jack and Evie watched the time tick away on the control panels in front of them. Both astronauts were strapped in tightly and hovering just above the surface of the asteroid's rocky terrain. They were near the southernmost pole of 2021CF02 and inverted (not that it mattered in space which direction was up or down). It only seemed strange because the asteroid was small in comparison to the size of a planet or a moon. Jack's heart rate was slightly elevated. He knew that working on the asteroid would be impossible if he and Evie couldn't anchor their tethers to the surface. A malfunction now could doom the mission. Evie watched the seconds tick past as tiny beads of sweat began dotting her forehead. She licked her dry lips.

Three, two, one, zero.

Green lights flashed on the control panel. Both ion thruster engines powered down just as a loud blast rippled along the bottoms of the Pegasus crafts. Heavy vibrations rattled each fuselage and shook Jack and Evie in their seats. Both astronauts felt a violent jolt as their crafts rocked away from the asteroid as three spear-like pistons were fired from underneath Pegasus I and II. Essentially, the ships had just deployed pile drivers into the surface of the asteroid and drove three titanium spears about a meter deep into the surface. Next, a small reservoir of high-grade epoxy resin exited the spears through small pores in the metal and filled any cracks or crevices in the rock that might become unstable later.

"What's your panel telling you?" asked Evie.

"My bow and both stern anchors are green. I'm locked in. Looks like I'm superglued to this rock. You?"

"Bow is green. My port-side resin didn't deploy, but my anchor is in okay. I can inject the resin manually during our EVA. CAPCOM, this is Pegasus I, we are anchored and ready to retract tethers. Jack, you're a go for touchdown."

"Copy that," Jack said as he reached for and slowly turned a control dial on his console. Internal winches gently reeled in the anchor tethers until rubber cushions on the underbelly of the ship, which would later be discarded, fit snugly up against the rocky surface. Pegasus II and Jack Parker had successfully landed on the asteroid. A second or two later, so had Pegasus I and Evelyn Davis.

"Houston, Pegasus II here, I'm on the surface," Jack uttered with obvious relief in his voice. An inadvertent but audible sigh escaped from his lungs.

"Houston, Pegasus I, I have touchdown on the asteroid surface."

Evie knew she and Jack had just dodged the largest potential problem of the entire mission. There's no way to redirect an asteroid if you can't land on it. As she took a moment to savor the accomplishment, a small drop of blood floated in front of Evie's face. A tiny red sphere reflected the shimmering light from the control panels in front of her. She touched it and the liquid fell around her fingertips. Then she noticed a sliver of pain coming from her mouth. Evelyn had been so focused on the landing procedure that she didn't realize she had bitten down on her bottom lip. It was nothing really, but the blood reminded her that she was now operating in zero gravity. No ion thrusters, and no noticeable gravitational pull by the asteroid.

"Jack, you ready to get busy?" Evie asked as she began unbuckling her restraints.

"Yes Commander, Let's go kick some ass-teroid," came Jack's reply.

"Oh no you didn't, did you just come up with that one?" asked Evie while emphatically rolling her eyes.

"Negative Commander, I've been working on that line for weeks," said Jack smiling.

"Geez, man. Did you forget this feed is live?"

In Times Square, three hundred thousand people crammed shoulder to shoulder to watch NASA's video feed of the Pegasus vehicles make contact with the asteroid's surface. Nearly three minutes after Jack and Evie reeled in the tether lines that connected them to the asteroid, the transmission from the Pegasus crafts reached Earth. At that moment, the formerly silent crowd in the heart of the nation's largest city erupted in uncontrolled jubilation. There were hugs and high fives, tears of joy, and sobs of relief. Hundreds fell to their knees in prayer. A mere twenty minutes later, street vendors were selling t-shirts with Jack and Evie's picture on the front, underneath was the phrase, "Let's Kick Some Ass-teroid!"

CHAPTER 18

2029

FOLLOWING date night at the brewpub, and their epic collapse at trivia, the bond between Jack and Emily grew a little tighter. It was an important step forward. The couple had been sharing experiences, but only in the small safety bubble of their domiciles, not out in the world. Now, with Emily's help, Jack began to tiptoe into places he hadn't been in years. A convenience store here. A sandwich shop there. Always during off-peak hours when people were scarce and getting in and out quickly was essential. Jack had thrown caution to the wind when he and Emily had gone to the brewpub that night, but he admitted later that it had made him uneasy.

Lately, sleep had come easy for Jack. Since his return from space, he had become a chronic light sleeper and was rarely fully rested. But now, in his bed, Jack curled his body around Emily under a pile of Egyptian cotton sheets and merino wool blankets. Her body comforted him, warmed him, and freed him in a way he didn't understand. He slept soundly.

Emily quietly slipped out from under the covers as Jack slept. Her nightgown, which was one of Jack's old dress shirts, was mostly unbuttoned and hung loosely over the curve of her bottom. She tiptoed over to the bathroom, peeled off her nightshirt over the top of her head, and twisted the shower knob. She loved her morning routine at Jack's cabin.

It was early May and daily temperatures had been climbing into the 50's. In the U.P., that's shorts and t-shirt weather. For Jack, the warmer weather was welcome, but it came with a price. Hiding behind layers of clothes and snowmobile gear had given Jack more anonymity, and that was gone with the winter weather. In its place were ballcaps and sunglasses. Jack fancied a navy Detroit Tigers hat and aviator-style Ray-Bans. Emily thought Jack's massive amount of facial and head hair was plenty good enough to preserve his identity, but she let Jack do his thing. And why wouldn't she? She found it more cute than necessary.

Jack's Ford F-250, recently revived from its winter hibernation, had been seeing sunlight for the first time in months. It was cleaned, polished, and reflected the sun's rays as they broke through the tree canopy that circled Jack's cabin and outbuildings. The truck's black paint and tinted windows gave the vehicle an official governmental look. In fact, it *was* a government-issued vehicle, complete with appropriate license plates and registration to match. Although Jack had never actually appeared in person to obtain a Michigan driver's license, he had one. After all, the former astronaut wasn't in the witness protection program, he was hidden away by choice. Even still, he had connections.

It was a cloudless Sunday morning, and like most days, it was starting a little chilly. Jack's gray fleece would later be shed, revealing a clean, white t-shirt to go along with a pair of well-worn Levi's and Red Wing boots. His black, shiny hair was pushed back behind his ears, as usual, but his beard appeared a little grayer in the light of a non-winter day. Although the whiskers seemed to age

Jack somewhat, his dark head of hair didn't quite match the grey on his face.

The forecast called for a stellar day, so Jack and Emily were hitting the road. Jack filled a YETI cooler with bottled water, a six-pack of Lumberman's Lager, and a few sandwiches that Emily had picked up from Sal's. Lily waited patiently in the back seat of the truck, her furry face sniffing the morning air through a half-open window. Her energy had increased with the spring temperatures. Emily and Jack had begun taking regular hikes through and around the ridges and bluffs on Jack's property, while Lily led the charge. With her bushy tail, Lilly took on the appearance of a fox from a distance. She was certainly happy to be out and about with her humans.

"You ready?" asked Emily as she closed the mudroom door of the cabin and swiveled back toward Jack.

"Yep, we're all set to head out." Jack paused as his glance lingered a moment on Emily. "Well, look at you. You look like a North Face model."

Emily grinned. The top of her hiking boots cut just above a pair of tan, outdoor performance trousers. The fabric moved along with Emily and matched the push and pull of her leg muscles. Clearly, Jack thought, the frequent hikes were paying off. Her light blue guide shirt fell just below her waist while a white headband, which kept her curly hair at bay, topped off her ensemble. Emily stopped and spun slowly in a circle.

"Thank you very much, sir," she replied still smiling.

"How was the shower? Hot enough for you?"

"If I ever decide we can't be friends anymore, I'm still coming over to use that shower. Just so you know."

"That so?" Jack answered. "Good to know."

Jack walked around the truck and opened the door for Emily. She pecked him on the cheek and climbed up into the passenger seat. It had become kind of a running joke between the couple.

"Friends" was a euphemism for whatever it was Jack and Emily had become. Emily had occasionally stayed the night at Jack's cabin, and they were certainly much more than friends. They were grownups doing what grownups do, but both were quite comfortable without trying to put a definition on their relationship. For now, they were happy just being in the moment.

Jack and Emily, with Lily in tow, left Jack's cabin and were soon heading north on highway M-26 toward the tiny hamlet of Eagle Harbor. They were in no hurry and had no schedule to keep. Jack's truck hummed as it rolled over the asphalt, his right arm curled around Emily's hand. Plenty of snow and ice still dotted the landscape, and it would be weeks before summer would completely take hold in the upper peninsula.

Emily was excited to get on the road with Jack. Driving seemed like such a normal activity, but one they had just begun to explore. She had forgotten how nice it was to ride in a car and not always be alone, to be able to talk and have a conversation with another person.

"This truck smells brand new. I love that smell," Emily remarked as she took in a deep breath through her nose and exhaled. "Mmm, what's in new-car smell anyway?"

"Money. And various chemicals."

Now that Lily had curled up on the back seat, Jack raised the back window to reduce the road noise, the hum inside the truck seemed to lull Lily to sleep like a baby in a car seat. Jack tilted his rearview mirror a bit to sneak a peek at his snoring little girl. Her tail hid most of her snout as her body curved around in a ball. Jack smiled.

The couple talked about nothing of importance. Jack asked about work at the clinic, and Emily recounted the week's adventures in petland. Emily's parents would return in a couple of weeks after a winter of snowbirding down south. Emily was curious about how Jack would react to sharing her, at least a little, with other people. They gave each other plenty of space at times, but both of them found that they liked having less space better.

"My folks are coming home soon, just head's up on that, by the way."

"I figured as much. Have you missed them?" asked Jack.

"I'm always a little ready for them to go, but then happy when they come back. Winters get, well, you know."

"I do. Have you mentioned me?" Jack glanced over at Emily then back at the road, then back at Emily.

"No," Emily finally answered. "I haven't. I'm not sure what you want me to do about that."

"Would they be okay with keeping quiet about me...at least for the time being?" Jack asked with a hint of hesitation.

"They'd do anything for me," Emily said matter of factly.

"Good. Can't wait to meet them," Jack said as a smile moved across his face. "I'm sorry about having..."

"It's okay, Jack," Emily reassured him. "You've gone to a lot of trouble setting up your life a certain way and staying away from people. I get it." Emily squeezed Jack's hand.

The day was magnificent. The couple, and Lily too, of course, pulled into town around mid-morning and began the day at the Eagle Harbor Lighthouse. The red brick building was built in 1871 and sat on a rocky outcrop facing Lake Superior. The lake was choppy, and the chilly wind prevented the couple from shedding their jackets. Although the lighthouse didn't officially open until June, the grounds held a few items of interest, such as a massive great lake's iron buoy and an old anchor. But the lighthouse itself was the real attraction. The building's red roof and spire popped against the cloudless, blue sky and gave the structure a picture-postcard feel to it, only in real life. Jack and Emily strolled around the grounds holding hands, as Lily explored the area, poking her nose into various spots on the ground.

Later, after looking through the windows of an old, one-room schoolhouse and a well-preserved general store, neither of which were open for the season quite yet, Jack, Emily, and Lily settled themselves on a beach area that faced the town's namesake harbor. Emily spread out a red, tartan print blanket on the sand while Jack poured some water into a bowl for Lily, who lapped it up immediately.

"Sal's?" asked Emily as she emptied a tote bag and spread out their lunch goodies between them on the blanket.

"Definitely," came Jack's reply.

"When was your last picnic?" Emily wondered out loud.

Jack thought for a moment, "I honestly couldn't tell you. My childhood, I imagine."

"Really?"

"People don't go on picnics. People say they like picnics and they generally intend to go on picnics at some point, but they never do." Jack stuffed the end of a meatball sub in his mouth and chewed as a line of tomato sauce dribbled down his chin.

"*I* go on picnics," Emily announced.

"No, you don't. C'mon."

"I do! I go on picnics every summer."

"How often? Once a summer, maybe?" Jack sounded slightly incredulous.

"I'd say, oh, maybe ten picnics a summer."

"No kidding? Well then, you win the picnic prize." Jack smiled and took a swig from the bottle of a Lumberman's Lager he'd just opened.

"Do you really have a sister? I read that you do, is that true?" Emily blurted out semi-randomly, but semi-planned in advance.

Jack turned to face Emily. "I do, and a niece named Alice. Cute as can be, I must say."

"Do you see them ever?"

After debating whether or not she should ask Jack private, personal questions for quite some time, Emily finally concluded that it would be just plain rude not to inquire. Normal people talk about those kinds of things all the time. Besides, Jack and Emily were way past those types of conversations.

Jack swallowed, paused, then shrugged his shoulders. "For years, I didn't. Not really. My job was my life and that's how I lived. My sister, her name is Paige, was the only family I had, but even still, I let that relationship wither. I felt I had to. Looking back, it was a shitty thing to do."

"Now?"

Jack went on, "After I got back from," Jack nodded toward the sky, "things changed. I couldn't go back to my old job, not after what happened. But I got to start over in a way, too. I reconnected with Paige and Alice. Made up for lost time. It was great."

"That's wonderful. I'm glad, Jack." Emily played with her black curls with one hand and made circles in the sand with the other.

"After a couple of years though, it got too hard. I mean, you know. Just driving to their house was impossible. And when I'd get there, we'd be trapped inside. Photographers with cameras outside pointed at every window and door, hoping for another photo. I mean, there are thousands of photos of me in existence already. It's insane. But eventually, they started following Alice to school. Checking their trash for, God knows what. Stuff like that."

"Jesus," Emily held her hand over her mouth and winced.

"So, now I'm here. And they live in peace in Houston. But hey, it's not all bad. We talk on the phone pretty regularly. Alice is in high school now."

Emily smiled and took a swig of beer.

"I just bought her a Jeep. Paige was mad, but I didn't care. Besides, I'm Jack Fuckin' Parker."

Beer shot out from Emily's mouth and sprayed straight onto Jack's neck and chest. Coughing, Emily choked and wheezed and tried to take in air while also trying not to laugh. Jack patted her on the back gently, knowing it wouldn't help. After finally regaining her composure, eyes red and her breathing returned to normal, Emily sighed and took in a couple of extra deep breaths.

"Whew...okay. I'm fine," Emily managed to say. "You're a mess, aren't you?"

Jack flashed Emily a boyish smile.

After another beer and thirty more minutes on the beach, Jack and Emily packed up and made their way back to the truck.

"Can I drive your truck?" asked Emily.

Jack tossed her the keys, "Sure."

It was early afternoon when Lily and her humans headed south on the highway, back towards Jack's cabin. Emily found a mellow, classic rock station on Jack's Sirius radio, which served up a steady stream of Elton John, Fleetwood Mac, James Taylor, and the like. The light musical fare made Jack's eyelids heavy and before long, he was asleep with his head back, mouth slightly open.

Emily looked over at Jack and watched him breathe. In and out, in and out. She felt a warmness in her chest, a feeling of, she wasn't quite sure exactly, but as best she could describe, the feeling was...certainty. After years of living alone and digging into her work, Emily was finally able to share her world with someone. Someone that wasn't just the best a small town had to offer, or the best she could hope for, but a man that liked her before he had to love her. And although they hadn't said those words yet, she felt their meaning in her heart...and it made her happy.

Emily English watched the road. Jack and Lily slept. And the sky turned gray. After locating the correct switch on the dashboard, she flipped on the seat warmer and felt the leather warm against her butt and lower back. A relaxing wave rolled through her body and the grip on the steering wheel relaxed ever so slightly.

A familiar road sign caught Emily's attention, an advertisement for a local bar, not unlike the kind many Yoopers visited frequently. Emily cleared her throat and coughed a few times until Jack stirred.

"You awake?" Emily asked in a voice slightly louder than it needed to be.

"Mostly," Jack said as he stretched his arms. "I can't believe I fell asleep. "How long was I asleep?"

"Probably thirty whole minutes."

Jack had just regained his bearings when Emily slowed the truck and pulled off the highway and onto a gravel parking lot. She wheeled the truck around in a tight circle and backed into a parking space against the south side of a white, rectangular building. Jack looked over at Emily curiously.

Emily announced, "This is Pike's."

Pike's was a typical Yooper bar, famous for delicious homemade pasties and cold beer. An old wooden bar ran down one side of the room and a jukebox sat in an area in the back surrounded by brightly colored neon beer signs. It was a place Emily had been to a hundred times, but also one she hadn't visited for years.

There were memories for Emily here, fond memories that had been clouded and packed away along with a relationship that had ended abruptly and painfully. Memories of a man that walked away and left Emily wondering if they had even been real. How can you share memories of a life lived when the person you shared them with had decided those memories weren't worth keeping. For Emily, Pike's was a place that needed an emotional cleansing.

"Let's go in for a bit. You want to?" Emily asked with excitement.

Jack scanned the parking lot, which was about half full of mostly SUVs and pick-up trucks, almost all of them coated with the gray of road dirt and dust. He looked at Emily a little confused.

"I don't know Em, it looks kind of busy. How about another time? Plus, we have Lily," Jack replied, unsure about getting side-tracked, or worse, recognized.

"Just a quick stop. Lily will be fine. Let's peek in and check it out. I used to come here all the time, but it'd be fun to show you the place. It's pretty great, honest," Emily pressed slightly.

Jack paused for a moment and thought. Finally, he sighed and spoke up, "If I go in, and it becomes a whole thing, then we'd need to leave. Most likely, my truck gets made, and I'd never make it home. I'm totally exposed out here." Jack figured his explanation would make sense to Emily and that she would understand.

"Jack, no one will recognize you. You are practically unrecognizable. C'mon, it'll be fun. I promise."

"Em, let's make it another day. Seriously. Maybe in a week or two," Jack said not wanting to hurt Emily's feelings.

"Please?" Emily asked with a big grin.

Jack's face fell a bit. He looked at the floor of the truck, not knowing what exactly to say next. His voice sounded stern when he finally replied, "I said, no. Another time."

The smile dropped from Emily's face. In one motion, she turned her head toward the windshield and put the truck in drive. She pulled out of the parking lot without saying a word, gravel spraying out from behind her.

Emily was disappointed, but her disappointment felt more like anger and she wasn't sure why. Jack hadn't done anything, and she did spring the unplanned stop on him quite suddenly. But she just so wanted to walk into Pike's, grab two ice-cold Rolling Rocks from the bar, and then walk to the back of the bar and press B13 on the jukebox. In her mind, she had imagined Jack pulling her close to his body and doing that thing where you move around in circles, not quite dancing, more like…being. Emily wanted to feel weak in the knees and a lump in her throat. Emily wanted B13 back. Was that too much to ask? She wanted to be able to give the song to someone else, someone that she…was in love with. She wanted to give B13 to Jack Parker.

"Fine," was all she could say.

CHAPTER 19

2021

T-Minus 54 Days

THERE WAS a lot of housekeeping to do before Jack and Evie stepped one foot out onto the asteroid. Each ion thruster, eight in total, would need to be readied for deployment. For months, the engines had been carefully stowed away as cargo. Each one would need to be unpacked and the delivery system for the thrusters would have to be assembled ahead of time. The engines were to be removed from the Pegasus vehicles using a small crane attached to the cargo section of the space crafts' hybrid interiors. On Earth, each engine weighed around six hundred pounds, but in micro-gravity, the weight would not be an issue.

That wasn't to say the engines could be carried about by the astronauts effortlessly. Far from it. The crane was one part of a transfer system designed for work in deep space, much different from working on a large body, such as on the moon, where some gravity comes into play. For Jack and Evie to move and work about the asteroid, they would need a force to keep them anchored to the rock. The lack of gravitational pull was a good thing when moving heavy ion thrusters, but not so much for an astronaut trying to walk on the surface of an asteroid.

NASA had to keep the astronauts anchored down, or they might simply float away under the right conditions. Large jet packs were out of the question. They would be difficult for the astronauts to control with accuracy while working, although two small thrusters with a very limited amount of compressed air had been integrated into the ORBIX suit in case of an emergency. It was a small failsafe. Besides, the amount of thruster gas Jack and Evie would need to complete the entire mission would be impossible to transport.

The solution had been in design for years, mothballed, brought back, tested, and updated as the technology improved over time. The EVA Anchoring System, or EVAAS, used a series of three tethers, designed to work in unison, that diverted and modulated the amount of pull the system delivered to the astronauts as they moved around on any surface in microgravity. Computers controlled the tethers, constantly adjusting the length of the line and the force needed for each astronaut individually, to "pull" them downward, mimicking gravitational force. The lines would be anchored to the asteroid and spaced approximately a hundred feet apart, in the shape of an equilateral triangle. The resulting triangles would overlap slightly so the astronauts could work together and cover the area between both Pegasus vehicles and the ion thruster field, where they planned to deposit each engine.

Jack and Evie had trained for hours rehearsing the protocols to detach and maneuver the thrusters from the vehicle cranes and across the asteroid to the thruster field. Over and over and over. Evie grabbed a handle here; Jack would clip and unclip various support clamps there. Their teamwork looked more like dancers moving over a dance floor than hauling equipment, except for the fact that they were operating on an asteroid in deep space. There was that.

With the help of a modified harness, the astronauts could easily move themselves and the ion thrusters anywhere they needed to go, so long as they were operating inside the perimeter of the triangles. The coolest part of the whole system was the control mechanism. The astronauts controlled the tethers via an eye-tracking system located inside their helmets. The visors were completely computerized with distance scales on one side and a video feed of their partner in the lower left-hand corner. A tracking system followed each astronaut's eye movements and automatically adjusted the tethers to where the astronauts wanted to go. It was amazing technology. All Jack and Evie had to do was merely glance at the spot they wanted to plant a thruster, and the tethers would retract, tighten, and move them along to that exact location. A series of eye blinks would activate or deactivate the system after the planned movements were locked into the computer. The EVAAS was probably the most reliable piece of equipment onboard the ship, practically foolproof.

The veteran astronaut Evelyn Davis would deploy EVAAS. She had over a hundred hours of EVA experience in microgravity, and her skill in operating in such an environment was essential to the mission's success. EVAs hadn't changed much in over forty years.

Evie cleared her mind and concentrated on the upcoming task. Jack, she assumed, was doing the same. The radio chatter between them had turned to silence, for now at least, as Evie began to build the layers of the EVA suit over her body. She looked at her smooth legs and laughed. They were going to get pretty hairy on the trip home. Shaving in microgravity was a complicated process and she hated it. The tiny hairs had to be carefully vacuumed and collected, or they would float around the spaceship like dust and get into every nook and cranny. With the artificial gravity provided by the Pegasus vehicle while en route to the asteroid, shaving had been much easier. She had taken the chance to shave one last time the day before she and Jack landed the Pegasus vehicles on the asteroid.

Evie put on her diaper, every astronaut's little EVA secret. There are no potty breaks in space. Next came a layer of long johns made from special wicking fabric, then the ventilation unit that managed her body temperature. Communication cap, under gloves, and several various-shaped pads and shields completed the inner layer of the unit. After slipping into the lower assembly of the spacesuit, Evie lowered herself and stepped up and into the upper torso assembly that had been attached to the wall of the craft. She twisted her body several times before the two sections clicked into place, and the self-locking mechanism sealed them completely. Before putting on her gloves and helmet, Evie made sure her tool pack was securely fastened to her body. She was ready.

"Jack, do you copy?"

"Affirmative."

"I'm entering the airlock. How are you looking?"

Jack replied quickly, "I'm on the flight deck looking out the window and waiting for the show to start. I'm ready to join you after EVAAS is deployed."

Jack wasn't the only one watching the preparation maneuvers. NASA's feed was coming in from the asteroid in high-definition and color. Although in reality, black and white footage would have worked almost as well. The only color visible came from a couple of valves on Evelyn Davis' spacesuit, as well as the US flag patch on the shoulder. The HD video transmission made the view spectacular. Earth had come to a complete standstill. Billions of people had stopped doing whatever it was they were supposed to be doing and were now squarely focused on video screens of all sizes. Cell phones, televisions, computers, even the big screen monitors inside nearly every arena and stadium on the planet broadcast a scene to the masses that was truly otherworldly.

The black and white colors of the Pegasus vehicles stood in stark contrast against the dark gray surface of the asteroid. Occasionally, minerals embedded in the rock caught the sun's light just so and sparkled like cosmic glitter. The terrain was fairly even, but a small crag was visible behind the space crafts. The outcrop rose about ten feet, then fell off and hid the rest of the area surrounding the asteroid from the view of the cameras. As far as the footing was concerned, Jack and Evie would have workable access in the EVAAS field. There were only small ridges and a handful of larger bumps and dips to navigate during thruster deployment. The angle of the sun's rays gave depth to every feature on the asteroid's surface, casting shadows that produced images on the screens with a vivid three-dimensional quality.

CAPCOM engineers could only watch the astronauts, just as everyone else. Although the distance between the Earth and the asteroid had been decreasing with every day, the distance between Earth and the Pegasus vehicles had been increasing. Right now, the transmission time for radio communications was around three minutes each way. NASA could problem-solve issues that weren't time-critical, but again, Jack and Evie were on their own if they had an emergency.

Captured from the cams on Pegasus II, Evelyn Davis emerged from the airlock and became visible to the entire world, not unlike the unveiling of a marble statue. She stood motionless as she waited for the footholds to unfold from the hull of the ship's undercarriage. Her helmet hid her face behind a golden visor, and the creases of the spacesuit at the joints gave her the appearance of a biker leaving a bar to take to the road. In a word, she appeared badass.

Evelyn blinked several times as her eyes adjusted to the natural light outside of the Pegasus cabin. She checked her safety clip and moved down the ladder slowly, the EVAAS system in tow. The unit was the size of a small trunk divided into three separate parts, one for each tether. Each tether unit held a retractable line, guidance mechanism, and anchoring system. Weightless, Evelyn's first order of business was to attach tether number one of EVAAS as soon as her foot hit solid rock. She was fully prepared.

"Jack, I'm setting the firing pin for the first tether now."

Evelyn fired a remote trigger and a foot-long titanium rod shot into the asteroid.

"The rod is set. I'm going to secure the unit and clip my harness to line one."

"That looked like a decent bang from here. Did you catch any debris from the blast?" Jack wondered.

"Nothing major. Didn't feel a thing." Evie attached the tether line to her harness and activated the EVAAS controls from inside her helmet. She jumped up and down slightly, testing the line. "Man, this tether feels great. It's moving right along with me." Evie took a couple of steps in each direction, marveling at the tether's ability to simulate gravity.

With just a few blinks, Evie had initiated the EVAAS display on the inside of her helmet. The red LED indicators showed the tension control override system for each tether in case she needed to manually adjust them. The unit displayed a distance finder that continuously adjusted to focal points set by the user. As she stood next to the anchor for line one, she continued to test the pull of the tether downward toward the surface of the asteroid. Of course, she couldn't stay in that one spot forever, and setting the next two tethers would be more difficult. But once set, she was convinced the EVAAS would make working on the asteroid a piece of cake. She was starting to get excited.

Then Evie felt her eyes tear up slightly. The sun was brighter out here than she thought.

"Okay Jack, I'm setting my visor for a good anchor spot for line two. Looks like I can go on either side of that small rocky outcrop.

It's only about two feet tall, not a big deal, but I think I'm going to the outside of it so that our thruster field will be big enough."

"Copy that. You're making it look easy, Evie."

Back home, inside of the cavernous confines of AT&T Stadium, home of the Dallas Cowboys and one of the largest video screens in North America, a crowd of people had gathered to watch Evelyn set the EVAAS system into place. Most of the crowd had been there well before the Pegasus vehicles had touched down on the asteroid some ten hours earlier. With all the dead time in between, a lineup of country music stars had been assembled and a massive stage set up in the north endzone. Tickets for the event were not cheap, neither was the beer, but the attendees didn't seem to care one bit. It was a party. Luke Combs had finished his set just as Evelyn Davis had exited Pegasus I. Despite the tens of thousands of people in the audience, it was remarkably still inside the stadium as every eye watched Evelyn move across the giant jumbotron. The scene was the "realist" of reality shows, and the people watching knew what was at stake. Every movement on the screen had happened nearly three minutes ago, and close to thirty million miles from Earth. There was, without a doubt, a lot of tension hanging in the air.

"Jack, I'm headed out to the anchor spot for tether two. Let's see how moving with only one tether feels."

"Copy that, Evie. The view from here is amazing. Looks like you've done this a million times."

Jack truly was mesmerized watching Evie work. To get to the second tether point, Evie would have to use some of the propellant in her suit to travel there. She couldn't be guided to the spot by one tether alone. Two tethers could help guide the astronaut some, but three provided resistance in a 360-degree field of play. One tether wouldn't be effective unless the astronaut was practically standing on top of it. Evie floated across the surface of the asteroid; much like a white dove floating across an Italian plaza. Stunningly graceful.

Evie closed her eyes and squeezed. Her vision blurred slightly as she read the visual display inside her visor screen. She focused on the controls and blinked to set the EVAAS locator. After the second line anchor was set, she attached the tether array and clipped the line to her harness. Two down, one to go.

Evie again closed her eyes and squeezed them tightly. A small tear fell from the corner of Evie's right eye and, because of microgravity, the droplet clung to her eyelid. Evie tried to blink it away, but a searing pain was now tearing through both her eyes.

"Jack, I'm having a problem here!"

"Come again, Evie?"

Her natural reaction was to wipe the tear away with her hands and rub her eyes, but behind her space helmet, that was impossible. At first, Evie thought that an eyelash had lodged itself under her eyelid, but an eyelash in both eyes seemed unlikely. And then there was the burning.

With concern now crossing over into fear, Evie winced in pain. "Jack, I can't see! Something's wrong with my eyes!"

Suddenly, Evie felt as if she'd been maced. She clawed at her helmet helplessly as the pain seared through her eye sockets. Tears poured out of Evie's eyes and formed a bubble that moved and collected on the bridge of her nose. She was beginning to panic.

"Fuck! What is happening? Jack, I need help! I can't see anything! I'm blind out here!"

"I'm on my way, hold on!"

Jack jumped out of his seat and headed toward the airlock while he simultaneously attempted to click his gloves and helmet into place. One glove in his teeth, his helmet floating unlatched on his head, he got one glove on and used it to pull on the handles inside the cabin. He flew across the crew compartment and past the cargo hold, all the while hearing Evelyn struggling with the EVAAS system.

"Hang on, Evie! I'm opening the airlock! I'm on my way to you!"

"Uhh. I'm trying to, Ahh. Crap, I can't…"

Without her sight, Evie had lost the ability to control the tethers. With her eyes on fire, she struggled to open them just enough to disengage the tether controls, but it was hopeless. The more she tried to control the tethers, the more they pulled her this way and that. Soon she was jerking back and forth in short spurts, causing her arms and legs to flail in all directions.

When the airlock was finally fully open, Jack couldn't believe what was happening. The two tethers that Evelyn had secured were now playing tug of war with her helpless body. She looked like a rag doll. For a moment, Jack stood motionless, in shock.

After two or three seconds, Jack yelled, "Evie! Manually vent your helmet. There is some sort of toxin in your suit. See if you can clear it!"

"I'm trying. I can't grab the valve." Evelyn tried to get her glove up to the back of her helmet. A pressure vent was located there, but each time she reached up to grab it the tethers would pull her torso up and her feet down, spinning her into a sort of cartwheel.

Jack used the emergency propulsion unit on his suit to cover the sixty feet or so between Pegasus II and his partner. It was too damn slow, but using excessive velocity would send him past Evelyn, forcing him to backtrack and waste time.

"Evie, I'm forty feet away. Hang tight. I'm almost there." Jack tried his best to sound reassuring. He couldn't be sure Evie could even hear him. Her fight to regain control of EVAAS was so loud and frantic that Jack could barely hear his own voice through the com system.

Twenty feet.

Ten feet.

Five feet.

Jack reached for both tethers in an attempt to stabilize the drag. Just as he was wrapping his hands around the lines, Evelyn's knees were pulled up by the tethers, causing her to hit him squarely in the chest. Like a basketball glancing off of the backboard, Jack bounced head over heels backward toward Pegasus II.

"Dammit!"

Evelyn didn't respond. Her body hung limp between the jerking tethers. There was no longer any sign of resistance or fight coming from the astronaut.

Jack quickly righted himself and headed for the first tether's anchor point. He'd have to release the line there. By doing so, the other tether would either go limp or pull Evelyn to anchor spot two and that would be the end of it. In his haste, he overshot the spot of the anchor and had to reverse course. He grabbed the base of the unit with one hand, extended his other toward the tether release mechanism on the far side of the unit, and he pulled up a safety plate covering the release and hit the button.

In one motion, the remaining line unreeled out of the unit toward Evelyn, shooting off into space like a kite's tail. The second tether, now in complete control, pulled Evelyn sharply in the direction of its anchor position. Just then, and in what seemed like slow motion to Jack, the only remaining EVAAS tether shot Evelyn Davis straight toward the lone rocky outcrop on the asteroid.

"Nooo!" Jack screamed.

Evie's helmet hit the asteroid with enough force to shatter the visor into a thousand pieces. Shards flew in all directions out and away from the astronaut. Evie, still alive at the time of impact, never screamed, but her communication system managed to capture one last muffled breath rush out of her body and into the void of space. She was dead within seconds. The water in her skin and blood vaporized and turned to gas almost instantly, causing her body to immediately expand. But the actual cause of her death was asphyxiation. Evie's lungs had instinctively gasped for oxygen that wasn't there as her eyes were being pulled from their sockets. A few moments later, Evie's grey corpse stood stiff and frozen in the vacuum of space. She was unrecognizable.

The EVAAS system, now finally disabled when Evie's helmet shattered, had stopped functioning. The lone tether now floated gently above the surface of the asteroid with the lifeless astronaut still attached.

"No goddammit! NO!" Jack yelled as he beat the rocky surface beneath him with his gloved fist. "Nooo..."

Suddenly, unexpectedly, and several minutes too late, Jack heard the crackle of his com system come to life.

"Evie, this is Houston. Advise you to return to Pegasus I immediately. Jack, stay on board Peg II. Wait for the next step instructions. We guess that the defogger on the inside of your helmet is going airborne in microgravity. We'll have a cleaning procedure for you in a moment. Again. Please, return and stay inside your spacecraft for the time being."

Jack said nothing. He didn't need to. The three-minute delay was finally catching up with real-time events on the asteroid. CAPCOM, and all of Earth for that matter, would see the horror that had just occurred soon enough.

Defogging solution? Jack thought.

Twenty years before, after an incident during shuttle mission STS-100, NASA had stopped using a certain chemical defogger because one astronaut had suffered an adverse reaction to the chemical during an EVA. It was an isolated event and wasn't critical, but it was enough for NASA to reformulate the defogger's formula for future use. ORBIX never got the memo. A small thing. It was a detail missed completely and by everyone that mattered. As engineers raced to ready two ships for launch into outer space to save the world, fifty cents worth of defogging solution was being applied to the inside of Evie's visor by a nameless ground support crewperson following procedure.

Back at AT&T stadium, a stunned crowd gasped and screamed as they watched Astronaut Evelyn Davis die a horrific death on an asteroid millions of miles away. The massive HD display captured every awful second of the astronaut's struggle to survive. When it was over, there was a brief silence followed by a panicked and stumbling dash for the exits.

CHAPTER 20

2029

HEY EMILY, *this is Jack...again. I'm not trying to bother you, I just wanted to talk. It's been a few days and you're probably busy at the clinic. Anyway, call me if you want. Or, when you're ready. I miss you, Em. Anyway, take care and hope to talk soon. Bye.*

Emily played the voicemail again. And then again. It had been almost a week since she and Jack had driven to the end of the peninsula. It was a wonderful day, but it had also been a bit of a wake-up call for her. By getting comfortable with Jack, she had been fooled into thinking that they could be a regular couple. Now, she felt silly. It wasn't Jack's fault.

Emily stuffed some old wrapping paper between a few logs that lay stacked in the fireplace. The days were warming up, but the nights were still cold. Emily was always cold. She lit a match and watched the fire move across and over the paper. The dry wood crackled and took the flames easily. Her hands automatically rose to catch the warmth of the fire. It was late, but Emily couldn't sleep. The heat spread over her arms and chest as she shifted the fabric in her pajamas to spread the warmth to the rest of her body.

Just then, without fair warning, a wave of sadness traveled through Emily. She put her head in her hands and let out a long sigh. The sadness didn't bring tears though; it wasn't that kind of sadness. Emily's feelings had been brought on by the reality of her situation. Loneliness in a town full of acquaintances. Love for a man that seemed too broken to love her back the way she deserved.

Emily moved over to the sofa, pulled her knees to her chest, and hugged them close to her body. She'd be fine. Like always. Jack hadn't done anything wrong, other than get her hopes up, and that was on her. After pulling a lime green afghan around her shoulders, she tilted her body prone on the cushions and watched the fire grow and dance around the logs. Eventually, her mind finally settled into a bit of calm, and she fell asleep.

Light rain was making its presence known against the upstairs windows. Emily, still asleep on the sofa, had never made it to her bedroom. The predawn light made its way through the clouds and past the window glass, casting faint flickers of light throughout the grey shadows of the living room. Dying embers were all that remained from the fire, but the room was still warm and comfortable.

Knock, knock, knock.

Emily lay undisturbed and fast asleep upstairs as the knocking on the back door of the clinic repeated a second, then a third time. Louder and more resilient, the fourth set of knocks startled Emily awake and reality slowly sharpened her senses. Thinking there might be an animal in need of emergency care, the veterinarian bolted off the couch and down the stairs to the clinic. As she got closer to the back entrance, a familiar shape took form through the glass panels of the wooden door.

It was Jack.

After hesitating for a moment, she slowly walked the last few steps to the door and opened it.

"Jack, what are you doing here?" she asked softly.

Water cascaded off the brim of Jack's hat, his rain gear shiny and wet. She studied him momentarily, noticing something in his demeanor that almost looked like...vulnerability.

"I know it's early. I'm sorry about that. I just wanted to catch you before you got too busy with your day." Jack looked down at his feet for a second, then straight at Emily.

"It's Sunday," she muttered.

"Oh, right." Jack paused. "Can I come in?"

Emily wasn't going to say no, but she wanted to. It was not that she didn't *want* to see Jack. She did. And although she'd gone over their looming conversation a million times, the words she had fashioned in her mind never sounded quite right.

After another moment, her reply came hesitantly, "Yeah, sure. I'll make some coffee."

"Thanks."

Jack hung his gear on a hook inside the door and kicked off his boots. Emily was already making coffee by the time he made it up the stairs and to her kitchen table. He took a chair and thought about what to say to the woman who was only ten feet away, but suddenly seemed out of reach. He had not thought about this conversation as much as Emily had.

She handed Jack a mug of black coffee and sat down at the table across from him slowly, warily.

"You look terrible," Emily remarked, noticing the bags under Jack's eyes and the general disheveled condition of his long hair.

"Listen, I know you're mad at me and I..."

Emily interrupted him, "I'm not mad at you, Jack. I'm not." She pushed her curls away from the sides of her face and looked squarely at Jack. Confident. Resolute.

"Okay. Well, something's up and I'm confused. I know I should have gone into Pike's with you. I'm sorry about that."

"Jack, you had a perfectly good reason to not want to go inside Pike's. You did nothing wrong. Honestly. It's not even about Pike's."

"Then what is it, Em? Tell me," Jack reached out and took Emily's hand from across the table, desperately wanting to touch her. Feel her skin. She withdrew it and put it in her lap.

"I can't be with you anymore. Not in that way. I'm sorry." She paused, "I let myself get sucked into this thing, and it wasn't fair to you. But I can't be with you, Jack."

"Why not?" Jack asked through parched lips, his mouth suddenly dry and sticky.

Emily smiled softly. She cared for Jack deeply, and she knew her words would sound harsh. "Jack, I can't live...wait." She started over. "I don't *want* to live like you. I don't want to work all day and then be with you in secret, tucked away somewhere hiding from the world. I like the world..."

Jack cut in, "That's not it at all. I'm not trying to hide you away. It's just that..."

Emily's voice rose slightly, "Not on purpose. I know that, Jack. Listen, I understand why you live the way you do. You're not wrong about it. I get it. But, I'm not going to do it with you. I want more, and I'm not wrong for wanting more out of life. Do you understand what I'm saying?"

Jack didn't know what to do or say next. He was in uncharted waters and sinking miserably.

Emily went on. "Jack, it's not your fault. Hear me? It's not your fault. You didn't do anything wrong. Okay? It. Is. Not. Your. Fault."

The former Guardian turned astronaut, turned hopeless recluse, felt his eyes getting moist. What was happening to him? A wave of heat rolled over his body and his chest felt hollow and empty. The words spilled out before he could stop them.

"Em," Jack whispered, "Emily, I love you."

"No!" Emily barked as she stood up and pointed a finger at Jack. "You don't get to say that to me. Not here. Not now. You don't get to say that, Jack!"

"But I do. I didn't plan for it, but I do. I love you, Emily." Saying the words felt like a weight had been lifted from his shoulders. Jack stood up and faced her straight on.

Energy coursed through Emily's body. Electric charges fired from nerve ending to nerve ending. She met Jack's challenge without hesitation. As she moved around the table to close the distance between them, she pulled up just short of Jack, extended her arms, and shoved him in the chest.

"Get out!"

Surprised, Jack fell back a step and his eyes widened.

"Get out, Jack!" Emily yelled as she gave Jack another push backward.

"Tell me you don't love me. Tell me that, and I'll go. Tell me that, and I'll understand."

Emily froze for a second, then put her hands over her face and took a breath. Then another. She brought her tone down a notch, but just barely.

"You think this is about love? Is that what you think? Love? Jack, the whole world loves *you*! They adore *you*. How is that working out for you?"

"That's not love, Em. That's insanity."

"That's what love is! It's irrational. It's insane. You know what I want, Jack? I want to hold your hand and walk down the street. I want you to tell everyone you meet how wonderful I am. I want you to be my biggest fan and I want everyone to know it." Emily was crying now, but she went on. "I want to show you off to my friends and say, 'This is my guy,' and not because you're Jack Parker, but because you love me so much it makes you stupid. That's what I want!"

Emily pushed her hands against his chest and kept them there for a second. She sniffed away a few tears and then looked up at him.

"Jack, you want to live alone. And that's okay. But I didn't choose to be alone, being alone found me, and I don't want to be alone forever. Now, please go. Please." Emily felt as though she was about to throw up, and she wanted Jack gone.

Numb, Jack let her words sink in. She was right. Of course, she was right. Jack let out a breath and his shoulders sank in defeat.

"Okay. I'll go," Jack said softly as he slowly turned away and headed for the stairs. Pausing at the top of the stairwell, Jack turned and looked at the woman he was leaving from across the living room. He wasn't done pleading his case.

"Emily," Jack said out loud and with authority. "Emily, I wish I could forget every second I spent on that god-forsaken asteroid. It was a miserable place. Horrific. I wish I could have lived a different life. You know, found you under different circumstances. I wish I could have been better for you. Truly. But all those things *did* happen, and they brought me here," Jack looked around and raised his hands. "And it all led to you."

Emily's lower lip trembled as she wrapped her arms around herself, eyes squinting to hold back a flood of tears.

"Before I came up here, people would walk up to me, all the time, and thank me. Constantly. They would come up and thank me for "saving the world," for saving their family. For saving their lives. They'd touch me, pat me on the back, or shake my hand. Once, I spent a week doing Make-A-Wish visits to dying children all over the Eastern seaboard. Did I "save the world" just so those kids could die miserable deaths later? Many had cancer eating away at their little bodies, some were suffering from diseases with names I couldn't pronounce."

Emily was quiet. Jack had never talked about the life he escaped in any real detail.

"Countries still fought wars," Jack paused. "A lot of them. Sometimes a school would get shot up by some maniac. No one was any nicer online or behind the wheel of a car. And yet, people still thanked me. People still crowded around me wanting a photo or an autograph. Somebody always wanted something from me. But not you. You never asked me for a thing, except once, and even then, you wanted something *with* me, not *from* me. I'm sorry, Em. I'm truly sorry I didn't understand that some things you give because you want to. This is my fault. All of it."

Jack turned and left. Emily waited until she heard the back door shut before collapsing on the floor, sobbing. Her mind was racing with both regret and reality, and she couldn't reconcile the two. She did love Jack Parker; she just couldn't tell him.

Back at his cabin, Jack slumped into a brown leather chair, his feet resting on either side of Lily, who had settled herself between his legs and lay sleeping on the matching ottoman. He gently squeezed his legs together to make her feel cozy. It was still cold and rainy, and the pair seemed to know there was nothing outside for them today. Jack's mind was at work, but it wasn't racing in all directions, not now. He was planning.

Slowly, Jack reached over and picked up his satellite phone from the end table next to him. He brought the antennae up to his mouth and lightly chewed on its rubber coating as he continued to think, turning things over in his head. Later, when he was finally satisfied, he pressed a well-memorized set of numbers and hit the send button. Almost immediately, a woman's voice at the other end of the line picked up and greeted him warmly.

"Hello, Jack. It's good to hear from you. To what do I owe the pleasure?"

"Madame Guardian, how're tricks?"

"Tricks are the same, yet different, as you are well aware."

"I bet. Listen, I'm going to get out a little and I'm going to need a few things. Can you help me out?" Jack wasn't asking a question, but he formed his words as one out of courtesy.

"Tell me what you need?"

When Jack was finished talking to The Guardian, he made two more phone calls, then slowly and carefully rose from his chair so as not to disturb Lily. He had things to do.

CHAPTER 21

2021

T-Minus 50 Days

"HE'S EXHAUSTED MR. PRESIDENT, but he is making progress."

Robert Blane looked at a large video screen showing the President's face staring back at him intently. The NASA director spoke calmly and used the fewest words possible to explain the mission's current situation. Blane intended to talk facts, not conjecture. Behind the President, a briefing room full of faces formed the same expression as the Commander-in-Chief. Everyone was on edge and worried. And, for one of the first times in history, "everyone" meant everyone. The President and his cabinet, as well as the joint chiefs, took in every word Blane delivered to the group.

The President pressed. "Robert, I need more than that. I have China readying a launchpad with a hydrogen bomb sitting atop a Long March 5B rocket. They are planning a launch targeting the asteroid, if necessary, and I don't blame them. The National Guard has been deployed in every state to try to keep things orderly, and unless there is good news, things will get worse, and that's saying something. So, is there any *good* news?"

Blane answered emphatically, "Yes, Mr. President. There is quite a bit of good news. As I mentioned previously, Parker was able to finish securing the first EVAAS to the asteroid. The engineers developed a new delivery system for the ion thrusters using lines from the second EVAAS. That took a little time, but Jack needed to transport the engines to the thruster field by himself."

"How many ion thrusters has he deployed on the asteroid's surface?" asked the President.

"Three," replied Blane.

"Three!? That's the same as it was four hours ago. Why isn't there more progress? Doesn't he know what's at stake here? Jesus." A low mumbling quickly spread throughout the room, which could be heard by Blane. Philip Chernier and Andrea Clark, who flanked the director, heard it too and exchanged glances.

"Mr. President, with all due respect, Jack Parker knows very well what's at stake. The man had been awake for fifty hours straight. The flight surgeon demanded he rest, and I agreed. We forced him to return to Pegasus II so he could eat and drink something. After that, he slept for a total of three hours. But, he's back at it as we speak."

"Okay, very well." The President sighed and the room settled down. "Can you tell whether the asteroid has shifted at all? Are the thrusters making any difference?" The President asked hopefully, clearing his throat and waiting to hear an answer.

"Sir, the amount of thrust generated by three ion engines isn't enough to affect an asteroid that size. We would need seven thrusters operating at full capacity to begin any course adjustment. There are eight on the Pegasus vehicles. We'll get there."

"Okay, well, tell me this then. Are we still on schedule? There was extra time built into the mission parameters. Does Parker have enough time to redirect this thing?"

That, indeed, was the million-dollar question.

Robert Blane paused, giving himself a moment to choose his words carefully. He looked over at Andrea Clark, who acknowledged his glance with a slight wince and a tilt of her head. "We are hopeful, yes, that there is enough time for the ion thrusters to do their job. For now, we can't be sure, but it looks very promising according to our calculations. That said, we won't know until the thrusters start to take effect and we can measure a change in the asteroid's velocity."

The President realized there was nothing more to discuss. He thanked Blane and abruptly ended the conference call. POTUS had plenty to deal with, and frankly, so did the NASA director.

Philip Chernier was the first to speak. "You painted a fairly rosy picture for the man, don't you think?"

Blane wasn't amused, "What would you have said differently, Philip? Seriously? We have one dead astronaut and another all alone on a rock several million miles away from home, doing the best he can to fucking move an asteroid that will most likely hit the heartland of this country if it can't be redirected. And yes, it may not be enough, but we're all working on it here, for chrissakes."

Chernier raised his hands as if he wanted to apologize. "I know. I know. But the fact remains that we don't exactly know the mass of that asteroid, and without that nugget of information, we don't know if this plan will work at all."

Andrea Clark chimed in, "We know a lot. The spectrometer has given us the general composition of the asteroid. Plus, we know its size fairly accurately. Pegasus I scanned and relayed the information back to us during its approach. But you're right, we don't know for sure if the rate of the course correction will be enough once the thrusters start to take effect."

Without saying a word, Blane tapped a few keys on his laptop and switched the video stream, which had become a black screen, to NASA's official online feed. There, in full HD, was Jack Parker, working to attach the fourth ion thruster to a set of delivery cables leading from the cargo bay of Pegasus I to the thruster field in the distance. Visible were three bluish rings of light emanating from each of the thruster engines. They were all fully engaged and glowing brightly. As a result, the area around the engines had been cast in a strange metallic hue. An arc of charged ions burst from the thruster engines like neon fire. The machines, modern marvels to be sure were mesmerizing-a campfire of barely shifting energy and flame.

Andrea Clark spoke first and with an almost wistful tone, "Look at those engines." She spoke softly, shaking her head in disbelief. "They're, they're...beautiful. The whole scene is surreal."

And it was.

Chernier shrugged and remarked casually, "Well, let's hope that cowboy can get the other engines on the ground before we all grow old."

Robert Blane stood up so quickly that his rolling chair sailed across the room behind him. Philip Chernier flinched and looked up at Blane, who proceeded to grab the ORBIX director and CEO by the collar and lift him out of his seat and a foot off the ground. Next, Blane turned his shoulders and threw Chernier away from the table and onto the floor. Chernier landed with a resounding thud. The poor man, clearly shocked by Blane's actions, let out a small yelp.

"Listen here, you little twerp!" Blane yelled, standing over Chernier and pointing a finger in his face. "You fucking shut your mouth right now! That man has met every challenge we've thrown at him. He's sure surprised the hell out of me, I'll give him that. But, you? What the hell have you done? You solve your problems by throwing money at them, making other people do the work. Then you stroll in and take all the credit. That's not how NASA works, Philip. We fix our shit here! As a team!"

Robert Blane wasn't finished.

"Where's *your* family, Philip? Where are they?"

"What do you mean? What are you talking about?" Chernier croaked, still flat on his back.

"You know exactly what I'm talking about. Your family is safe and sound, all tucked away on your estate in New Zealand. Solar and wind-powered. Fully stocked with what, ten years of food? Armed guards probably. Private runway. Fuel tanks topped off. Fuck you, Philip! We're working folks here. We don't have that option! If we fail, we pay the price. But not you, so fuck off!"

Slowly, and breathing heavily, Blane backed away from Chernier as he picked himself up off of the floor. After taking a moment to compose himself, and tuck his shirt back in his trousers, Chernier looked at Robert and Andrea Clark. The two of them had just taken the whole incident in with a feeling of satisfaction, and Chernier replied defiantly. "You'd do the same thing, Robert! For your family!"

"The hell I would. That's not how things work here. We don't plan for failure. And besides, when this is all over, when we do this right and everyone writes a book about it, including you, don't forget to tell the world how *you* hedged your bet. Do you hear me? Because if you don't, I will."

"So will I," Andrea Clark added with a slight smirk.

"Fine. Point taken, but I'm not apologizing for what I did." Chernier paused a moment, then added, "I'm leaving. And try to calm down, Robert. Jesus."

After Philip Chernier scurried out of the conference room, Andrea Clark turned to Blane and slowly clapped her approval.

Clap. Clap. Clap.

"What was that all about? Don't get me wrong. The guy can get annoying, but still," Clark said as she tapped the top of the table with her fingertips.

"Oh, nothing. I'll apologize later. Just a little alpha dogging, I guess. The guy is brilliant, but not in a way we need right now," Blane remarked as color returned to his face.

"Look at him," Andrea said as she nodded toward Jack on the video feed.

On the screen, Jack was slowly guiding a thruster engine over the uneven surface of the asteroid. Step by step, slowly, methodically. The machine, held three feet above the asteroid by guide wires, slowly followed Jack as he made his way to the thruster field. Once there, he would attach the thruster to the surface and ignite the ion beams, just as he had done three times previously. Three blue rings would turn into four, and eventually, all eight would be firing at full capacity with just enough force, God willing, to nudge the massive asteroid in a slightly different direction. Just enough, he hoped, to skip it past Earth and back into space, to be some other world's problem a billion years from now.

"Where is Evelyn Davis' body? I don't see it on any of the camera feeds?" Andrea asked in a whisper.

"He clipped her to Pegasus I, in the shade. Without direct sunlight, her body will be perfectly preserved. He smashed the only camera lens that would have made her visible to anyone. CAPCOM cut the entire transmission for a while, but it's back up now. The President demanded it." Blane sat down and leaned back in his chair. He let out a heavy sigh and rubbed his temples gently.

Andrea changed their focus back on the mission. "We can start calculating the asteroid's orbital changes about two or three days after all the engines are running. I'll let you know as soon as I know something."

"Okay. I'll have our guys run the numbers, too. Let's hope we get good news." Blane looked at Andrea Clark. They both were operating on little sleep and looked haggard. The death of Evelyn Davis had been a gut punch to the NASA family. Her horrific demise had been the most-watched event in television history. But they had little time to dwell on it. Jack Parker needed all the focus and support NASA could give him.

Several million miles away and closing in on Earth, Jack Parker's mind was lost in the moment of the task at hand. He was tired and alone, but he was still moving, still working.

At a roadside bar, about as far away from Jack Parker as one could be, a mostly packed house watched a bank of television sets all tuned to what had become known simply as the Jack Parker Channel. The bar, and thousands of bars just like it, had become unofficial community gathering places, places where rural Americans checked on one another and made sure if their neighbors needed anything, they got it. Men bartered goods such as vegetable seeds, ammunition, fuel, and fishing line. In places like these, to the surprise of many, the sense of community had strengthened.

Supply chains, for the most part, failed to deliver the many items people sought. Americans looked to Amazon or UPS trucks to deliver the goods they needed, versus the luxuries they wanted: Solar cell phone chargers instead of eyeliner. Flour and sugar rather than video games and specialty cupcakes. America's biggest cities, famous for industry and their sports teams, did not have the kind of soulful fabric needed to instill anything but selfishness into the competitive nature of their lives. Since the death of Evelyn Davis, crime in populated areas had risen by three hundred percent. The past few days had been rough on people. When Evie Davis died, many just assumed the NASA mission would fail.

But then, Jack Parker got to work. With every ion thruster he secured to the surface of the asteroid, the more hope he delivered to humanity. More hope meant more people watching Jack Parker save the world, live and in person, on their television screens.

What helps people settle in and restore hope better than watching their favorite show on television?

The bar was full but not crowded. It was Sunday. After a good hour and a half of church praying and looking to God for answers, the folks in this small community came out for a beer and something to eat.

"Two," a man said as he held up two fingers to the woman working on the other side of the bar.

"Need anything to drink with those?" she asked.

"A couple of Millers," came the reply.

After the bartender pried the caps off two bottles of cold brew, she handed the man his beer and two baskets of food. The guy made his way through the crowd and to a table where his wife sat waiting for him to return.

"Oh, those look delicious!" said his wife as she pushed her black frames up onto the bridge of her nose. Her wild curly, black hair sprang from her head and fell with a bounce on both sides of her head. She carefully picked up the food from her basket and took a bite. "Hot!" she whispered between breaths, then chewed and swallowed as fast as she could. "Look at that guy, that Jack Parker up there." The woman nodded toward the screen mounted on the wall behind the bar. "Poor guy's barely slept in over two days."

"Um, yeah, best pasties in the U.P. for sure," said the man in a flat voice. "Listen, I need to talk to you about something."

"Like what?" the woman asked between chews. The tangy beef along with the potatoes and carrots inside the flaky crust made her want to eat, not have a conversation.

"Well, this is hard to say, so I'm just going to say it...I'm leaving." The man paused, knowing he was delivering a hammer blow to his unsuspecting wife. He coughed and shifted uncomfortably in his chair. "I'm sorry," he said quietly, "this isn't what I want."

Thirty minutes later and numb with the news she'd just been given, the woman sat alone in a pickup parked in the lot next to the bar. She stared in front of her at the white wall of the building she'd just left. Slowly, she lowered her head until it rested firmly against the top of the steering wheel. She cried softly, barely making any noise, as if she wanted to hide her emotions, even from herself. Tears rolled down her cheeks.

After several minutes, the woman started the car and put it in reverse. She left the parking lot in such a hurry a cloud of dust shot from under the tires and hung in the cool air behind her. The dust cloud drifted and fell around a sign sitting atop a pole near the side of the road. The sign, in bold blue script, said "Pike's."

CHAPTER 22

2029

RED and blue flashing lights puzzled the man behind the wheel of
the motorhome. He hadn't been speeding; he was sure of it.
Slightly confused, but still confident he'd done nothing wrong, he
veered the RV off the road and onto the shoulder of the interstate.
The Oklahoma border was about thirty miles north, and just
beyond the state line was Turner Falls, his destination for the
night.

"Why are you being pulled over, Thomas? What did you do?"
asked the man's wife.

The woman, tan from the gulf coast sun, was slim; her hair was
mostly dark, save a few streaks of silver. She was in her mid-sixties
but could have passed for a woman ten years younger. She and her
husband were headed back home after having spent a fine winter
on Padre Island, the crown jewel of Texas' beaches. The couple had
planned several stops on the way back to Michigan's Upper Peninsula, but this wasn't one of them.

"Nothing. I didn't do anything," the man protested as he

shrugged his shoulders. He looked at his wife and repeated his reply, "I didn't do anything."

A short time later, they heard a knock from the passenger side door of the motorhome. When the man opened it, a crisply dressed Texas State Trooper, adorned with a Stetson hat and aviator sunglasses, stood before him. He tipped his hat and smiled up at the driver.

"Afternoon, sir. I'm officer Patrick. May I see your driver's license and registration please?"

Anticipating the officer's request, the man handed over the items and stood waiting at the door of the motorhome. His wife was close behind him, peering over his shoulder. Both waited silently and quite anxiously for the officer to tell them what was going on.

The trooper looked down at the driver's license in his hand, then up at the man standing in the doorway. "Sir, just to confirm, can you give me your name and home address, please?"

"Thomas English, 624 Pinehurst Street, Hancock, Michigan."

"Is this your wife, Jillian?" the trooper asked.

After a brief hesitation, the man replied, "What is this all about officer? How do you know my wife's name?

"Sir, will both of you step out of your vehicle for a moment, please?" the officer asked, and took several steps back away from the door. The couple complied.

"Officer, can you please tell me what's going on here? Did I do something wrong?" Mr. English was beginning to get annoyed. He stood facing the trooper, who was standing directly in front of him.

"Mr. and Mrs. English, you did nothing wrong and there isn't any type of emergency going on. There is nothing for you to worry about. I want to make that clear. That said, I have been asked to have you follow me to a secure location a few miles from here. Not far in fact."

Perplexed, Thomas English replied, "And if we refuse?"

"Then nothing," the officer said, "You go on your way, and I report back that you took a pass on my request." The trooper smiled slightly as if to convey to the couple that behind his persona was just a nice fellow, trying to be of service.

Thomas looked at his wife, their confusion now hedged with a bit of curiosity. "Do you know *why* we've been asked to follow you?"

"I do not. Honestly, I'm the lowest link on the chain here, sir. But where we're headed is not far from here, and then you can find out for yourself."

The officer waited as the couple exchanged glances, trying to gauge what the other was thinking. Jillian English shrugged her shoulders and whispered to her husband, "Let's go."

"You sure?"

"Yep. Otherwise, we'll be wondering about what this was about the whole drive back to Michigan, so let's find out for ourselves." Jillian turned, hopped through the motorhome door, and was back in her seat before Thomas had returned his driver's license to his wallet.

Half an hour later, the motorhome followed the state trooper up a slight hill and past a set of chain link gates onto what looked like some sort of military compound. At least, that is what it appeared to be, except there was no uniformed personnel anywhere in sight. After parking the RV, the couple was immediately met and escorted through several sets of doors by a man in a black suit and tie. The structure, strange as it was, had once been a cold war era nuclear fallout shelter. Massive orange blast doors remained and they would be perfectly functional if necessary. Impressive as the underground bunker was, the building was currently serving as a regional FEMA command center, essentially, it was an underground office building.

Thomas and Jillian English sat alone in a small meeting room fifty-eight feet below ground waiting patiently but nervously, for someone to come in and tell them that they had won the Powerball or perhaps the King of England had requested a private meeting. But what happened next was even better.

The door opened and in walked a man who needed no introduction. His hair, neatly trimmed and slightly peppered with gray, was parted on the side and curled in a wave over the top of his forehead. Freshly shaven and with his signature square jaw and dimpled chin, the fellow standing before them was both ruggedly handsome and instantly recognizable. Jillian English's mouth fell open. Her husband rose excitedly to greet the man's extended hand.

"Mr. and Mrs. English, my name is Jack Parker. Thanks so much for indulging me and meeting here today. I must apologize for all the drama involved with it. Old habits die hard with me."

Stunned, Thomas English spoke, almost without thinking, "Mr. Parker, it's…it's very nice to meet you. By all means a pleasure," he said weakly as he continued to shake Jack's hand. Jillian English stood up slowly and proceeded to take her turn shaking the astronaut's hand.

"Yes, hello, Mr. Parker, it's so nice to meet you!" said Mrs. English, smiling broadly. "I can't believe it's you! What in the world are you doing here? With us?" Thomas and Jillian looked at each other in total amazement and confusion.

Jack sighed and took a moment. Then he began, "Mr. and Mrs. English, I've been living up north, not too far from you in fact, for quite some time. Secretly. Alone by choice and perfectly content. Content, but as it turns out, not necessarily happy. Not miserable by any means, but I realize now I wasn't exactly happy, either. That is, until recently. Recently, things changed for me in a big way."

Jillian English stared at Jack intently, hanging on his every word. Thomas, feeling the surrealness of the situation at hand, rubbed his chin subconsciously as Jack spoke.

"What happened?" the parents of Emily English blurted out, almost in unison.

Jack paused and a smile came over his face, "Well...I met your daughter."

"You met Emily?" Jillian asked.

"I did. And...I fell in love with her," was Jack's reply.

Twelve hours earlier, Jack had parked his truck in an alley behind a small, two-story red brick building that stood in the city's main business district. He rapped sharply on a metal door, and it opened almost immediately. Inside stood a thickly built man in his mid-fifties. He was of average height, balding, but solidly built like a battering ram. The man was a former All-Big Ten wrestler who had parlayed his athletic success into a career in public office. Affable yet pragmatic, Mayor Charles Dunning was in the middle of his fourth term in office when he received a call from a man claiming to be *the* Jack Parker. The man had politely asked for a private meeting, and for now, stressed the need for complete discretion.

Dunning stood at the door and eyeballed the man before him. Jack's long hair and beard were doing their job to hide his identity, but after a closer examination, coupled with a little imagination, the mayor's eyes lit up.

Jack spoke first, "Mr. Mayor, I'm Jack Parker. It's a pleasure to meet you, and thank you very much for doing this for me today. I truly appreciate it."

Suddenly sparked with unbridled enthusiasm, Mayor Dunning smiled broadly and ushered Jack through the door.

"Please come in, Mr. Parker!" he said, shaking Jack's hand vigorously as the two moved into a dark, narrow hallway. "It's a pleasure to meet you, sir! Surely it is. Here, follow me."

Charles Dunning moved down the corridor, past an office and a restroom, then into a large open room that looked out over Huron

Avenue, one of the city's main thoroughfares. The large plate-glass storefront revealed an unobstructed view of the city's historic businesses lining both sides of the street. Dawn would break soon over the city, but for now, the only light showing through the front window was from the pale-yellow street lamps still buzzing with electric current.

"Here you go, Mr. Parker, have a seat," the mayor said as he waved his hand at one of three identical chairs placed along one side of the room.

"Jack."

"Excuse me," Dunning said in return, as he took the chair closest to Jack.

"Call me Jack, please. Just call me Jack," said the former astronaut in the friendliest tone he could muster. After all, Jack Parker was here on a sales call.

"Sure thing...Jack," Dunning said happily. "Tell me. What can I do for you? You said over the phone that you needed a favor. And let me tell you right now, whatever you need, consider it done!" Charles Dunning swiveled back and forth nervously in his chair.

"Charles, I appreciate that. Sincerely. But, I need *two* favors." Jack leaned back in his chair and stretched, hoping his relaxed repose would ease Dunning's anxiety. The man appeared ready to pop. "First," Jack sighed, "as you can see, I need a bit of a trim... and a shave, too."

Jack twisted around the heavy-duty barber chair he was sitting in until it faced a counter scattered with the usual tools of Dunning's trade. A tall glass cylinder full of blue disinfecting liquid was pushed off to the right side of the space. Next to it, laid out in order by size, was a neat array of high-quality barber combs along with several pairs of scissors. Each item was perfectly spaced apart on a crisp white towel. A large mirror stretched along the length of the wall in front of him. Jack studied his reflection as he ran his hands through his thick mass of hair. After pulling some strands

175

straight down over both ears, the length fell just below the jawline. Dunning, who both served the town as mayor and local barber, beamed at the request from his esteemed visitor.

"That's no problem at all Mr. Parker, er, I mean Jack. I can give you a haircut and a shave right now, if you'd like."

"Excellent," Jack answered.

"How do you want me to cut it?"

Jack looked toward the wall to his left and nodded. Hanging proudly next to a picture of the 1984 World Series Champion Detroit Tigers and above a photo of famed University of Michigan coach Bo Schembechler, was an official NASA photo of-none other than Jack Parker.

"Cut it like in the picture, if you don't mind."

"You got it!" Dunning said with a little too much excitement.

The mayor/barber had his work cut out for him, but he was up to the task. Slowly and methodically, Dunning worked his way around the chair, pulling locks of hair up between his fingers and snipping them cleanly with a shiny pair of stainless-steel scissors. Tufts of hair rained down past Jack's face and collected on his lap and shoulders. Occasionally, Dunning would kick away the hair that had accumulated at his feet.

Jack noticed that Dunning's tongue slipped out the side of his mouth as he meticulously worked around Jack's ears and neck. Slowly, an image started to emerge in the mirror. It was a person Jack hadn't seen in years. As his armor was chipped away by the barber, the former Guardian appeared, and Jack stared at his reflection. There he was, like a ghost flickering in and out of focus just before the dawn. More flesh than vapor as the morning light started to stream in through the windows of the shop, Jack's famous and familiar appearance was reflected in the mirror.

Just as the morning sun started to give depth and color to the various objects in the shop, the barber went to work on Jack's beard, carefully using his scissors to remove the largest masses of whiskers, then turning to an electric trimmer to cut closer to the skin.

There he was, no longer an anonymous face, but easily recognizable. Completely uncovered. Exposed.

"Let's give you a nice, close shave to finish the job. That okay?"

Jack responded with a nod.

Dunning tilted the barber chair back and gave the handle on the side several back-and-forth pumps. As he did, Jack felt his body gently lift upward from the floor, higher than he had expected.

The warm lather felt good on Jack's skin, and he allowed a relaxed sigh to escape from deep within his lungs. The mayor took great care as he shaved around the contours of Jack's face, slowly working as if he was gently restoring a renaissance era masterpiece, a fresco by Raphael or Michelangelo.

When the job was complete, Charles Dunning dried Jack's face with a towel and wiped off the straggling bits of shaving cream that remained. He returned the chair to its upright position and let Jack examine his handiwork. The two men let a moment of silence hang in the air.

Other than a few more flecks of gray hair, Dunning had transformed the once rather scraggly man into a replica of the one in the picture that hung on the wall of his shop. He was handsome and rugged, but noticeably less stoic, less...serious looking.

The Jack Parker in the picture in Mayor Dunning's barbershop was not unlike the many like it hanging on walls all around the world. But, the neatly groomed Jack Parker sitting in the chair of the dimly lit barbershop was different. He was...*smiling*. It was small, a slight upturn on one side of his mouth, but a smile nonetheless. He rubbed his smooth chin and jaw.

In the NASA photo, Jack had been carrying the weight and future of the planet on his shoulders, and it showed. The Jack Parker in the mirror was done with all that. Today, the reflection that looked back at the two men carried only the promise of Jack's future, not everyone's. The difference between the two Jack's was palpable, to both barber and former astronaut.

"Well, what do you think?" asked Dunning.

"It's perfect. Thank you," Jack said as he welcomed back the man in the mirror.

"Sure thing, um, Jack," the mayor replied just before pausing a moment to gather his words. "So, tell me. You said you need two favors. What's the other?"

Jack stood up and turned to look at the mayor. He put his hand on his shoulder and asked with a smile, "I'd like to speak to the good people of your city. When's your next city council meeting?"

CHAPTER 23

2021
T-Minus 36 Days

"MR. PRESIDENT, as I've said before, the ion thruster engines should be working. It's just too early to tell at this point what effect they are having on the asteroid."

Robert Blane had said these same words repeatedly over the last several days. Any change in the asteroid's velocity, its speed or direction, would take time to measure. Hopefully, those minuscule changes would, over the next several weeks, build enough for the asteroid to change course enough to skip past Earth. But measuring that tiny amount of change wasn't possible...not yet.

The President wanted answers. "Robert, the American people deserve to know if we've done our job here. The whole world is watching. And, of course...waiting. The thrusters have been firing now for a week! Are you saying that you can't measure whether or not they are working yet?"

Blane continued, "Sir, imagine a large man going on a diet and losing a few ounces a day. You wouldn't notice such a small change, even if he got on a scale, but then, maybe a few days later, he steps on the scale and, boom! He's down a pound. One pound. But, he didn't lose that pound all in one day, he just lost the last few ounces he needed for the loss to register on the scale. The diet was working all along. It's the same principle. It *will* work. I guarantee it."

Blane looked confidently into the computer camera. He didn't blink. Everyone on the other end of the conference call had to trust him and have the utmost confidence in what he was reporting to the President.

"Okay, Robert. Okay. Tell you what, call me the moment you register any change. I want all your calculations to be fluid and up to date." The President paused, "And I trust you are not sugarcoating any of this. Understand?"

Robert Blane replied immediately, "I would never do that, sir. NASA doesn't do that. Our work is based on numbers. Facts only. We don't guess."

"Very well."

Then, the screen went black. POTUS was done talking.

Philip Chernier, on his best behavior since the NASA director's gently applied attitude adjustment, spoke up. "A fat guy losing a pound. That's a really good analogy. So, just between us," Chernier nodded at Andrea, "when do you think our asteroid out there is going to shed that first pound?"

Blane sighed, "Any moment. It's got to show up soon, or this whole mission will have been a complete folly. Oh, and *we're* all gonna be screwed as well."

"I thought you didn't sugarcoat things?" Andrea asked as she turned to give Blane her full attention. "Why did you tell the president it was working. We don't know if it's working yet. It might not be."

"It's working!" Blane replied, slightly raising his voice, not in anger, but as if he were trying to convince himself that his words were infallible. "It's working," he said again in a whisper.

Andrea Clark's team at LINEAR had been tracking 2021CF02's path since Brody Falls had sent them its location when what now seemed like ages ago. They were the people waiting for the scale to show that first pound of weight loss. Jack Parker had fired up the eighth and final ion thruster on the asteroid's surface almost seven days earlier, and the waiting game was excruciating. But three hours after Blane's conference call with the president had ended, Clark's cell phone vibrated. She dug into her back pocket and took the call.

"Yes," she answered.

Clark listened intently, nodding occasionally. The person on the other line was giving the LINEAR director a massive amount of information. Sitting a few feet away from Andrea was Brody Falls, her red hair pulled tightly behind her head into a ponytail. The two had set up shop in a large storage closet turned makeshift office just outside of mission control's main entrance. Brody, dressed in a dark pantsuit and flats, appeared to have latched onto the most intense internship ever created in the field of aerospace.

"Got it. Let me call you back in ten. Thanks," Clark said softly. She terminated the call and turned to look at Brody.

"It's moving, isn't it?" Brody asked.

"It's moving," Andrea answered.

Brody watched as the director collapsed in her chair. In one motion, she bent over and buried her face in her hands. Quiet sobs escaped from deep inside and her hunched back bounced with each breath. A tremendous sense of relief rolled through her body in waves. Composing herself as quickly as she could, Andrea lifted her head, straightened, and looked directly at Brody. Her eyes were red and watery, but she was smiling.

"You okay?" Brody asked.

"I'm great. Let's go deliver the good news."

Jack hadn't been able to sleep. It had been days since he had finished anchoring the thrusters to the surface of the asteroid, and like everyone else, he sat around and waited for NASA to report that the thrusters were working. Since Pegasus was anchored to the asteroid, and not moving through space, Jack floated around inside of the vehicle in microgravity. That meant more time on the ARED would be necessary to keep up his fitness and strength, but he often exercised out of boredom anyway.

An astronaut on the International Space Station always had plenty of work to do, but Jack didn't. There were systems checks and daily routines to follow, but his mission had a singular purpose, one that had been completed. There was nothing more for him to do but wait, then ride the asteroid back to Earth. Home. Hopefully, home would be a place worth returning to.

The radio suddenly crackled and came to life.

"CAPCOM to Pegasus II, come in. Over."

Jack pulled on a grab handle fastened to the hull of the ship to propel his weightless body across the vehicle and toward the radio transmitter. He was hoping for good news.

"Peg II to Houston, come in Houston," responded Jack, and then he waited. The travel time for each transmission was still close to two minutes.

"Jack, Robert Blane here to give you a bit of good news..."

Jack's heart rose and thumped heavily in his chest as he took in the director's words.

At that very moment, billions of television viewers around the world also heard NASA's Robert Blane tell Jack that the asteroid's orbit was shifting. He'd done it! Alone and against the odds, he'd done it. And with that news came the tears.

Parents around the globe sobbed with relief and hugged their children tightly. Loved ones embraced each other, and friends, well they hugged each other, too. Enemies forgot their petty grievances. Countries rejoiced and church bells rang out in glorious celebration. In small towns across America, people drove their cars and trucks around quaint town squares and historic downtowns, honking horns and shouting with delight.

Virtually every television screen on Earth was tuned to the Jack Parker Channel, and every screen showed a man sitting quietly, alone. Still. Motionless. He didn't say a word, or clap, or pump his fist. Then slowly, Jack turned his head and looked directly at the camera mounted on the back wall of the crew compartment. Finally, and for the first time, he allowed himself to imagine the millions of faces of people watching him from Earth. Faces that previously had been blank and meaningless in his mind suddenly became very real and brilliant with color and light and *hope*. From over twenty million miles away, Jack Parker looked through the camera at the people of Earth and...waved.

And the folks watching back home went wild.

T-Minus 28 Days

Philip Chernier and Robert Blane had each given around a hundred interviews during the previous two weeks. The components of the mission had been broken down and explained on every level; the subtext was translated into over thirty languages. The United States was basking in the glow of unprecedented achievement, one far greater than Armstrong's first lunar footsteps, rivaled only by its contribution to ending the second world war. The US stock market had doubled in the last week, adding to the monstrous gains it had made the week before. Breweries across the nation ran dry. To no one's surprise, almost exactly nine months later the country would see a rather sudden jump in its birth rate.

Despite the sudden shift in the pulse of America, Andrea Clark and the entire team at LINEAR continued to closely monitor the path of 2021CF02. When the engineers first ran the data and as they continued to analyze the effects the thruster engines were having on the asteroid, the numbers showed a thin but reasonable possibility for error, one that could be as much as several thousand miles.

But now, the numbers began to show something else.

Blane and Chernier crowded inside Andrea Clark's office and looked over a set of printouts. Everyone was tense and on edge.

"Jesus Christ, are these numbers accurate? Are you sure about this?" Robert Blane said softly. The color had drained from his face. And because of his boasting to the press, Philip Chernier looked even worse.

"Best we can tell, yes. Give or take a hundred miles," the LINEAR director answered as she looked down at her computer screen worriedly. "It's the Earth's gravity. It's pulling the asteroid with more force than we had predicted."

"How's that possible, Andrea? We had a margin. There was room to spare." Blane leaned against the wall behind him. He seemed defeated by the news and was aware that he needed to regroup. Chernier was completely out of his element, unable to understand the complicated data they were seeing, and he said nothing.

"The computer models can only give us back data based on what we know, and we *didn't* know how much the gravitational pull our planet would have to steer the asteroid's path. There's no model for that. Not for an orbit like this, and not for an object that big. It doesn't exist, Robert. You know that." Andrea Clark sat stone-faced looking at the NASA director.

"So, explain to me, what will happen now?"

Clark looked puzzled, "You mean, like worst-case scenario?"

"Yes."

"Okay. Well," Andrea paused and pulled up a 3D model of the Earth on her computer screen. "At first, the impact zone was here, basically the center of the country. With time, the thrusters shift the trajectory north. Like this." Clark ran her finger along a dashed line laid out on a graphic map of North America. "The projected impact zone gets slowly moved towards the North Pole. And then, according to our original projections, the path of the asteroid skips up and over the top of the planet." With that, Clark threw her hand out and over the top of the computer screen.

Blane nodded, "What do the calculations tell you now?"

"The orbital shift is stalling. If we can't move it further, our best guess is that the impact is about here." Clark marked an "X" just *below* the North Pole, squarely in the center of the Arctic Ocean.

"Oh my god," Blane whispered.

Chernier finally spoke, "That's okay, right? No one lives there; it's unpopulated. That's better, isn't it?" No one answered him. Clark and Blane hung their heads and tried to breathe.

Still looking down at the floor, Blane finally responded, "No, Philip. It is not better."

Sparing Blane the agony of explaining to Chernier why it was worse, Andrea began speaking. "Philip, we are talking about an extreme rise in temperature within the Arctic Circle. Massive polar cap melting. A rise in sea levels threatening every coastal city on the planet. The warm water would cause sea currents to change. The jet stream would shift. Climates could change violently, practically overnight. Freshwater supplies would become unreliable, and crop production would, well, who the hell knows?"

The threatening chain reaction of a polar impact began to impact each person in the room.

"Oh, god," Chernier croaked, then added, "Can we get more thrusters to the asteroid in time?"

"I don't see how? Even if we had a vehicle that could get there, it would be too late," Blane responded.

As small as Andrea's office was, the two men had never noticed Brody Falls sitting quietly in the corner of the room. Who could blame them; their thoughts were elsewhere. But the young girl heard every word that was said, and her mind was on the problem instantly. In her view, the solution was obvious.

"They're already there," Brody said without looking up from her computer.

The two gentlemen stood up and stared at Brody, saying nothing but looking a bit confused.

"What do you mean?" Andrea asked.

"The Pegasus vehicles. Each one of them has a big ass thruster engine on the back, right? Use *them*." Brody Falls looked up from her computer just in time to see the lights turn on in each of the other so-called "adults in the room." And she smiled at them politely.

The air in the room seemed to suddenly return.

"Jesus Christ, Mother Mary, and all that is holy," were the only words Blane could manage to say.

————

T-Minus 24 days

After hours of meetings, presidential briefings, procedure development debates, and consultations with the ORBIX engineering team, a plan was devised and transmitted to Jack Parker.

Since he would be untethered briefly, Jack had to recharge the limited volume of pressurized gas in his EVA suit for navigation purposes. Then, he would leave Pegasus II and perform an EVA over to the Pegasus I landing field. Next came the grisly task of stowing Evelyn Davis' freeze-dried remains inside of the vehicle she had once piloted. NASA's video feed would go dark for the removal of her corpse...nobody needed to see that, but it had to be done in the event something went wrong firing up the ion engines while the spaceship was still anchored to the asteroid. There were many unknowns.

The ORBIX engineers repeatedly voiced their concerns about starting the thrusters while the craft was tethered to the rock's surface. "It's not built for that!" was the phrase heard most often during NASA's interactions with ORBIX.

"Philip, just tell me, can the anchor points take the stress?" Robert Blane demanded.

"Theoretically, yes. But more likely that 'yes' is a 'probably'," Chernier finally relented.

"That's good enough for me."

It was decided that Jack would rotate the thrusters downward fifty-seven degrees, just shy of the maximum, and ignite the engine. Next, he'd set the autopilot to gently increase the thrust up to seventy percent capacity. It would take some time for the engines to get to that point, so to assure his safety, Jack would return to the Pegasus II vehicle and observe. If the procedure worked on Peg I, then Jack would fire up the thruster on his ship.

By the time Jack returned to Peg II and extracted himself from the EVA suit, the blue light from Peg I's thruster engine had cast the area behind the ship in a steely light. Jack watched the vessel through the flight deck's main window, while he cautiously tried to relax in the co-pilot's seat.

A short burst of static broke the silence just ahead of a voice from mission control. "Peg II, Houston control, nice job out there. We are monitoring the video feed and are going live minus the delay, over."

The delay, or the time it took for the audio and visual transmission to travel back and forth between home and Jack's ship, had been decreasing every day as the asteroid got closer to Earth. Currently, the gap was around seventy seconds, still long enough to cause fairly awkward conversations, but much better than it had been. And, at the insistence of the President, NASA's feed was now being transmitted around the world. POTUS had pledged full transparency, and there was no turning back on that promise.

"Copy that, Houston. I can see the thruster's firepower increasing nicely. The blue light is getting brighter as we speak. How long do we have to wait to fire Peg II's thruster? Let's keep pushing this thing, over."

Expecting NASA's reply momentarily, Jack took the opportunity to float over the crew compartment and get a drink of water. He filled a pouch with 500 ml of water and slowly emptied it through the straw. He was filling it up for a second time when he heard a panicked voice over the com.

"Jack, are you seeing this? What's happening out there?"

Jack quickly turned and grabbed the nearest handle hold in front of him. He pulled and flung himself through the crew cabin and toward the flight deck of Pegasus II. He grabbed a second handle and pulled again, arching his back and raising his torso to see out and over the window just ahead of him. When he reached the front of the craft and looked out to see what was happening with Peg I, he gasped.

The area where Pegasus I had been just a few moments ago was empty.

The ship was gone.

In the roughly two and a half minutes it had taken for the video feed to travel home and for NASA to send back a response, Pegasus I had endured a catastrophic failure.

An anchor line, the very one that Evelyn Davis had intended to secure with resin manually after it had failed to deploy on its own, broke loose. The engine's thrust, as it slowly increased, soon caused the craft to gently shimmy from side to side. The wobble was slight in the beginning, but quickly picked up momentum as the untethered side of the craft began bouncing erratically. In mere moments, Pegasus I was shaking and moving about violently as the ion thrusters applied more and more pressure to both the hull of the ship and to the two remaining tethers straining to secure it to the asteroid's surface. Finally, much like a wild animal being released back in the wild, Pegasus I broke free from its inter terrestrial chains and shot off into outer space, spinning wildly in circles and out of control.

The ion thruster engines would provide enough power to fuel the spaceship for decades, maybe longer. And with that, the people of Earth saw the last of Pegasus I as it flew off into the nether regions of the galaxy…carrying Evelyn Davis' body away with it.

CHAPTER 24

2029

THOMAS AND JILLIAN English had been home for about a week. It was nearly June, and the couple was settling into their summer groove, spending the first few days back home unpacking from their trip and restocking their kitchen with groceries. As much as they loved leaving the U.P. during the winter months, that didn't mean they disliked being up north. Far from it. After decades of harsh winters, they had opted to leave all that cold weather living to the young folks. Besides, summers on the southern coast, with the humidity and hundred-plus temperatures, were worse. At least they thought so.

Summers in northern Michigan are glorious. Crisp morning walks along the river or warm hikes through the jack pines and birches in the afternoon are every bit as beautiful as any stroll on a Texas beach, which no doubt pale in comparison to the hundreds of freshwater beaches lining the Great Lakes. Gazing out over the vast horizon on Lake Superior isn't much different than looking out over the Gulf of Mexico. The awesome beauty and enormity of both are simply majestic.

Since her parents' return, Emily spent nearly every night after work at her folks' house, catching up and reconnecting. She loved her parents, but she was always ready to see them leave for the winter. By summertime, though, she was more than happy when they came back home. Such was the cycle Emily had grown accustomed to expect. Also, she was an only child and often felt her parents were sometimes a little too involved in her private life.

During the last few months, Emily had called to check in with her mom and dad routinely, as was her custom. But she never talked about her dating life with her parents, although her mom would sometimes ask. Jillian English wasn't prying, just making conversation, but Emily didn't always see it that way. Regardless, there was never anything to report. The single men in the area represented a rather thin slice of the population, and for the most part, Emily found the slice unappealing.

Of course, Emily didn't realize that there was a reason her mom hadn't broached the subject, that reason being Jack's rather interesting way of introducing himself to them. However, after their meeting in Texas, her parents were anxious to find out a few details from their daughter. They played along at Jack's request and pretended they didn't know a thing, but it wasn't easy to do.

"What do you do all winter down south anyway? Don't you get bored?" Emily wondered out loud as her mom poured them each a glass of red wine (a rather large pour, but Emily wasn't complaining). She took a sip and sat with her mom on the back patio. The sun was finally dipping below the tree line, transforming the forest into a black silhouette against the orange and yellow colors on the horizon. Emily was wearing the rather odd combination of shorts and a hoodie. After the sun went down, she often needed a little extra something for warmth.

"It's not boring at all. Your dad and I walk every morning. We cook. We read a lot and listen to music. I sketch birds…"

Emily cut her off, "You sketch birds?" she asked rather surprised. "Can I see?"

"Eventually," Mrs. English replied smiling. "I'm almost good enough to share some of them."

"Okay, well that's actually kind of cool, I have to admit. What else?"

"Oh, you know, sweetie, it's just the usual stuff. Stuff you can't do in three feet of snow," said her mom as she crossed her legs and rested them on the bench in front of her. "What about you? Don't *you* get bored in the winter?"

Emily let out a short chuckle, "Well, I wasn't bored *this* winter." As innocuous as the remark was, it hung in the air between mother and daughter, then drifted away in the cool night breeze. "I mean. I always keep busy. You know that."

Emily took another sip from her wineglass. Mrs. English noticed that her daughter seemed to stare out at nothing, lost in her thoughts. She felt she was betraying her daughter's trust a little by keeping Jack's secret, but Emily's private business was her own, and if she wanted to confide in her mother, she could.

"You okay?" she finally asked her daughter.

"I'm good, mom," Emily replied, her face without expression.

Jillian looked at her daughter and pressed a little, "Em, listen, I'm sorry I haven't been very helpful to you, with, you know. Relationships. But you should put yourself out there a little more."

"Mom, I know you mean well…"

"But that's just it. I'm not much good in that area." Her mom paused to sip her wine, "I got lucky. I fell in love with your dad when I was in college, and it's been wonderful. Truly. But I know it rarely works out that way. I'm not good at giving you advice on matters of the heart and how you should feel. I have no clue. I wish I knew what to say to help. I honestly do."

192

JACK PARKER SAVES THE WORLD

"Mom, do you think I'd even listen? Even if you gave me the best advice, I wouldn't take it." Emily laughed. "You know me."

Her mom smiled. "That's true. But I wish I could tell you anyway. That way, I could say 'I told you so'."

"Ha!" Emily scoffed. "You're hilarious."

Emily raised her glass and waited for her mom to match the gesture. "Cheers, mom. You somehow manage to find the right words."

After another healthy swig of wine, Emily felt the warmth of the alcohol rise slowly in her chest. A moment or two later, Emily broke the quiet and cleared her throat.

"Mom, I wasn't bored this winter because I met someone." Emily paused while her mother looked at her, waiting for her to continue. "But it didn't work out. It wasn't anybody's fault. He's a good and decent man, and he didn't do anything wrong."

"So, you *aren't* good, then?" Emily's mom finally asked.

"Not so much."

———

Jack parked his truck just inside the tree line that shielded his property from the road. After twisting the top off an iced cold Lumberman's Lager, he flipped down the tailgate of his Ford and took a seat. Lily jumped up and sat beside him. His jeans were dusty and the trucker hat he was wearing was damp with sweat. It had been a busy morning. Thirty yards in front of him, the disjointed sound of vehicles whooshing past his driveway muted the calls of the nearby robins and sandpipers.

At Jack's request, and with help from Guardian and the resources at her disposal, Jack had had his property secured in a way that someone of his stature both needed and required. If he were to step out of his self-imposed exile and back into any semblance of public life whatsoever, he needed to take precautions.

193

Jack hoped that the community would embrace the notion that he could live a simple life among them, but there was certainly no guarantee that he would be able to do so safely. And if Emily saw her way clear to share her life with him, then he would need to protect her as well. Besides, he figured if his plan went sideways, he could always find another place and, once again, retreat into isolation.

The cold beer was refreshing, and Jack sipped it slowly as he stared out at the road. Although the entrance to his property was certainly visible from the main road, the turnoff wasn't something a person would necessarily notice, particularly if they were looking for it. It wasn't marked. There was no mailbox out by the road, either. Anyone passing by would probably think the path was little more than ingress into a parcel of uninhabited land. Eventually, over time though, if he began leaving and returning to the cabin enough, someone would notice.

The Guardian had sent a rather industrious construction crew to secure the property. They had arrived in two white panel vans with a mountain of supplies loaded on a flatbed truck. After seven days of laying concrete, carpentry, and laying cable lines, they were gone, but what they left behind was nothing short of amazing.

In all of the country, only Camp David's safeguards could compare to the safety net built around Jack's cabin. Motion sensors, video monitors, thermal arrays, and various alarms had been placed at strategic locations around the perimeter of the property. A gatehouse had been installed just inside the main entrance, far enough back from the road that it remained unseen by passing motorists. It was large enough to be comfortable, heated and air-conditioned and with running water and a restroom. Jack made certain that the structure was extremely well camouflaged, to blend in with the natural surroundings. For now, the gatehouse wouldn't be manned by security personnel, but he could easily add them later if needed.

Another larger guardhouse had been erected near Jack's cabin to monitor all of the video and sensor feeds. This building had over 600 square feet of room and included a bunk area, a kitchenette, and a full bathroom. Jack's computers were also upgraded to receive the data as well, just in case any alarms were triggered. Jack's cabin and the land surrounding it had become a secure compound.

Lily sat upright next to her companion Jack, watching the tree limbs shake with the movements of a squirrel she couldn't see, but knew was there. Her ears perked up.

"Lily, what do you think?" Jack asked as if he expected an answer. Lily turned toward Jack and tilted her head.

"You know, this is all your fault, you know that, right?" Jack rubbed the scruff of her neck and leaned over to let her lick his face. "Yeah, this is all your fault. But you know what? I'm not complaining."

After a few rubs behind the ears, Jack hopped off the tailgate and Lily followed close behind.

"Let's go do this. C'mon girl."

Jack and Lily hopped in the truck and headed back toward the cabin to get cleaned up. The former astronaut slowed down when he approached to the newly installed gatehouse. He reached out of the cab and pressed his thumb against a glass scanner. A heavy iron gate swung open to let him pass, then quickly closed behind him.

———

Charles Dunning had spent nearly two weeks preparing for an "emergency" city council meeting. He had explained repeatedly that there was no *real* emergency, no important or urgent issue that needed the council's immediate attention, but he assured everyone he came in contact with that they wouldn't want to miss it. An uncontrollable smile usually accompanied his "warning." and his efforts to drum up curiosity and enthusiasm for the meeting were contagious. So much so, that plans were made to move the meeting from the city's council chambers to the high school gymnasium.

Tuesdays don't have much of a flavor, not like Fridays or even Mondays, but this Tuesday felt like an unofficial holiday of sorts. The people from the city and surrounding area filed into the gym by the hundreds. The air conditioner did its best to fight the rising temperature of the room, but with so many bodies crammed together, it was losing the battle. Mayor Dunning checked his watch. It was 6:45, fifteen minutes until the meeting was scheduled to begin.

A wooden podium had been placed at one end of the room underneath a basketball goal that had been cranked up toward the ceiling. Bleachers on each side of the court buzzed with chatter as the crowd waited for the meeting to begin. Rows of folding chairs placed evenly inside the lines on the basketball court were also filled to capacity. In the back of the room, more people without seats stood and waited. Some folks thought Charles Dunning was going to announce a plan to run for governor. Others considered the notion that the mayor wanted to reveal his plans for a performing arts center, a pet project of his for quite some time. Wild guesses were the main topic of conversation.

Suddenly, Mayor Dunning tapped on the microphone to make sure it was live. The screeching noise quieted the room in anticipation. Several tables had been set up next to the podium, where eight council members sat looking more annoyed than curious. Although the mayor could call an unscheduled meeting anytime if he saw fit, the council was usually given briefings on such matters ahead of time. Now, however, they had no inkling of what Dunning was up to. The crowd of people didn't know why they were packed in the rather hot, stuffy school gymnasium, either. Nobody knew anything. Well, almost nobody.

A few blocks away, Thomas English rang the bell at the back door of his daughter's clinic. While his wife sat in the gymnasium in a folding chair twenty feet from the mayor, Emily's dad was stopping by to give Emily one last chance to come with him to the mysterious council meeting. Emily had no interest. She didn't see what all the fuss was about. After several more rings and a few knocks, Emily opened the door.

"Hey, dad. I thought you were over at the school. What's up?"

"Em, I need to you come with me over to the gym. Your mom is waiting, saving us a couple of seats, and I want you to come and see what this is all about. Okay?" Mr. English said, trying hard to hide, at this point, what was a terrible poker face.

"Why do you keep asking me to go to that thing, Dad? Seriously. It's no big deal to me. Sounds boring, in fact," Emily said as she gave her dad a little smirk.

Thomas, knowing that he had few options left if he wanted to get Emily over to the high school, was grasping at straws.

"Emily, there's going to be a speaker there tonight. Someone that wants to talk to the town, and it's pretty exciting. I think you know him."

"What are you talking about? I know just about everyone in this town. So what?" Emily asked, still not understanding the reason her dad was making such a fuss about the whole thing.

Mr. English sighed, then hedged his bet and said in a whisper, "Mayor Dunning told me to keep this a secret, but he swore to me that Jack Parker is going to speak tonight to the city council. He wants to address the whole community about, well, something important."

Emily looked at her dad, mouth agape. Finally, she asked, "What's going on, dad?"

"Are you coming or not?" was his only reply.

CHAPTER 25

2021
T-MINUS 23 DAYS

THE WORLD'S sentiment could have easily turned against NASA. The most accomplished space agency in history had fought long odds to intercept a dangerous and problematic asteroid in deep space; had successfully landed not one, but two space crafts on its surface; had deployed eight ion thrusters on alien terrain, and had done all of that in an incredibly small time frame. But, all of that was forgotten.

Billions of people had watched Evelyn Davis perish because the wrong chemical defogger had been applied inside her helmet. Pegasus I had detached from the asteroid and cartwheeled out into space because CAPCOM neglected to have Jack fully secure one of its tethers. Those two errors might have doomed the mission. Not only that, but redirecting the asteroid's strike to the arctic would undoubtedly set off unimaginable consequences for the entire planet. NASA and ORBIX had made things worse.

Americans watching events unfold at home didn't know how to

react. There were pockets of people that wanted to take out their frustrations on the government, and a few did, but most people didn't know exactly where or how to direct them. The National and State Guards had been deployed for months to help calm the worried population, so their presence had been normalized. Community policing had been ramped up, and for the most part, had been interacting with citizens without major issues. Parents didn't want to frighten their children, so many soldiered on as if nothing bad was going to happen. Surprisingly, many people conducted their lives as if everything was normal. Psychiatrists referred to this as Optimism Bias, a condition where a person thinks the danger at hand doesn't really apply to them, or won't affect them in a significant way. However, after the loss of Pegasus I, Optimism Bias soon gave way to the reality of the likely failure of the mission, along with overwhelming anxiety and dread.

Interestingly, an unforeseen run on telescopes had occurred and virtually none could be found for sale anywhere. Online retailers had been sold out for months, and even the supply on eBay and Craigslist had gone dry. As the asteroid moved closer and closer to Earth, it became visible to the naked eye. At first, it appeared as a dot in the night sky, faint and still. The image of a streak of light blazing across the heavens is all Hollywood. In reality, the pinpoint of light simply got slightly brighter with each passing day, slowly changing position against the backdrop of the night's starry constellations.

Observatories around the world focused their telescopes on the greatest celestial show in recorded history. Each of them put stunning images on their websites. Observing the oncoming asteroid from Earth was nothing short of amazing, but *terrifying*, and there was nothing anyone could do to change the likelihood of the oncoming disaster. Nobody that is, except Jack Parker.

Hours after the loss of Pegasus I, Jack went back to work. He was no longer waiting for NASA's help. It's not that he didn't need their assistance; it was that he knew they couldn't provide him a quick resolution. Pegasus II's ion thruster was on deck, even though firing up Peg I turned out disastrous. There was no other option.

Jack felt horrible, and he was angry. He blamed himself for the loss of Pegasus I. Evie's voice echoed in his head as he recalled her informing NASA about the failure of the resin injector to completely seal one of her anchor points. How could he have missed it? Shortly after Pegasus I had disappeared, Jack readied himself for another EVA. A voice from CAPCOM crackled through his communication system.

"Houston to Pegasus II, do you copy, Jack? Our monitors indicate you are a "go" to commence EVA activity."

"Copy Houston, I'm entering the airlock with the resin injector now. Standby to secure EVAAS."

Jack planned to shore up Peg II's anchor points. If his ship became untethered as Pegasus I had, even with him in the pilot's seat, the asteroid would simply continue toward Earth without him. The loss of momentum would be so great that Jack would not have enough time to catch up to the asteroid. Besides, there would be no way to repair the anchoring system if it failed. The mission could not sustain any more errors. Every action was now mission-critical. Zero fail.

Jack left the airlock and made his way underneath the ship. Slowly and methodically, he inspected each of the tethers that kept Pegasus II connected to the asteroid. They were rock solid. But taking no chances, Jack used the manual resin injector to layer more adhesive resin onto each attachment point as an added precaution. Brown resin oozed over the titanium anchors and onto the asteroid itself, creating a globule reminiscent of a quickly cooled lava flow. The material was a hundred times stronger than concrete and it instantly solidified when exposed to the vacuum of space.

"Looking good Jack. Our engineers are confident those joints will hold up. Over."

"Houston," Jack paused to catch his breath, "that's just great. Tell them all thanks so much for me."

Jack's sarcasm dripped through the microphone, and it was as biting as it was unexpected. Jack paused and waited for a response. As he did so, he turned and looked out past the asteroid's scraggly, uneven terrain. The sun never sets in space, its light shines throughout the solar system like a star atop a Christmas tree, crystalline in nature. The shimmer from millions of distant stars was swallowed by the Sun's presence. The astronaut admired its beauty through his tinted visor, then raised it to take in its full effect. Jack squinted, then turned his head slightly. That's when he noticed, for the first time, a tiny bluish light in the distance, only recognizable if one knew what to look for. Earth.

It was a sight Jack hadn't seen in months, his *home*. Finally, after so much time in space, he could see what he had been fighting for. Overwhelmed and overcome with emotion, Jack stared at his home planet, mesmerized by the tiny ball floating in a sea of blackness. Alone and quiet. A world that was so ordinary in the distance, but teeming with color and sound and life in Jack's mind. He closed his eyes and imagined as many miracles of nature and human accomplishments as he could. Back home, a voice filled with almost childlike wonder and awe came over the radio.

"I see Earth," Jack whispered. "Houston, I can see it."

NASA's video feed, which followed Jack's every movement, showed a single astronaut standing tall, tethered tightly to an alien surface, all alone, looking out into space. The image was breathtakingly poignant, and as usual, the world was watching.

Jack, forgetting himself, continued to speak into his com without measure. "I'm here looking at you. I'm here and you're all there, so far away. But I see you." Jack paused. His voice had started to tremble slightly, but he continued, "You look magnificent. I can't believe it. I don't think I've ever seen anything as beautiful as what I'm seeing right now."

Most of Earth's eight billion people were watching a man they had never met, but at that moment they knew exactly how he felt. Over the past few months, every man, woman, and child old enough to know better had, at one time or another, imagined what it would feel like to *be* Jack Parker. They listened to and hung onto his every word. Mankind watched silently with their hands over their mouths, biting their fingernails, or slowly lowering their heads in prayer. Jack stood on the asteroid, population of one, and looked out at a planet that was thirteen million miles away from him. Yet at that moment, somehow, it was as if everyone was connected, humanity grasping tightly to the common thread that weaves through everyone. Jack remained outside Pegasus near the airlock, watching Earth. Thinking. Wondering...

Instead of unclipping the EVAAS harness and climbing the steps back up into the ship, Jack moved around and under the Pegasus vehicle. The camera angle was such that his actions couldn't be seen by NASA, but he clearly lifted the resin injector and began working on something.

A few moments later, Robert Blane's voice came over Jack's com, "Jack, we can't see what you're working on from our angle, please advise, over."

"I'm adding resin to the other end of the tethers, the ends connected to Pegasus."

When the message came through Blane's radio, he replied instantly, already knowing it was too late.

"Negative, Jack. Do not shore up the Pegasus side of the tethers. You will not be able to release them if you add the resin. REPEAT, do not add resin! You will not be able to disconnect from them effectively."

Blane shook his head in disbelief. He knew that the Pegasus vehicle would need to unsnap the tethers under the belly of the ship, so it could leave the asteroid's surface and return to Earth. With enough force, the line could break. Nothing could prevent that possibility. Even so, loose tethers whipping around wildly under the Pegasus craft would undoubtedly cause catastrophic failure to the heat shields, making reentry impossible. Jack was essentially stranding himself on the asteroid.

CAPCOM's radio sprang to life, "Robert, it's fine. I've got to shore up the tethers. If Peg II breaks off from the asteroid, we're screwed. I won't have time to chase it down, and even if I did, I couldn't land on it. Besides, I'm planning on ejecting as I fly past Earth. So be ready."

Jack used the remainder of the resin, then worked his way back toward the airlock. He disengaged the EVAAS and entered Pegasus II. He was in the process of taking off his helmet when Blane's urgent voice came in over the radio.

"Jack, ejecting at that speed is not assured. And that's if you're in close enough to pull it off. The ejection capsule is built for abort on takeoff and at low orbit only. If you're not in low orbit, you'll skip right off Earth's atmosphere. Do you copy? Jack…"

Jack stowed his EVA suit while Blane continued to talk. Making no mind of the camera, he proceeded to strip down to his boxer briefs. Jack's body was muscular but thin. His time on the Advanced Resistance Exercise Device had been paying off. He pushed his way to the crew compartment and filled a pouch with water. When Robert Blane had finally stopped talking, Jack looked at the camera and laughed.

"Robert," Jack began with a chuckle. "Do you honestly think Pegasus can move this asteroid to any level above low orbit altitude? Really? We'll be lucky to track this thing over the pole and out into space. I'm not worried about that."

Jack paused and took on a serious tone, "Listen. If I can eject safely, then fine. If not, I'm going down swinging. I cannot return home a failure. If I can't succeed, then why come back, right?" Jack looked straight into the camera, "Don't worry about me."

Jack shrugged his shoulders and slammed down the pouch of water. He was tired but resolute.

As the people of Earth watched and listened to Jack's exchange with CAPCOM, they all realized the same thing.

Jack was going to redirect the asteroid or die trying.

———

T-MINUS 19 DAYS

Andrea Clark's team was running the numbers and clenching their teeth, just as they had earlier while measuring the effect the original thrusters had had on the asteroid's orbital redirect. Over the last few days, Jack had cautiously raised the thruster power on Pegasus II from five percent to forty percent. The tether lines were holding firm as the spacecraft strained against them. All Jack could do at this point, along with everyone else, was wait.

Pegasus' thruster engine was succeeding in changing the path of the asteroid, but only slightly. At the current rate of redirect, it wasn't going to be enough. Jack would have to continue to increase the thruster's capacity slowly. But NASA's team was working on a math problem with too many variables to successfully predict the outcome.

Andrea Clark and Robert Blane had just finished another video briefing with the President and his cabinet. The news presented was encouraging, but hardly definitive. Nevertheless, the tone of the exchange seemed acrimonious. The President was tired and irritated.

"Well, that went well," Andrea said aloud after the screen went black.

Blane wasn't fazed, "Oh, it was fine. The President's just frustrated like the rest of us."

"How so?" asked the LINEAR director.

"Lack of control is incredibly frustrating, wouldn't you agree?"

"Yes. I would, no doubt," Andrea said nodding her head. She leaned back in her office chair and sighed.

Blane went on, "For the most part, we've lost control of the mission. All that's left is to calculate how much and how quickly we need to increase the thruster output on Peg II. Then we cross our fingers. It's not much of a plan at this point, especially in our business."

Clark thought for a moment, then asked the million-dollar question: "What are your guys telling you? Can we fire the ion engine at a hundred percent?"

"We think eighty percent, tops."

"Okay then, at eighty percent, you're going to have to get there pretty quickly for the engines to have enough time to reach assured orbital redirect. Right?" Andrea was quickly making the estimates in her head.

"Eight days, five percent a day. Eleven days left until possible impact." Robert Blane checked the computer on the table in front of him. On the corner of the screen was an envelope, and on it, a red number that read 10,489,799. It was Blane's official NASA email inbox. Messages from all over the world had stacked up for months, making his email account unusable. The NASA director clicked his mouse a few times, opening an alternate email account that had been set up for him, and scanned a handful of new emails.

"A message from Philip. How nice. I wonder where he's been hiding." Blane's eyes moved from side to side as he read Chernier's message.

Andrea scrunched her face, "You haven't seen him?"

"Not in a couple of days, but he's around. At least I think so.

Maybe he took off. Hell, I don't even care at this point," Blane replied matter of factly.

Blane continued to read Chernier's message, his focus steadily intensifying. He made a few more clicks on the computer and stood up.

"What did he say?" Clark asked.

"Ejection capsule protocol. I sent it over to CAPCOM. Jack's window is going to be tight. Very tight."

———

T-Minus 10 Days

Jack thought about dying. He wasn't afraid of death, but the dying process was a little disconcerting. There were options, though. If the ejection capsule skipped off Earth's atmosphere and out into space, then he would simply run out of oxygen. Breathing air with high levels of carbon dioxide and little oxygen would cause him to pass out and eventually die. A breach in the Pegasus vehicle was also a possibility as he neared Earth's atmosphere. The craft was inverted under the asteroid relative to its position to Earth. With no heat shield, the craft would break apart. The speed of the Pegasus vehicle encountering that kind of atmospheric friction would either roast Jack alive or shred him to bits as Pegasus disintegrated. Both seemed less appealing to Jack than running out of air. He could always open the airlock in a pinch. But again, less appealing.

One hundred and fifty days ago, NASA sent two crafts into space to change an asteroid's path just enough to avoid a global apocalypse. And while they hadn't succeeded just yet, they were still in the game. Pegasus' thruster engine had achieved eighty percent capacity, and NASA's numbers looked good. Good but not great.

Peg II was approximately six million miles from Earth, and while the lag time between radio transmissions had been reduced to half a minute or so, the spacecraft was still farther away from Earth than any other manned spaceflight had ever been, by far. The general public considered Jack close to home. He wasn't. Not yet.

"Peg II to CAPCOM, over."

Jack waited for a response. Yesterday was wash day for Jack. That meant his clothes were too funky to keep wearing, so he simply changed into a new flight suit. It's impossible to do laundry in space, so astronauts pack plenty of underwear, socks, and jumpsuits. And, if an astronaut changes flight suits, they'd better shower first. For Jack, a shower on Pegasus meant using a few disposable washcloths and a clean shave.

The personal area in the crew compartment was the only place on the ship where there weren't any cameras, and Jack enjoyed its privacy. Unfortunately, if he stayed there too long, everyone watching made assumptions about what you were doing. In that way, even private time wasn't strictly private. Regardless, Jack was clean and freshly groomed and looked remarkably well, all things considered.

"Houston to Pegasus, we copy. Sending you a slight thruster increase now, over."

Jack received the message and read it carefully. NASA was asking him to exceed what many felt was the thruster limit as it sat tethered to the rock. That meant that the asteroid needed even more redirect. He didn't hesitate.

"Copy that, Houston. Increasing thruster output to eighty-three percent."

A digital readout on the ship's console changed from eighty to eighty-three as Jack adjusted a dial on the flight deck. The thruster output would adjust to match the new setting.

"Jack, we feel that the thrusters can handle..."

Without waiting for the message to finish, Jack talked over CAPCOM's signal.

"That's fine. Whatever you need. No explanations are required. Just do the math," Jack said bluntly.

Blane, Chernier, and Clark, all standing in the heart of mission control, looked at each other with trepidation. Chernier was holding a set of computer printouts, studying a few lines of data in front of him.

"It's going to be close. Jesus."

Blane replied softly, "It's razor-thin. Even at a hundred percent thruster output."

Andrea Clark didn't say a word.

CHAPTER 26

2029

JACK PARKER SAT in a storage closet with piles of paper towels and toilet paper stacked on shelves to his left and an empty mop bucket on his right. He'd been sitting on a metal folding chair for almost an hour. For the last twenty minutes or so, he held a large can of OdorBan absorbent granules, or as the manufacturer described them, "Fairy Dust for Life's Big Messes." The *messes* included mucus, vomit, and excrement. The directions for use and ingredient list fascinated Jack as he read over them, again and again. He was thinking about how underpaid custodians certainly must be when a light knock brought his attention back to his current situation.

Charles Dunning opened the door slowly then quickly stepped inside and shut it behind him. Jack stood up still holding the can of vomit granules in his hand as Dunning spoke.

"Everything is ready, Mr. Parker," the mayor said quietly. "It's a full house, just so you know."

"Emily and her parents?"

"Emily and her dad just sat down. Jill must have fought off a hundred people trying to save those two seats for them. It was a thing of beauty I must say. The woman is fierce."

Dunning straightened his tie, then extended his hand. Jack shook it. "Remember now, just walk straight across the hall and through the double doors. I've blocked an area off so you can walk right up to the podium and speak. I'll make a few remarks, thank everyone for coming, that sort of thing, then you'll have the floor."

"Thank you, Charles. I appreciate it." Jack said. He placed his hand on the mayor's shoulder and repeated himself, "Sincerely, thank you."

"Mr. Parker, you don't have to thank me for a damn thing. It's the least I could do." Dunning was so awestruck by Jack's graciousness that he almost started to cry. After a moment's hesitation, he turned and exited the storage closet leaving Jack nervous and alone.

Jack chuckled to himself. After his mission, as much as he wanted to keep a low profile, it hadn't been possible. The United States had accomplished the improbable, if not the impossible, and Jack felt it was his duty to embrace the legacy of the achievement. NASA and ORBIX both deserved credit for their contributions. And if nothing else, the details of the intercept and his time in space were important for the historical record. That was something important to the former Guardian, turned astronaut, turned hopeless recluse. History always matters.

The mayor began his speech and Jack could hear his muffled voice through the closet door. He looked at the can of vomit granules one more time and took a deep breath. Not that long ago, Jack Parker had spoken to arenas full of adoring and grateful citizens. He'd been on cable news shows, late-night shows, even on Sesame Street. Not long after he returned from space, he appeared in front of a joint session of Congress to accept the Presidential Medal of

Freedom. Jack Parker had done it all, but never in his life had he been *this* nervous.

———

2021

T-Minus 5 Days

Andrea Clark looked at her computer screen. The world had access to photographs from the most powerful telescopes on the planet, and every observatory that could get a clear view of the oncoming asteroid had posted amazing photographs online. But no one saw what she could see. Thanks to the Hubble Space Telescope, the LINEAR director sat looking at one of the most astonishing pictures she had ever seen. Pegasus II, clear as a bell, stood firm on the underside of 2021CF02. A blueish light cast small shadows on the uneven terrain near the ion thruster field. If for some reason Jack needed to leave Peg II and perform an EVA, she would have been able to see his tiny body moving about on the surface.

Incredible, she thought.

Andrea Clark picked up her phone and dialed. Robert Blane answered on the first ring.

"Yes Andrea," said the NASA director.

"Hello, Robert. Have you seen the images from Hubble?"

"I have."

"Will they be released to the public?" Andrea asked.

"Not yet. Listen, Andrea, this is a bad time. Let me call you right back?"

Blane hung up the phone.

Clark looked over at Brody Falls, sitting quietly in front of her computer loading the latest data into LINEAR's tracking program. NASA updated the asteroid's orbital estimates constantly. Velocity, gravity, and thrust from the ion engines were always at odds, but one thing was clear, the mission's slim margin for success was getting slimmer. Brody scrunched her mouth and wrinkled her nose. Her hair was pulled tightly behind her into a bun, revealing a brow furrowed with concentration. She whistled quietly and tapped her pencil on the desk rhythmically.

"I don't think this orbital adjustment could be any tighter," Brody said as she continued to study the data in front of her. "Think about it. If NASA had launched one day earlier. If the ion engines were a tad more powerful, or even if we could have loaded more engines onto the Pegasus vehicles in the first place. Or, how about this, if the asteroid had one percent less mass..."

"Brody," Andrea Clark interrupted. "What's your point?"

"It's fascinating, that's all. A million little pieces fitting together just so." Brody paused and thought for a moment. "Andrea, did you know that in 1985 a Lockheed L-1011 crashed on approach to DFW Airport killing 163 people on board plus one guy who was driving his car on the freeway. The plane just dropped down on top of him. Probably never saw it coming."

Clark looked at Brody curiously, "I've read about that crash. A microburst brought it down."

"Correct. But think about the one guy on the ground that died. Missing one green traffic light would have saved his life. Or he could have poured himself one more cup of coffee, which might have pushed his departure back a few minutes. That would have saved his life for sure. Suppose he'd gotten a phone call or had broken a shoelace. Point is, even if he knew in advance the plane was coming down at that moment in that exact spot, he couldn't have planned for his car to be there on purpose. Just too many variables out of his control. It was horrible luck."

The LINEAR director looked at Brody and smiled. Then she asked, "What does all this have to do with the orbital redirect if I may ask?"

"Ms. Clark, we are dealing with exponentially fewer variables here, and the ones we do have are all set. Either this planet is going to have an asteroid hit it, or it won't. There is nothing more we can do. Am I wrong?"

Surprised by the girl's demeanor, she decided to ask Brody about how those variables played out in her head.

"Okay then, what do you think the odds are that we're safe? Give me odds?"

"I'd say, maybe sixty percent. Give or take."

Andrea winced a little then said, "That doesn't sound so great, Brody."

"Any gambler would take those odds."

"Brody, they'd take those odds with money, not with their lives." Andrea looked at the girl a little confused. Brody was extremely smart, gifted really. But sometimes her observations puzzled Andrea.

"Where's my phone?" Andrea said out loud to herself.

"It's under there," Brody replied as she pointed a finger at a stack of papers.

Andrea picked up the phone and dialed. She looked at Brody Falls and gestured to her as if she wanted the girl to listen to her conversation. A moment later, someone on the other end picked up.

"Hey, babe. Did I wake you?"

Andrea smiled. Her face wore exhaustion with a touch of sadness.

"No, I'm fine. I just wanted to hear your voice for a second."

Brody looked at Andrea Clark curiously, wondering why she chose this moment to make what was obviously a very personal phone call.

"I know. Me too."

Andrea's eyes suddenly reddened, even as her smile broadened.

"Listen, I have to go. But I wanted to tell you how much I love you, sweetie. You're everything to me."

There was a long pause, then Andrea put the phone down on her desk. She sniffed and wiped the corner of her eyes with the back of her hands. Brody continued to watch the LINEAR director closely. She'd never seen her even the least bit vulnerable before now.

After she'd composed herself, Andrea looked directly at Brody Falls to make sure she had her full attention.

"Brody, it's time for you to leave here to be with your family."

"But why?"

"It's time for you to be with the people that love you."

———

2029

Mayor Dunning oozed enthusiasm. His wide grin and peppy demeanor seemed odd to many in the crowd. Dunning had always prided himself on being cool and collected. At the moment though, he seemed anything but. No matter, the folks in the gymnasium would soon know why the mayor had set up the meeting and what all the fuss was about.

Emily sat between her parents trying to catch her breath. Not only had she run the three blocks from her house to the gym, but she was also more than just a little nervous about what was happening. Her dad had played dumb well enough that Emily had finally stopped asking questions. Thomas and his wife exchanged looks as he gave her a subtle wink of accomplishment. Just then, the microphone sprang to life with the squeal of feedback.

"Oh, sorry about that folks," the mayor said apologetically.

He waited a moment for the noise to subside, then Charles Dunning started speaking with a tone just above that of a eulogy. Heartfelt, but reverent.

"Thank you for coming today." Dunning hesitated and cleared

his throat. "Councilmembers, thanks for indulging me in calling this meeting. I'm sure you've been wondering why and I'm sorry about all the mystery."

The crowd was silent.

"I'm proud to be a part of this community. It's unique. Special. The people here, your neighbors and mine, are resilient and compassionate. We support each other and come together when we need to, but we also value hard work and contribution. Our community is passionate about life and the way we love our families. There is no better place to live anywhere on Earth. I believe that and I know you do as well."

The people in the room hung on Dunning's every word.

"A few weeks ago, I got a call from a man who asked for a favor. He wanted to speak to the fine people of this city. And, he wanted to ask something from this community. I set up this meeting for him to do just that. You see, I owe this man a debt of gratitude. For me, it was an honor to help him out any way I could."

Jack quietly opened the door of the storage closet and stepped out into the hall. The mayor's words, no longer muffled, reverberated through the walls of the gymnasium and moved through the air around him. Jack stood still and took a deep breath. He let it out slowly. Six years had passed since he had excused himself from public life. Six years of isolation and self-imposed exile was going to end in a few seconds, and the man holding a can of vomit granules felt as though he was going to need them any moment. He stood up straight, cleared his throat, and ran a hand over the top of his neatly trimmed hair. The mayor had stopped talking. That was his cue.

The man who had so bravely fought to save the world from a catastrophic disaster took two long strides to the heavy door of the gymnasium and pulled it open. With all the courage he could muster, Jack walked into a room packed wall to wall with people, and he walked up to the empty podium. A stunned crowd collectively gasped as they watched the most recognizable face in history step up to the microphone. After a moment of whispered 'oh my gods' whooshing around the room, Jack awkwardly set the can of vomit granules on the floor next to his feet and smiled.

"Hello. Thank you for coming here today. My name is Jack Parker."

———

2021

T-MINUS 24 HOURS

Philip Chernier had just finished a briefing with the ORBIX team regarding the capsule ejection protocol. Pegasus was designed to save the lives of the crew in the event of a catastrophic failure, but it had never been deployed in a real-life emergency. Soon, that would change, and no one was certain of the outcome. Parker had a small window of time, mere seconds, to make his ejection from the Pegasus vehicle or risk bouncing off of the atmosphere and out into space. He'd be lost with no return capabilities. Everyone was aware of the risks. All of the waiting would be over soon enough.

Leading climatologists had given the United Nations their best estimates on the thermodynamic repercussions of an asteroid strike anywhere near the polar cap. Philip Chernier wasn't taking any chances. If the mission failed, the ensuing chaos couldn't be quantified, and the ORBIX director was a human being whose entire adult life was data-driven. Uncertainty was a bad thing in his book, something he wasn't willing to accept. Chernier had done all he could do. There was nothing left. It was time for him to leave, to be with his family.

Chernier took quick strides out of the building and over to his candy apple Tesla Roadster, got in, and took off toward the base's front gate. Soon, he would be cruising at 40,000 feet in a Gulfstream G650. His family, neatly tucked away at his New Zealand compound, were anxiously waiting for him.

The roadster navigated through a double set of guard posts, then weaved around several airplane hangars that lined both sides of the executive airport's runway. Chernier entered his spotless private hangar through a large set of double doors and parked behind the waiting jet. The crew was patiently waiting for his arrival near the plane's entrance.

The ORBIX director fished his phone out of his front pocket and dialed.

"Hey babe, it's me. I'm about to get on the plane and I wanted to let you know. I'm coming to you and the kids now."

Chernier smiled and listened, holding an index finger up to the crew waiting for him, as if to say he'd need a moment.

"We aren't sure. It could go either way, but there's nothing more we can do here."

Another pause.

"I know. I know. We'll be okay, I promise."

Finally.

"Listen, I have to go." Chernier paused, then added, "I love you. You know that, right? I always have. Tell the kids I love them too, and I'll see you soon. Okay...bye."

A large breath escaped from the Chernier's chest. He needed sleep. His head was clouded from exhaustion and worry. After a moment to collect his thoughts, the director walked over to the pilot of the Gulfstream and said just three words.

"Let's fucking go."

———

2029

Emily English stared at the handsome man standing at the podium. Her heart felt heavy, thumping wildly in her chest and causing her blouse to shutter slightly with every beat. She'd never seen Jack Parker looking like, well, like Jack Parker. Before, long hair and a scraggly beard had given Jack the appearance of either a hippie or a hipster, neither of which resembled the man that everyone else recognized and stood in front of them now. It was difficult for Emily to reconcile that the man she had fallen in love with, and *this* man, were the same person.

Jack scanned the first few rows of people in front of him, found Emily sitting with her parents, and smiled at her. It was a quick, sweet smile, one that matched his eyes. Emily smiled back, then covered her mouth with her hand as she trembled.

The entire crowd was silent. Jack continued.

"Several years back, as you certainly must know, I left public life and retreated from a world that had become difficult for me to live in."

Jack stopped to catch the eyes of several people in the audience. Some looked at him slack-jawed. Others leaned forward slightly and blinked as if they were seeing an apparition. As for the others, they simply stared at Jack, waiting, wondering what was happening and what their hero was going to say.

"I came here. Just me and my dog, Lily. We tucked ourselves away up the peninsula and stayed there. As you're well aware, this is a special place. It's sometimes harsh, always beautiful, and definitely peaceful. And I needed *all* that; for a long time, I needed that."

Just then, Jack noticed a young girl with long blonde hair, maybe fourteen years old, raise one arm to about chin level. She was holding a cell phone. Without saying a word, the girl's mother gently pushed her hand back down to her lap. Jack looked at the mother and smiled.

"Ma'am. Thank you for that. I can't tell you how much that simple act means to me. And I'll tell you why."

The woman nodded her head but couldn't find the breath to talk. After all, Jack Parker had just spoken directly to her. The others took notice and followed suit. Cell phones and cameras were tucked away in respect.

"I would like to stay here and live a quiet life. I'd like to go to Sal's and eat a meatball sub and sip a cold beer."

Sal, who was sitting near the back of the gym, let out an audible gasp.

"I'd like to go to Pike's and shoot a game of pool and play songs on the jukebox."

Jack looked directly at Emily, whose eyes had turned red and narrow.

"I'd love to play trivia at the brewpub on Wednesday nights and hang out with you guys. The onion rings are delicious, and the beer isn't so bad either."

Erin Flynn instantly made the connection from Jack to the long-haired, bearded friend Emily had brought to the brewery a while back. She had been oblivious to what now seemed so obvious: this fellow was *the* Jack Parker. Flynn smiled and chuckled to herself.

"Maybe I could join a snowmobile club and hit the trails with some of you folks, that would be fun. But, most of all..."

Jack paused and took a breath.

"...most of all. I'd like to do these things with someone who's become very special to me. Someone who shouldn't have to share her life with someone who's been living in the shadows, far away from the real world. Hopefully, if you don't mind, I can do these things here, with her at my side."

Jack turned toward Emily and caught her eyes. Then he smiled.

"Because I'm in love with Emily English, and I want everyone here to know it."

––––––

2021

T-Minus 30 Minutes

Twelve US Navy ships, as well as a dozen more from Italy and Great Britain, dotted the North Atlantic, hoping for a timely capsule recovery in the event Jack Parker could successfully eject from Pegasus II. Chinese and Russian ships were not aiding in the recovery of the ejection capsule. Their leaders wouldn't jeopardize the safety of their ships or crew in the event the asteroid struck Earth, nor would Russia permit US planes to maneuver anywhere in its airspace in the event a recovery was needed on Russian soil. If Jack survived and was successful in redirecting the asteroid, Russia announced that they would make "every effort" to recover Jack's capsule promptly (whatever *that* meant).

For the last twenty-four hours, Robert Blane and Jack had rehearsed the ejection protocol repeatedly. By routine, the procedure wasn't difficult, just a simple two-step operation, but the timing was everything.

CAPCOM would give Jack the "go" for abort. Due to his velocity, his estimated window for ejection was around ten seconds. After a hundred and sixty days of safe travel in deep space, Jack's life and his successful return came down to ten seconds. Ten seconds.

Blane stared at a bank of large screens lining the wall across the room; several dozen men and women sat at computers in between. Most of the staff were texting or calling their loved ones, and hushed whispers pattered around mission control.

Husbands, wives, children, parents, lovers, brothers, sisters, friends.

I love you. Everything will be alright. I'll call you as soon as I can.

Robert Blane sighed, then picked up his phone and dialed his wife.

"Hey sweetie, it's me."

"I know. It's all happening now, but I wanted to tell you... just how much I love you, okay?"

"Me too," Blane smiled slightly, nodding as if his wife could see him. "Bye for now."

The NASA director then cleared his throat, took a deep breath, and called his crew to order.

"Okay everyone, we are going live in five minutes. Let's get video feeds from Eureka and Barentz science stations up on full view, and get the B-2 pilots on standby. They'll know something first. Ladies and gentlemen, whichever way this goes, every one of you has accomplished something no one thought possible. We have a lot to be proud of, no matter what happens."

Robert Blane's voice had cracked slightly. After a moment's pause, he straightened himself and stood resolute and tall in front of dozens of exhausted engineers and technicians.

"Each of you is a credit to NASA, our proud nation, and all of mankind. You are all heroes."

CHAPTER 27

2021

ARRIVAL

"NOW, JACK! DO IT NOW!"

Robert Blane's voice bellowed through the microphone and off the walls of mission control. The NASA director didn't realize he was screaming. Harsh radio interference, possibly caused by the asteroid's proximity to the exosphere, was making communication difficult. No one knew what, if anything, was getting through to Jack on his end. Blane, the cords on his neck bulging, had been yelling through his headset for over a minute. The window for Jack to safely eject and re-enter the atmosphere was far less than sixty seconds, but Blane repeated the directive anyway.

"Now Jack! Do it now!"

Pegasus II had gone silent. Either Jack wasn't talking, or his transmissions weren't getting through. For now, everyone in flight control held their collective breaths and waited for the escape pod's GPS to activate and transmit its location.

Suddenly, Robert Blane stopped yelling. The room fell utterly silent.

A live video feed from Eureka Science Station, the northern most research facility on the planet located in the Canadian territory of Nunavut, seized the attention of everyone in the room. An image was slowly coming into focus on the screens. There, above the dimly lit arctic horizon, was a reddish-orange line of light slowly moving across the sky. At first, it looked like a thin thumbnail scratch, red and growing longer with every second. Moments later, the streak had widened, with little bursts of orange and red and yellow. Before long, it looked as though God Himself was unzipping the sky.

Asteroid 2021CF02 had arrived.

"...ow...do it..."

Jack reached out in front of him and lifted a glass cover in the center of the spaceship's expansive control panel. After checking one last time to make sure his helmet was securely fastened, he struck a large red button with a closed fist.

ORBIX had developed the first-ever ejection system designed for use in low orbit. It was a brilliant design but had never before been tested in a real-life situation. The engineering team never had the chance to do so and had never intended to. Activating the ejection pod would separate the flight deck from the rest of the spacecraft, destroying the Pegasus vehicle in the process. It was a last-ditch fail-safe by design.

The instant Jack hit the red button, all kinds of things began to happen within nanoseconds of one another. Heavy nylon straps automatically tightened around Jack's body, pushing him back in his seat as the entire flight deck swiveled its position to better absorb the upcoming g-forces. A titanium and resin shell closed around the crew compartment, encapsulating Jack in a protective casing that would shield him from the intense heat of reentry. Thunderous concussions reverberated throughout Pegasus II as an array of explosions separated the escape pod from the rest of the spaceship. The entire forward section of the Pegasus vehicle splintered away, and a snowglobe-shaped cocoon hurled itself away from the rest of the ship and toward Earth.

Jack Parker, suddenly free of the rock he had called home for nearly two months, sucked in oxygen in rapid breaths. Through a small viewing portal, he saw the asteroid slowly shrink in the distance as Pegasus II left a trail of debris in its wake. The pale blue light of the ion thrusters continued to glow in the darkness of space. The ejection of the flight deck had been successful. Now, Jack hoped the escape pod would enter Earth's atmosphere and not skip off like a stone on water.

"Mission Control, separation successful. Do you copy? I repeat, separation complete. Computer reentry program activated. I am in your hands, over? Do you copy?"

There was no response.

For whatever reason, atmospheric interference or possible damage to the radio during ejection, no one at Mission Control was receiving Jack's transmissions. Neither were the billions of people watching NASA's live video feed. No one knew Jack's condition, and at the moment, they weren't concerned with the capsule. Their attention was completely focused on the rather large asteroid that was entering the atmosphere.

People around the world gathered in front of television sets. Humankind was exhausted. One hundred and sixty days of uncertainty is detrimental to the psyche. So, people held hands. They hoped. And more than ever, they prayed. News organizations, together with teams of scientists and astronomy experts, broadcast a riveting and detailed play-by-play of NASA's video feed. Bold and colorful graphics framed screens with such gloom and doom titles as "Killer Asteroid Arrives," or "Northern Hemisphere Apocalypse."

Most just wanted the whole thing to be over with, one way or another. Some trembled. Others cried and turned away from their screens. Nearly all were silent. Many were prepared to "meet their maker." Others counted boxes of freeze-dried meals and ammunition stacked on shelves in basements and bunkers. Families and their loved ones came together, to see things through to the very end. They huddled together on sofas and held each other close. And they all wondered just how it all would end.

One such family tucked away on the upper peninsula of northern Michigan sat transfixed and nervous in front of their television. Thomas and Jillian English, along with their daughter Emily, were nervous, but they were also hopeful. They had to be. An asteroid strike near the pole would flash-melt trillions of metric tons of arctic ice that would eventually wash into the Great Lakes and over the very peninsula they called home.

Thomas pointed to the TV, "Look, it's getting thinner, right? The path of the asteroid. Is it getting thinner?"

A fiery streak of light cut across the television, wider on one side, thinning as it moved across the dark blue of the northern sky, then disappearing altogether. The heavens, burnt and smoldering from the asteroid skimming across its back, seemed to fade out, much like the remnants of holiday fireworks-a final explosion of light and color before the sky returned to its previous state of calm. Nobody spoke. Not just yet.

A few moments later, this family, like millions of others, would realize that, after months of anxiety and uncertainty, fear and worry, and a roller coaster ride of emotion, they were going to be safe.

It was all over.

Emily English wrapped her arms around her knees and leaned

forward. She pushed her glasses up on her nose and whispered, "It passed by. Look." She paused, then spoke a little louder, "It *missed* us."

Emily put her head between her knees and started sobbing, softly at first, then harder and louder, as her curved back flexed up and down with her breathing. Her parents leaned their heads on their daughter's back and wrapped their arms around their only child in a tight squeeze.

The asteroid had kissed the top of Earth's atmosphere and moved on like a ship in the night, shadows dancing across the rock's uneven surface. Glistening in the sunlight, with the blue and white of Earth standing close in stark contrast to the grayish color of its celestial visitor, the asteroid now appeared more beautiful than threatening, a wonder of the galaxy living on until it would, someday far in the future, meet its inevitable destruction.

———

2029

Jack walked over to Emily and held out his hand. She stood up slowly, paused, then placed her hand in his. The room was uncomfortably quiet, especially considering the number of people packed inside. After maneuvering her in and around a couple of rows of onlookers, Jack pulled her close to him and whispered something in her ear. She nodded slightly, then buried her head into his chest. Jack wrapped his arms around her and held her firmly. Lovingly. Happily.

The gymnasium erupted!

————

2021

NASA was tracking the escape pod. Although it had managed to enter the atmosphere, it was traveling at an extremely high rate of speed. Earth's atmosphere created massive amounts of friction, which causes two things: it slows the capsule, which is good; and it generates incredible heat, which is problematic when an astronaut is traveling inside of a fireball.

There was some good news, however. Jack's angle of descent wasn't awful, meaning, it could have been worse. Technically speaking, his descent was well under what is termed as "ballistic" reentry. G-forces during a ballistic reentry are crushing. At seven Gs, a 190-pound astronaut weighs 1,330 pounds. Currently, G-forces were pushing Jack into his seat to the point that he had to remind himself to breathe. That is, of course, if Jack was in the escape pod to begin with. Mission Control did not yet know.

Certainly, he was. He *had* to be.

CAPCOM assumed Jack was inside the capsule. There was no way to perform the ejection sequence without sitting on the flight deck, but NASA had not heard from Jack since well before the pod separated from Pegasus II. There was no confirmation that the pod had successfully protected him during separation from the space-craft, or if the heat shields had protected him during reentry. No one knew if Jack was alive inside the pod. Or if all that remained of Jack Parker was his corpse.

Meanwhile, the world had turned its attention away from Eureka's video feed of the asteroid to a jerky video broadcast of Jack's capsule in the upper atmosphere, somewhere over the North Atlantic. As the video stabilized, it became clear that the Pegasus escape pod was intact and plummeting back to Earth. Every news agency picked up the broadcast, which held the collective attention of the world. Dozens of studio talking heads explained what was happening, and what was *supposed* to happen, to viewers with palpable anxiety in their voices. Jack's survival, as they repeatedly pointed out, was still uncertain.

Blane's voice cut through the broadcast as NASA's audio feed was picked up and played alongside the visual. All the cable hosts and news anchors immediately stopped talking, to watch and listen, just like the rest of the planet.

For the fifty-second time since reentry, the words, "Mission Control to Jack Parker, come in, over," were spoken, with no reply.

Blane continued to monitor the capsule's descent.

"Stand by for Forward Bay Cover jettison."

At thirty-five thousand feet, the top of the escape pod that had shielded Jack during reentry was jettisoned. An onboard altimeter activated seven exploding bolts and blew the cover-up and away from the capsule.

"Jettison of the Forward Bay Cover is complete. Drogue Parachutes released."

At twenty-two thousand feet, small drogue parachutes were released, helping stabilize the capsule, and more importantly, helping to slow down the rapidly moving pod.

"Fifteen-thousand feet. Drogue Line away. Pilot and Main Parachute deployment."

As the drogues cut away from the Pegasus capsule, smaller pilot chutes helped pull and release massive main parachutes up and over Jack's capsule. Slowly, three bright orange and white checkered canopies unfurled and blossomed against the blue of a cloudless sky. As the parachutes caught the air, the escape pod slowed abruptly, leveling out to an easy twenty miles an hour.

Robert Blane continued his commentary, "Three good main chutes...five thousand feet...two thousand feet."

It took several minutes for the Pegasus II escape capsule to complete its fall back to Earth. Water splashed over the capsule's small viewing port as a ring of yellow flotation buoys inflated around the perimeter of all that remained of the mighty and heroic spaceships. The sea pushed the blackened capsule up and down gently as if it was cradling and taking special care of its occupant.

"We have splashdown. Splashdown confirmed at 2:47 PM Central Time."

The USS Anchorage was twelve minutes away.

———

2029

Hours later, the gym was almost empty. Jack and Emily had visited with dozens of people, shook hundreds of hands, and received even more well wishes. They sat exhausted in metal folding chairs at one end of the gymnasium, as Mayor Dunning and Emily's parents stacked dozens more chairs on carts at the far end of the room. The clanking echoed loudly in the empty space.

Jack twisted in his chair and faced Emily. A half-smile formed on one corner of her mouth as she looked at Jack, shaking her head slightly.

"You may have to grow some of that beard back, and the hair too. At least a little."

Jack gave her a curious look, "Why's that? I thought you'd like all that stuff gone."

"Well," Emily paused and tried to push a bit of his black hair over the top of his head, but it was too short and sprang back into place. "The Jack Parker *I* know doesn't look like this. The old one was just for me. *This* guy belongs to everyone...I don't know how I feel about sharing him."

"You won't have to. I promise."

"Oh, it's okay. I don't mind sharing him a little bit."

Emily took Jack's hand and held it between hers. She brought it up to her cheek and held it there a moment, her eyes closed, lost in the moment.

"You okay?" Jack asked.

"I'm *so* good. But nervous. And a little scared."

"You don't have to be. Remember, I'm Jack Parker. I'm the guy that saved the world, or something like that."

"True," Emily paused, then added, "And who's the girl that saved you?"

Jack placed a finger under Emily's chin and raised her head just enough to look into her eyes.

"That, without a doubt, would be Emily English."

2021

The USS Anchorage, a 684-foot amphibious transport dock with a top speed of 25 mph, managed to reach the Pegasus ejection pod in just under fifteen minutes. The ship's bridge team had been specially trained for such recoveries and quickly positioned Anchorage alongside the ORBIX capsule. The crew quickly dispatched two dive teams in small inflatables and, after attaching a series of guidelines, they hauled the entire capsule onto the back deck of the vessel.

The captain of the Anchorage spoke to the NASA director on a secure line.

"Director Blane, the capsule is secure and on the recovery dock."

"Captain, we have not had radio contact with our man in over an hour. Can you confirm his status?"

Blane and his crew waited nervously for a reply.

"Sir, how about I let you see for yourself."

The ship's onboard camera zoomed in on the hatch just above the upper curve of the space capsule. The video feed was sent straight to Mission Control via satellite, then after a six-second delay, relayed to well over six billion people worldwide through nearly every broadcast channel on the planet.

In the decades that followed, images from deck cameras aboard the USS Anchorage would grace the covers of thousands of books in a hundred languages. Video of the Pegasus capsule's opening would become the second most-watched footage in history, second only to the Zapruder film. The resulting uproar from major urban centers around the globe would be loud enough to move nearby seismometers. And it was all due to the love and gratitude for one very special human being.

Jack Parker popped the hatch and stepped out unsteadily onto the deck of the ship. He closed his eyes and filled his lungs with crisp ocean air. Then, as if scripted, he asked the question everyone on Earth but he knew the answer:

"Did it work? The asteroid...did it hit?"

Over four hundred navy seaman packed tightly around Jack's capsule roared with approval.

————

2032

"Sal, take the money. That's the deal, remember?"

"Mr. Parker..."

"Call me Jack. We've been over this a hundred times."

Sal laughed. "Mr. Jack, I can't charge you. I just can't."

Emily smiled at Sal, then looked over at Jack standing next to her holding a large meatball sub in each hand.

She cleared her throat and said, "Sal, if you don't take this money, I'm going to create a Twitter account and tell the world to never eat at Sal's because they make crummy food. You'll be out of business in a day. Do you understand?"

"You wouldn't?"

Emily placed a twenty-dollar bill on the counter, her expression now serious. "Of course not, silly. But you're taking the money. See you next time."

Emily and Jack turned and headed for the door.

"Goodbye, Sal," Jack called out over his shoulder. "Thanks, my friend."

Lily barked a welcome as the couple walked out of Sal's Sub Shop and to the truck parked just opposite the front door. Jack gave Lily's head a rub through the back window, then, like the gentleman he always was, opened the passenger door for Emily. He handed her the subs, closed the door, then walked around the front of the truck and took his place in the driver's seat. A man walking down the sidewalk passed in front of Jack, gave him a nod, then went on his way. A woman and her teenage daughter smiled at the pair but kept moving. Jack returned the smile and waved.

"Let's eat in the truck. I'm starving." Emily started to unwrap the sub resting in her lap.

Jack laughed.

"What's so funny?"

"It's nearly impossible to eat a meatball sub, dripping with sauce mind you, and drive at the same time without making a mess. No?"

Emily took a big bite and started chewing.

"Is it harder than moving a large asteroid in deep space all by yourself?"

Jack smirked and let out a sarcastic grunt. He steered the truck with one knee and unwrapped the sub with his hands.

"Damn, these are good," Jack almost moaned with pleasure. Then he turned his attention to Emily, still tearing into her sandwich with determination. Sauce was dripping down both sides of her mouth.

"You have sauce on your chin, sweetie."

Emily smiled, then managed a laugh between bites.

"Yeah, well. I make no apologies."

Lily nosed her head through the gap between the front seats and waited patiently for a meatball. Jack licked the marinara off one and handed it to her. She gently took it from his hand, and happily ate it in one bite.

"Tell me," Jack began, "do you think that when Neil Armstrong got back from the moon his wife had to pester him to take out the trash? You think she did that?"

"Most definitely," Emily instantly replied.

Jack nodded.

A few minutes later, Jack turned off the main road and rolled slowly up to an automatic security gate. He rolled down the window and pressed his thumb firmly on a thermal scanner. The gate rose and Jack continued past an empty guard shed and up toward the cabin.

Emily gathered the sub wrappers and carefully crumpled them around a pile of used napkins she and Jack had completely defiled on their way home. Jack parked next to the side door of the house and got out to open the passenger door for Emily. He held out his hand and Emily grabbed it, then carefully eased herself out of the truck and onto solid ground.

"Easy there, Em," Jack said as he helped guide her out of the truck.

Emily smiled and stood still for a moment, still holding Jack's hand. She let go only so she could place both hands around Jack's neck and pull him closer.

She kissed him softly, but let her lips linger on his for an extra moment or two. Emily looked into his eyes and smiled in a way only truly happy people can do, then whispered. "Thanks for taking me to Sal's. I was *so* craving it."

Jack looked down at Emily's rounded belly, the top of which was covered in marinara drippings from her sandwich. She freed one hand long enough to push her glasses up the bridge of her nose, then smiled at him.

Jack Parker looked at Emily with a grateful heart and whispered back.

"Anytime."

EPILOGUE

1955

THE GUARDIAN HAD JUST FINISHED construction on what would become one of the most important research facilities in the history of the modern world. Later, and quite unintentionally, it would also be clouded with more mystery and intrigue than nearly any other location on Earth. Groom Lake, which would later be known as Area 51, was now complete.

Seven years earlier, the Guardian had brokered the exchange of five alien bodies, the result of a nasty crash in the New Mexico desert some years prior. In return, the Guardian received ten metric tons of alien mined rare earth metals. Over the next hundred years, the spherical ingots of platinum, osmium, ruthenium, and rhodium that the aliens had mined and processed from a far distant asteroid would be worth over one trillion dollars. The Guardian had successfully financed the construction of the brand new facility, as well as guaranteed his agency's viability...forever. He would never have to ask the United States government for future funding.

The Guardian removed his grey hat and hung it on a hook

mounted on the wall next to a set of shiny metallic elevator doors. The doors opened and he stepped through, pressed a round button which read "LL" printed in red letters, and patiently waited for the elevator to descend some one hundred feet below the surface. After a thirty-second elevator ride, the doors opened and he stepped out quickly and with purpose.

A crew of twelve specially chosen individuals sat at desks spread out over an expansive workspace. Vacuum tube television sets littered the worksite. A gargantuan early-era supercomputer sat behind glass doors on the far end of the room. Ten men and two women looked expectantly at the man, known simply as The Guardian, and awaited his directives.

He scanned the room, nodded to his crew, then simply said, "Let's get to work."

———

2022

Jack Parker sat in the Oval Office on a chair opposite the President of the United States sipping a glass of Pappy Van Winkle over ice and enjoying a casual conversation with the Commander in Chief. The atmosphere was relaxed, even celebratory. It had been six weeks since he had splashed down and was recovered by the USS Anchorage on live television. It was the first time he had met with the President since his return.

"So Jack, tell me. Why not just go back to your old job? We need good men like you. You understand that."

Jack took a sip of bourbon, then paused to enjoy it. "Mr. President, you know my old job requires complete and utter anonymity. That's impossible now, there's no way. We both understood that from the beginning."

The President grimaced, "Well, I suppose that's true. Still, there's no replacing you. That's for sure."

Jack put his glass on a fancy presidential coaster and leaned back in his chair. There was no gray suit, not anymore. Jack was wearing a white button-down shirt, no tie, under a sharply tailored blue suit and brown loafers. He paused a moment before he delivered his news.

"Well, sir. I have someone in mind for my old job."

"Is he any good?" asked the President.

"*She* is going to be excellent," Jack replied with a grin.

————

2025

The secret service agent escorted the woman through the West Wing and directly into the Oval Office. The new President stood waiting for the visitor to arrive, not quite knowing what to expect, but very curious. The new president had been thoroughly briefed. The Guardian entered the Oval, and the door was quickly closed behind her. The woman, wearing a gray pantsuit, rotated her arm and pulled up her sleeve to reveal a brand. A puffy red raised scar, shaped like a cross inset into what appeared to be a shield, marred The Guardian's skin. The two shook hands.

"Madame President, it's a pleasure to meet you."

"Likewise," the President paused, then continued. "I'm sorry, how would you like me to address you?"

"I'm just The Guardian, ma'am," answered the woman, the woman formerly known as Brody Falls.

———

2029

Jack and Emily held hands as they walked into Pike's. It was late on a Monday evening and the crowd in the bar was light, sparse really. Emily ordered two Lumberman's Lagers and a couple of beef pasties for her and Jack.

"You're going to love these; they're the best anywhere," said Emily confidently.

The bartender gave Jack and Emily a nod of recognition, opened the two bottles of suds, and rang them up at the register.

"Ketchup?" Emily asked the bartender.

The man nodded, "Bottles are at the end of the bar. The pasties will be out in a couple of minutes. That'll be twelve bucks."

Jack handed the man a twenty and told him to keep the change.

"Appreciate that, sir," said the barkeep as he gave Jack a knowing smile. "You guys can sit anywhere. I'll bring the food to your table."

"Ketchup. Really?" Jack remarked. "Why bother?"

Emily wrinkled her forehead, "What do you mean?"

"Well, if you pour ketchup over something, that's all you'll taste. What's the point?" Jack wondered out loud.

"Some folks prefer gravy, but don't ask for any. Not here anyway." Emily said softly.

Jack seemed to understand immediately, "Oh, it's like being in Texas and putting beans in your chili. I get it."

"Why wouldn't you put beans in your chili? It's chili."

"Not in Texas it isn't," Jack said shaking his head.

"Hmm. Well, okay, then," said Emily. She decided to change the subject. "How about a game of pool?"

"You're the boss," replied Jack, "I'm here to please."

Emily and Jack played several games of pool in between bites of the pasties. She beat him every time. It was almost comical. It was as if he had never played pool before.

"How it is that you're so bad at pool?" Emily asked with amusement and genuine curiosity.

"Maybe I'm sandbagging you? Ever think of that?"

Emily tilted her head and scrunched up her face in mock surprise.

"I think it's time. Are you ready?"

"I am," replied Jack

Emily walked over to the jukebox and slipped in two quarters. She pressed B-1-3 and quickly took Jack's hand and led him over to a corner of the room that served as a dance floor. Jack put his hands on her waist and waited for the music. This was the dance she had planned to ask him for last Spring, the one he had flatly denied her. It was long overdue. Emily laced her fingers behind Jack's neck and smiled up at him.

"I'm sorry it took me so long to dance with you," Jack whispered as he tilted his forehead down to meet hers.

"That's okay. I love you anyway."

The music began just as Emily asked Jack if he believed in fate. Before he could answer, "Rocket Man" by Elton John started playing through the jukebox speakers.

"You're kidding," Jack said with a laugh.

"I know. Weird isn't it?"

ACKNOWLEDGMENTS

While this book is a work of fiction, I owe a tremendous amount of gratitude to the fine men and women of NASA for all they accomplished during the golden age of space flight and beyond. Neil Armstrong and Buzz Aldrin walked on the moon the day after my sixth birthday. My first GI Joe action figure came dressed in an orange flight suit. I have always had a special fascination with space exploration, and this book contains references to real-life events that took place during several NASA missions.

A special group of people helped me fashion and form this story into its final version. Jill Carlton, Erin Mendoza, my wife, Allison Crow, and my mom, Elaine Flanigin, were kind enough to read this book, one chapter per week, and help me sort through the direction of the story. Paul Berg, Joe McSpadden, and Susan Mayes also gave me valuable input that guided the story's final form.

Ray Bellant's experiences in Michigan's Upper Peninsula convinced me that Jack Parker needed to live in that fascinating part of the country.

Jim Robinson's detailed knowledge of ham radios and how they operate was a vital component in helping me keep the storyline authentic.

Jo Linda Crow's editing skills were, once again, greatly appreciated and extremely helpful.

Finally, I'd like to thank everyone that read my first book, *Hollywood, Texas*, and told me how much they enjoyed it. Their kind words gave me the encouragement I needed to move forward with another story. My heartfelt gratitude goes out to you all.

.

Made in the USA
Columbia, SC
29 December 2021

52709179R10135